TILL DEATH DO US PART

ALEATHA ROMIG

NEW YORK TIMES BESTSELLING AUTHOR

Book #2 of the Brutal Vows series

New York Times, Wall Street Journal, and USA Today
bestselling author

COPYRIGHT AND LICENSE INFORMATION

TILL DEATH DO US PART

Book two Brutal Vows

Copyright @ 2024 Romig Works, LLC
2024 Edition
ISBN: 978-1-956414-89-9
Editing: Lisa Aurello
Proofreading: Stacy Zitano Inman
Sensitivity reader: Danielle Sanchez
Spanish editor: Telma Santos
Cover Art: RBA Designs/ Romantic Book Affairs
Formatting: Romig Works LLC

ALEATHA ROMIG'S MOST RECENT AND UPCOMING RELEASES

BOUND BY A PROMISE – Brutal Vows, book three - September 2024

Arranged marriage, age-gap, forbidden, mafia/cartel stand-alone romance

ONE STRING – July 2024

Aleatha's Lighter Ones - Second-chance, enemies-to-lovers, fake-date, little-sister's-best-friend, forbidden, stand-alone contemporary romance

NOW AND FOREVER – Brutal Vows, book one - May 2024

Arranged marriage, age-gap, mafia/cartel stand-alone romance

LIGHT DARK – April 2024

Cult, psychological thriller, forced proximity, romantic suspense stand-alone

*Previously published through Thomas and Mercer as INTO THE LIGHT and AWAY FROM THE DARK

REMEMBERING PASSION – Sinclair Duet book one – September 2023

Scorching hot, second-chance romance filled with the suspense and intrigue

REKINDLING DESIRE – Sinclair Duet, book two – October 2023

Scorching hot, second-chance romance filled with the suspense and intrigue

For a complete list of all Aleatha Romig's works, turn to BOOKS BY ALEATHA at the end of this novel.

SYNOPSIS~

*Arranged marriage, enemies to lovers, Mafia/cartel
romance*

As the only daughter of the Kansas City capo, at eighteen years of age, I was given to the son of my father's consigliere, a man who was expected to accomplish great things for the famiglia. Things didn't go the way we planned.

There wasn't love.

My husband was a traitor, taking part in a coup against the famiglia.

He's now dead.

I'm free.

Until the fateful night my brother, our new capo, informs me that I've once again been promised in marriage. He explains that as a childless widow and the daughter of the late capo dei capi, I am desired. Requested.

Aléjandro Roríguez is the son of the leader of the Roríguez cartel. My brother married a woman from the cartel, securing the Mafia/cartel alliance. He says that it's now my turn.

I've only met my future husband a few times, but I know without a doubt that I don't like him. Loving him is impossible. I've lived in a marriage without love. I won't do it again.

Aléjandro lives a dangerous existence.

Death saved me once before.

Maybe it will again.

Have you been Aleatha'd?

TILL DEATH DO US PART is a stand-alone dangerous Mafia/cartel romance in the new "Brutal Vows" series. Each arranged-marriage story is filled with the suspense, intrigue, and heat you've come to expect from New York Times best-selling author Aleatha Romig.

*TILL DEATH DO US PART is a stand-alone Mafia/cartel, arranged-marriage romance within the interconnected world of 'Brutal Vows.'

PROLOGUE~

Mia

This time of year, a sea of green surrounded my parents' mansion tucked away in the Ozark Mountains. High above, the sun shone in a beautiful sapphire-blue sky. Workers milled about in preparation for my brother Dario's wedding. As a means of an escape from the hubbub or perhaps hoping to avoid the bride's incoming family, my cousin Giorgia and I lay by the pool, enjoying the solitude out of the way of the chaos.

Giorgia lay on her stomach, a magazine in her grasp, as she read news of celebrities and the type of people often envied. "I'm thankful all of our dirty laundry isn't published for the world to read."

"Like the fact Dario is marrying someone from the cartel?"

Giorgia laughed. "Catalina was nice enough at the bridal shower."

Closing my eyes, I remembered the shower. A plane full of my brother's family, mostly women and bodyguards, flew to Southern California for a one-day trip. Mom insisted that our family had a strong showing. It was all about an alliance the Luciano famiglia and Roríguez cartel were forming.

"Nice," I said, thinking of my future sister-in-law. "I think I may have scared her with the see-through teddy."

Giorgia giggled and rolled to her back, tossing the magazine to the travertine tile. "She was as white as a sheet."

We both laughed.

"She's marrying the future capo," Giorgia said. "She should get used to being outside her comfort zone."

I nodded. "I guess she's better than Josie, but" —I shuddered— "I don't envy Dario for marrying into that family. Rocco says the cartel will double-cross us. He doesn't trust them."

Rosa, one of Mother's maids, appeared, carrying a tray with two mimosas. "Mrs. Moretti." She handed one to me. "Mrs. Pesci." She handed one to Giorgia.

We waited until the maid walked away before bringing our glasses together with a giggle. "To the alliance," my cousin said.

After a sip, I shook my head. "Rocco would be furious to know I was even pretending to support it."

My cousin looked at the glass in my hand. "How would he feel about your third mimosa before noon?"

I pressed my lips into a straight line. "Since I'm on my period, he knows I'm not pregnant." I made a face. "It added to his wonderful disposition."

"You're wearing a bathing suit."

"I told him that Father would be furious if the cartel saw bruises on the capo's daughter." I laid my head back against the chair and lifted my face to the sunshine. "Holding that over him has been the best part of this farce."

We both turned toward the sound of male voices.

Father's gaze went disapprovingly toward the two of us. "Mia, Giorgia, go inside. Our guests have arrived." We might both be married adult women, but that didn't matter. My father's word, as capo dei capi, was law.

Giorgia and I stood and quickly covered ourselves with beach robes.

The three men standing with Father were obviously from the Roríguez cartel. The oldest was probably in his early sixties with a complexion darker than the other two. The younger ones were probably in their twenties or thirties, with haunting dark stares simmering unabashedly toward the two of us in our bathing suits.

Father's chin was raised as he explained. "Jorge,

this is my daughter, Mia, and my wife's niece, Giorgia."

The older man smiled and nodded. "Beautiful young ladies." He turned to the younger men. "My sons, Aléjandro and Reinaldo."

"Hello," I replied.

"Hi," Giorgia said.

Aléjandro and Reinaldo merely nodded.

"I'm afraid they're both married," Father said with a chuckle. If the information was supposed to stop the leering looks from Jorge's sons, it didn't.

Giorgia and I hurried away from the pool deck with our mimosas in hand. Once inside the safety of the house, we both gulped down the remainder of our drinks.

"Rocco is right," Giorgia said. "The way those two were looking at us gave me the creeps. I should tell Antonio."

Telling my husband that the drug lord's sons were leering at Giorgia and me like we were for sale would, one, result in my husband punishing me for being at the pool at the time of the cartel's arrival, and two, create a showdown between my husband, Vincent's son-in-law, and Jorge Roríguez's sons.

"I think we should keep it to ourselves. Over half of the famiglia is upset enough about this alliance." I shook my head. "Telling Rocco and Antonio about the Roríguezes would just add fuel to that fire." After leaving our now-empty glasses on a table, we went up the stairs toward our rooms. Lowering my voice, I said, "We'll be lucky if we get through Dario's wedding without bloodshed."

Despite everyone's concerns, the marriage ceremony came to a successful conclusion. The Luciano and Roríguez alliance was official, and my eldest brother was finally a married man. I almost felt sorry for Catalina. Every now and then throughout the wedding and now during the reception, she'd turn to Dario with a look of terror.

Part of me wanted to tell her that she'd survive. Despite Dario's reputation as The Blade, a man capable of killing without remorse, he had a kinder heart when it came to women, kinder than others in our famiglia, such as our father or my husband.

The men who arranged these marriages as if they were nothing more than business deals had no concept of the horror and anguish the new bride was forced to endure. To them, it was all about transactions, benefits, and cementing their roles. The fact that most women weren't even aware that their wedding was being planned until the deal was done went completely over the men's heads.

"You kind of want to give her a pep talk," Giorgia whispered in my ear during the reception, speaking of Catalina.

"She's probably thinking about her wedding gown."

My cousin covered her lips with her fingertips as

she laughed. "I thought she was going to faint this morning when we told her about that tradition."

We hadn't realized that Catalina was unaware that tonight Dario would cut her wedding dress from her body. The sheer fright in her eyes let us know of our mistake.

An expression of sympathy washed away Giorgia's smile. "It's not fair. Even if she isn't one of us, Catalina is nothing more than a sacrificial lamb."

"She's no different than you and me. We didn't have a say in who we married."

"But at least we married within the famiglia." My cousin shook her head. "I can't imagine being told I had to marry one of them."

It wasn't a concern we needed to worry about. Giorgia and I had done as we were told and married within the famiglia. There was no getting out of our vows except by death. My gaze landed on one of the cartel men across the room. I recalled he was one of Jorge's sons. Taller than Rocco, Aléjandro had wavy dark hair, a muscular build, and an arrogance about him as if he had the audacity to think of the famiglia the way we thought of the cartel.

He was talking with his brother and others from Catalina's family when he turned.

My heart beat in double time as his dark gaze landed on me, scanning me as if I were still wearing my bathing suit from yesterday.

Giorgia followed my line of vision. "Don't let Rocco see you checking out Jorge's son."

"I'm not checking him out. If anything, he gives me a weird feeling, like he thinks he's better than the famiglia."

Aléjandro's lips curled into a grin as he whispered something to his brother, and they both looked in our direction.

Giorgia reached for my arm. "Come on. I need more champagne if I'm going to survive this reception."

As Dario and Catalina took to the dance floor, Giorgia and I made our way to one of the many bars set up throughout the reception. The young redheaded woman in line in front of us didn't need an introduction. She also wasn't supposed to be at the wedding.

"Oh, Mia," she said as she turned with her drink in hand. "Hi."

"Jasmine. What are you doing here?" I was relatively certain my father had forbidden her presence.

"I didn't want to miss Dario's wedding."

"You weren't invited."

Aléjandro appeared from the crowd, placing his arm around Jasmine's waist. "Jasmine is my guest."

I sucked in a breath at his presence and predatory gaze.

"Surely, there isn't a problem with my guest."

Straightening my neck, I met his stare. "I shouldn't be surprised that the two of you found one another."

"Mia," Jasmine said pleadingly.

It wasn't her fault she was despised by the famiglia. It was who she represented and what—a time when Dario chose to follow his own rules instead of Father's.

Aléjandro's smile returned as he tugged Jasmine toward him. "I'll take that as a compliment." He scanned from my light brown hair to the tip of my shoes. "Jasmine is a rare find. Most famiglia women are cold as ice."

"She isn't famiglia," I said.

"Hi, Jasmine," Giorgia said, friendlier than I was. After Jasmine returned her greeting, my cousin looked at me and tilted her head. "Mia, Rocco is looking for you."

"Yet, from what I hear, they make such obedient wives," Aléjandro said as we walked away.

"Rocco isn't looking for you," Giorgia whispered as we walked away. "That guy gives me the creeps. What is *he* doing with Jasmine?"

"I don't know. I can't stand either one of them."

After Dario and Catalina made their exit, I looked around for Rocco. The reasonable answer was that he'd gone with the other soldiers into Father's office. That get-together was one last opportunity for the fruition of a red wedding—top officers from both the famiglia and cartel in close quarters with alcohol and weapons.

The other possibility was that he found someone

else to screw. A smile threatened my façade. If that was the case, I might get a good night's sleep.

Up in the mansion, I walked down a back hallway, trying to avoid any of the guests, when I made a startling discovery.

Aléjandro and Jasmine.

He had one arm against the wall, trapping Jasmine.

There was something about her body language that set off my alarms. I wasn't a fan of the young woman. That didn't stop the small hairs on the back of my neck from standing to attention at seeing her in what appeared to be an uncomfortable situation.

I raised my voice. "Aren't you supposed to be in the big meeting in my father's office?"

Both sets of eyes came to me.

Jasmine's blue gaze sent a silent plea my direction. Aléjandro's dark orbs were again scanning me from my head to my toes.

Steeling my shoulders, I went closer. "Jasmine, you should go."

Quickly, she nodded.

Aléjandro dropped the arm that had been preventing her retreat. As Jasmine slipped away, her predator turned his attention on me. His lips curled as he reached out, caressing my face. Without thinking, my palm slapped his cheek. The smack sent hot tingles through my hand and up my arm.

Instead of responding in kind, Aléjandro began to

laugh. "I like a woman with fire in her blood. Much better than a timid little girl."

"Go to hell."

He secured his arrogant grin. "There's no doubt. I just want to have some fun along the way." His deep, accented voice was like the prickling of rubbing velvet against the grain.

The heat of his stare singed my flesh even beneath my dress, finding its target at my twisting core. My body's reaction was not only inappropriate, but it was also downright wrong. This man represented everything I detested about my family and his.

Power.

Greed.

Misogyny.

"The next time you want to have *fun*" —I emphasized the word— "do it with someone who is of age and wants your attention."

"Jasmine is eighteen. Of that, I'm positive."

"If you think she wanted what you were trying, you have a warped sense of entitlement."

He took a step closer. "You're right."

His answer surprised me.

"Her fire wasn't near as hot as yours."

I took a step back. "Don't be ridiculous."

He shook his head. "I can smell your arousal, Mia. You want a man who knows what he wants and takes it."

"You couldn't be further from the truth."

Before I could say more, the rumble of voices caused both of us to turn.

"What the hell is happening?" Rocco yelled. My brother Dante was at his side.

"Aléjandro is leaving," I answered.

I supposed I should be happy my husband wasn't screwing some waitress from the reception. However, as our eyes met, Rocco's stare sent a cold chill over my flesh, the exact opposite of the effect Aléjandro's had.

"We'll show him out," Dante said. "Come on, Rocco."

Instead of watching them leave, I hurried toward my room, dreading my husband's return.

ONE

Two months later~

T he priest preached that death was a part of life. While I supposed that was true for everyone, it was never as true as it was for those of us born and raised in the famiglia. As the only daughter to the capo, I'd been immersed in it all my life. The reality that life would end was an ingrained truth that surrounded each and every one of us day and night.

One day, death would come for those we loved as well as those we loathed. I was no different. One day it would come for me.

The night both my brothers arrived at Rocco's and my door, I sensed the presence of death, a heavy dark cloud descending around us. It was as if the gates of hell were personified in my eldest brother's stare. At that moment, I didn't know, nor could I fathom, the changes that had occurred in the Luciano famiglia. I just knew that seeing Dario and Dante unexpectedly upon my doorstep filled me with trepidation. It was the knowledge that long ago, my eldest brother had taken over many of our father's duties—being the grim reaper was only one of them.

"Mia, let us in," Dario said. "We have news we need to talk to you about."

For a moment, I froze in place. If I refused them entry, would I also silence their news? That hesitation was barely a blip on the radar of time. I wasn't even certain my brothers noticed. I was in no position to stop their entrance nor their news.

Dario's dark stare swirled with emotions he'd never show. He couldn't, not as a male or as next in line to become capo and run our famiglia.

I took a step back, bidding Dario and Dante entrance.

My brothers and I had never been especially close. The seven- and five-year age differences were probably a factor. Our father's strict belief in the distinction between male and female roles was another. By the time I was old enough to be interested in the lives of my brothers, Dario was a teenager and a made man and Dante was on his way. They had little to no interest in their childish sister.

Dario's impending news filled the space between us in a dense fog.

"Rocco?" My husband's name was barely audible as I forced it from my lips.

They both nodded.

Tears filled my eyes, and my knees grew weak as I surrendered to the news.

My husband was gone.

The news was a blow to my world. Even being the capo's daughter, my identity was intertwined with my husband's.

Dario reached for my arm and led me to a sofa in the front room.

I'd been concerned when Rocco hadn't returned home last night. However, his absences weren't unusual. He oversaw the whores at Emerald Club, the famiglia's private club. Sometimes his work would keep him at the club at all hours. Recently, he'd taken a trip to New York, one that I didn't know about until he returned. Rarely was I ever told the particulars of his business, only that it was always in service to my father.

Even screwing the club whores.

"How? Who?" I tried to block out images of my husband's demise.

Had he suffered as I'd suffered throughout this marriage?

I was eighteen years old when my father had given me the news. I was to marry Rocco Moretti, the son of

Father's trusted consigliere, Tommaso Moretti. My feelings or emotions were never considered as Father and Tommaso plotted to continue their dynasty. To suggest that love was a factor in our ten-year marriage would be the furthest from the truth.

Rocco was a cold and calculating man who refused to accept responsibility for our lack of children. A child would have secured his role in the Luciano famiglia even after my father's demise. Yet throughout the last decade, Rocco never accomplished a higher rank than that of a trusted soldier. His dream of grandeur was continually thwarted by my brothers, Dario and Dante. Even his marriage to Vincent Luciano's daughter couldn't elevate him to the status of Vincent's sons.

Dario, my eldest brother now seated to my side, spent most of the last decade defying our father's wishes. Each time that Rocco thought Dario's disobedience would raise Rocco's stature, he was wrong.

We were nearly five years into our marriage when Rocco began taking his disappointment out on me. I hid the bruises well with makeup, sunglasses, and long sleeves. Only my cousin Giorgia was aware of the hell I lived. My mother would have sympathized but never would have spoken to Father about it. I'd long ago suspected that my parents' relationship had the same issues.

Dario sat taller. His lips pressed into a straight line. "The Russians?" I asked. The war between the famiglia and bratva continually simmered below the surface, never easing or growing cold. I opened my eyes wide, staring at Dario. "The cartel." It wasn't a question. Rocco loathed the alliance Dario had formed with the Roríguez cartel. My husband's disgust extended over to Dario's wife, Catalina, the daughter of one of Roríguez's top lieutenants.

"I killed Rocco," Dario stated without remorse.

I jumped from the sofa. "You?"

Dante came forward. "Mia, hear him out."

Dario stood, this time keeping his distance. "For you and your reputation, the extent of Rocco's crimes against the famiglia will not be made public. Know that he was involved in an attempted coup. He took from me and tried to take more. As capo, I cannot tolerate dissension."

My eyes opened wide. "Capo? You're capo? What about Father?"

"Gone."

My stomach lurched, doubling me over. Gathering my strength, I stood again, my gaze going from Dario to Dante and back. "Did you—?" *Kill our father*...I couldn't form the question.

Killing the capo was against the omertá. If Dario had murdered Father, he couldn't be capo. Did Dante?

"Alesia shot him last night," Dante explained.

Alesia—our father's mistress.

Dario went on, "Dante and I spoke with Father only minutes before. When we arrived, Alesia was screaming. Our dear father was in the process of beating and raping her."

I sucked in a breath.

"After Dante and I left, she used his gun. The KCPD has already taken her statement and ours." Dario shook his head. "Domestic violence is a sickness within the famiglia I would like to eradicate."

Crossing my arms over my chest, tears cascaded down my cheeks as I let Dario's words sink in.

My husband was dead.

My father was dead.

My father—the man who made me marry Rocco could no longer rule my life.

The epiphany hit me. My tears weren't for what I'd lost but for what I'd gained.

Inhaling, I lifted my chin. "I'm free."

"You will always be a part of the famiglia. Now, it's time for you to mourn."

A scoff passed over my lips. "In public, I'll do as you say." My smile grew. "In private, know that I'm rejoicing in my freedom."

Dario inhaled. "Mia, you're only twenty-nine. You're childless."

"I've been to every doctor. It was Rocco, not me." As soon as the words left my lips, I regretted saying them, especially to the man who now controlled my future. "Dario, please don't marry me off to some soldier. I've done as Father wanted. For ten years." My volume rose. "Ten years. I've paid the price of my heritage. Let me live."

He looked around my living room with judgment in his gaze. This townhouse was nothing close to the grandeur of his apartment or even Dante's. Our living arrangements were meant to reflect Rocco's standing. In other words, we lived as soldiers did. Our status was only elevated by association.

"After the funeral, you will move back into the mansion with Mom."

The mansion up in the Ozarks and away from Kansas City. That was also away from my friends and family.

"I can live on my own."

Dante shook his head. "Not in this shitty place."

"You're still a Luciano." Dario said. "You deserve better. And as a single woman, you need to be protected. The mansion is best."

Protected.

That was code for controlled.

Dario lifted his hand, silencing any attempt at a response. "Tell me, sister, do you support me as capo?"

It was a trick question. If I said yes, I was subjecting myself to Dario's rule. If I said no, I was committing myself to go the way of Rocco and Father. Dario was basically asking if I wanted to live. I suspected I wasn't the only member of the famiglia to be asked this question.

I nodded and stood straighter. "Capo dei Capi." I

bowed my head before looking up at his accepting gaze.

I'd choose life.

And after my mourning period, I would finally get to live.

FIVE MONTHS *later~*

STEPPING onto my balcony in the cool winter air, I wrapped my robe tightly around me. The cement chilled my bare feet, making my flesh pebble with goose bumps. In the silence of the early morning, I took in the view. Each day was better than the last. Winter was about to give way to spring. Redbud trees were bringing a hint of color to the leafless gray ones. In another month, in every direction, flowering trees would be popping with blooms, blanketing the mountains in a rainbow of hues. This was my fifth month living with my mother. To be honest, her home was large enough to go days without seeing one another. However, her wish was that we spend each evening dining together.

It wasn't too much to ask, and I appreciated that after the first few weeks, she'd lessened her requirements for formal attire. There was no reason to dress up. As two women in mourning, our visitors were few. Dario's guards made sure of that.

We also weren't privy to all the famiglia news, yet I had my secret source: Giorgia. Antonio, her husband, swore his loyalty to Dario and the famiglia. He would have done the same to Father and Tommaso if they had prevailed. That didn't mean that Giorgia's husband was a threat to Dario's new organization.

In my opinion it meant that like many of the other soldiers, he lacked the fortitude to rule. The soldiers were dangerous and deadly while also followers and subordinates. They didn't have the brutal leadership qualities Father and Dario shared. If I were to be honest with myself, Rocco had also been without those qualities. When it came to the famiglia, Rocco learned from his father. Tommaso was ruthless to the world. Yet in the privacy of my father's company, he never failed to grovel. Father liked that about him and others.

Dario didn't.

Tommaso saved his own life with his pledge of loyalty, yet he couldn't retain his status. Dante was now Dario's confidant—his consigliere. I had to give my brothers credit—both of them. Through Giorgia's updates, it sounded as if the alliance with the Roríguez cartel was working. Not only did the Luciano famiglia have more quantity and quality product, but the allegiance also gave our famiglia the resources to slow the bratva's efforts to infiltrate our territory.

My mourning would be over in another month, the acceptable amount of time for a childless widow. As the capo's wife, Mother's would last longer—an entire year of wearing black.

That was the extent of her bereavement—a black wardrobe.

In the privacy of her home, we'd worked to move on with our lives. The sad reality was that neither of us were exactly brokenhearted. We were also sheltered in the middle of nowhere. That didn't mean I didn't have plans.

I did.

I'd looked into attending college. Yes, I was older than many of the freshman students, yet my plans weren't for socialization but for education. Dario's wife had a degree. There was no reason to deny me one.

Mom's biggest ire was that Father's whore, as Mom referred to Alesia, was still living in Father's luxury Kansas City apartment with the protection of the famiglia. She even had the audacity to attend Father's funeral, wearing black.

Despite Mom's rants, Dario refused to budge on his decision. He'd given Alesia his word, and he wasn't going to falter. After a life of submission to her husband, Mom faced the reality that she was now under her son's rule.

Wearing my robe, I made my way down to the dining room. Breakfast didn't have mandatory attendance like dinner. Nevertheless, I was growing accustomed to a bit of conversation with my morning coffee.

Sunshine poured through the dining room windows. Mom sat at the head of the table, the seat she'd claimed after Father's death, with a plate of uneaten food and her cup of coffee. She peered up at me from behind the pages of the *Kansas City Gazette* and sighed.

"Good morning," I said as I took my seat and Rosa poured coffee into my cup.

"Breakfast, Mrs. Moretti?"

I scanned Mom's untouched meal. The eggs looked like rubber and the bacon was cold. "Fruit and an English muffin."

Rosa nodded and disappeared into the kitchen.

"Dario and Catalina are coming to dinner tonight," Mom said, folding the newspaper and setting it down to the side of her plate.

"To what do we owe the honor?" Sarcasm wasn't disguised in my question.

"He said he wants to show her springtime in the Ozarks."

I rolled my eyes. "I can't believe their marriage is still working."

"Before their wedding night, I wouldn't have given it six months."

Lifting the rim of my cup to my lips, I blocked out my mother's soliloquy, the story about Dario and Catalina's sheets. I'd heard it too many times to count. Each time she retells it, I can't help thinking of my own wedding night. It was the only wedding night I knew was not embellished. The memories made my stomach turn.

Once Mom was done, I turned to her and scrunched my nose. "Don't you think Catalina's sister was right? We have some savage traditions."

"They aren't savage."

"Did the old bats come into your bedroom after you and Father were married?"

Mom lifted her coffee cup. "Of course. It's tradition."

"And how did that make you feel?"

"I don't recall."

"I call bullshit."

"Mia," Mom exclaimed.

"It's true. We all hate it, and yet we make each new bride go through it. Surely, Dante will be marrying soon." Rosa entered with my breakfast. Once she was gone, I lowered my voice. "I just hope he marries an Italian. Dario and Catalina can bear the weight of this alliance."

"I spoke with Dario last night. There is to be another wedding."

My forehead furrowed as I lifted my eyebrows. "Dante. Let me guess..." I tried to think of unwed women from the famiglia. Now that he was Dario's consigliere, he would want more than a soldier's daughter. "Is it someone from the Chicago or New York famiglias?"

Mom pressed her lips together as small lines formed around them. "Apparently, the negotiations have been in the works for the last three months."

"I'm surprised Dante will wait that long if he has his mind set." I lifted my English muffin to my lips, taking a bite of the buttery goodness.

"Mia, it's you."

My throat forgot to swallow. I had the sensation of falling, as though the floor had just been taken out from under me. "No," I sputtered, finally swallowing the muffin. "No. I've done my part. I married Rocco." I wasn't a prized virgin nor the daughter of the capo any longer. "I won't be forced to marry another soldier."

I could admit that I'd enjoyed living in Mother's mansion with her servants. This was the life I'd been raised to expect. Another soldier would mean I was back to living in a townhouse or worse, some small house in a rundown area of Kansas City.

"Mom, please," I pleaded, "talk to Dario."

She shook her head. "Your brother doesn't listen to me."

"I'll call Dante."

"You can try that."

"Catalina," I said, a grain of hope springing to life. "He listens to her."

"Do you think she'll recognize that your sudden

interest in being her sister-in-law is to benefit from her position with your brother?"

Mom was right. I should have tried sooner to be close to her. "I've been in mourning and isolated in the mountains, surrounded by trees and guards."

"They'll be here late this afternoon. I don't think you're going to change Dario's mind."

"Who is it? Who does he want to marry me to?" I verbalized my fears. "I'm not a virgin. Who wants an older wife?" Surely not a man in line to work his way up in the famiglia. My thoughts went to recently widowed men. Oh God, would it be someone old, someone as old as my father?

Mom shook her head. "I'm not going to say. I've voiced my objection. The rest is up to Dario."

"Your objection." I pushed away my breakfast. "You're not in favor?"

"I can't imagine anything worse."

Anything worse.

"What does that mean?"

Mom inhaled as she stood. "We have few choices in our world. Yet we do have the choice to live or die."

The sunny day faded into the darkness of Mother's words. As I walked back up to my suite, my thoughts were in a downward spiral. There were stories of women who killed themselves to get out of loveless, abusive marriages. It was the way of the famiglia...

In alive.

Out dead.

Could I do that? Could I take my own life?

It depended upon Dario's announcement.

Would I have a life worth living?

CHAPTER
TWO

I didn't dress appropriately for dinner despite our honored guests.

As I looked at myself in the mirror, I saw a woman about to attend her sentencing. I knew the ropes. This wasn't the first time I'd had this conversation. Eleven years ago, I'd taken the news of my impending nuptials like the proper young Italian woman I'd been raised to be. Clenching my jaw, I peered into my hazel eyes. Twenty-four hours ago, they'd been filled with optimism for the future. Now they looked back at me with a blank stare, no longer filled with hope but void of emotion. If I let emotion take hold, I wouldn't be able to go on with this dinner.

Straightening my shoulders, I exhaled.

That proper girl no longer existed.

That well-bred obedience had been raped and beaten out of me. On the night of my wedding, I'd made the mistake of telling Rocco no—I was young, frightened, and believed in the hope of kindness and consideration. The memory of the way his lips curled at the challenge made me want to vomit. The blood I'd shed should have enraged my father, the man who was supposed to protect me. My heart died a little when along with the other men, Father laughed at the news and patted Rocco on the shoulder.

No. I wouldn't go willingly.

I wasn't dressing up for the capo dei capi when he was about to condemn me to another loveless marriage. Whoever Dario thought he could marry me off to would have a rude awakening. I'd done my time and grown stronger for it.

I made myself a vow.

Taking my own life wasn't in my future. However, I wasn't above murder. How could I have lived in this famiglia for nearly three decades and not embraced the idea of killing those who thought to control me? In the five months since Rocco's death, I'd experienced a new kind of freedom while simultaneously being held captive in the mansion. If killing was necessary to retain my freedom, I'd live that way in a federal prison. It had to be better than marriage.

Wearing tight black leggings, flat ballerina shoes, and a loose black shirt, with my dark blond hair pulled back to a ponytail, and very little makeup, I made my way from my suite down to the first floor, knowing that Dario and Catalina were due to arrive any minute. There were voices coming from below.

I paused at the second-floor landing, enamored by the vision. The setting sun shone through the high transom, drenching the chandelier with golden rays and sending cascades of color dancing over the marble foyer. Down below, Catalina's bodyguard stood near the front doors. Mother hugged Catalina as I made my way down the staircase. By Mother's exuberance, you'd never suspect the unkind things she said about Dario's wife in private.

My gaze went to my brother.

Nearly half a year of ruling the famiglia showed in the tenseness of his jawline and the tiny lines spidering from the sides of his eyes. The pressure was evident, making him even less stoic than before. Nevertheless, as Mom released Catalina, Dario went to his wife's side, wrapping his arm protectively around her waist.

Mother turned to me with a quick scan, her expression voicelessly objecting to my attire. Of course, everyone else was dressed more formally. It was as I neared the last step that I heard my sister-in-law's news.

Baby.

Catalina is pregnant.

The information caused my steps to stutter.

How old is she?

Twenty-four or twenty-five.

She and Dario had been married for eight months, and she was already carrying his child. A child who would be both Mafia and cartel. The news hit a nerve I wasn't expecting.

I'd yet to acknowledge that deep inside me, I grieved my lack of children.

As long as Rocco was alive, I'd told myself our childless status was his failure. It gave me another reason to detest him. It also made it easier for me to deal with the reality that deep down, I wanted children. After his death, I'd come to terms with the idea of never having a child of my own.

At Catalina's joyous news, I was unable to squelch the green ink of jealousy seeping into my bloodstream and coursing throughout my body. With monumental effort, I feigned a smile as my tone jumped an octave. "Did I hear you're pregnant?" I reached for Catalina's hands. "So soon."

A rose hue filled her cheeks, giving her a radiant sheen as she leaned into Dario and kept her green stare on me. "We wanted to tell you in person."

Catalina was no longer the terrified new bride from her wedding night. The way she sought Dario for support was but another reason for me to be resentful. Had I ever sought support from Rocco?

"When are you due?" Mom asked.

"July."

Five months away and yet, there was no visual sign of a baby growing within her. Under Catalina's slacks and blouse, her frame was as trim and slender as it had been on her wedding day. The only possible difference may be that her breasts were bigger. To be candid, I never before fully assessed Catalina's breasts.

"Congratulations," I said. I turned my attention to Dario. "So, this happy news is the reason for your visit."

"One of them," Dario said.

"Oh, I can't believe you haven't told me before now..." Mom continued her gushing as she led the four of us into the front parlor. "Your father would be so happy. Have you considered naming your son Vincent? It's a tradition..." Her words, phrases, and questions came a mile a minute as she asked about the baby and Catalina's health. "Are you going to learn the baby's gender?"

Catalina deferred to Dario, like the disgustingly submissive wife she was.

The answer to Mom's question was no—they didn't want to know the gender before birth. Despite Mom's desire for grandsons, Dario said they'd be happy with a boy or girl. Interestingly, no one had addressed Mom's question about using Father's name.

My own thoughts blared in my head, stifling the conversation around me. If I was going to enlist my sister-in-law's aid in stopping my marriage, I needed to pay closer attention to what they were saying. Yet with each passing minute, my mind was on *my* future or lack thereof, not on the upcoming bundle of joy.

When Rosa arrived with a bottle of prosecco, our mother's favorite before-dinner sparkling wine, and four glasses, Mom sent her away. "No alcohol. My daughter-in-law is expecting."

Rosa's eyes opened wide. "Congratulations, Mrs. Luciano." She was speaking to Catalina. "Would lemonade be appropriate? Or water?"

"Yes, lemonade," Mom said. "Good idea."

"Water for me," Catalina replied. "Acidic drinks and I are still not getting along."

"Of course."

"Rosa," I said as I tried to maintain a smile. "I'm not pregnant. Leave the prosecco."

"Mia," Mom chastised. "Don't you need to excuse yourself to go upstairs and put on something more appropriate for dinner?"

I looked down at my outfit, pressing my lips together. "Nope. Black is my new favorite color." My smile grew. "And we're all family, right?" I motioned to Rosa. "Bring the wine over here."

"Please," Catalina said. "Don't let me stop you from drinking whatever you want."

I gave Mom a *'told you so'* look as Rosa placed the tray with the open bottle and glasses on a nearby table. I waved Rosa away. "Go get Catalina's water. I can pour." I turned to Mom first. "Prosecco?"

Mom flattened her lips and nodded. "If you're sure you don't mind, Catalina."

Catalina shook her head.

"Dario?" I asked.

"No, thank you."

"More for me," I muttered as I filled my glass with a generous pour. Bringing the rim of the glass to my lips, I took a hearty drink before filling Mom's glass, handing it to her, and topping off my own.

When I looked to the rest of the family, Dario's admonishing stare was on me. "Perhaps our other conversation shouldn't wait until after dinner," he said.

I shook my head. "Or, better yet, it can wait longer than that. Maybe until hell freezes over."

Catalina paled.

Dario turned to Mom, silently asking if she'd shared the other reason for his visit. Mom nodded and brought her glass to her lips. After a sip, she spoke to Catalina. "It's a bit chilly outside, but we have a beautiful view from the living room. Come with me before the sun fully sets and see how stunning the mountains are in springtime."

Dario nodded, giving his wife permission to go on what could be best described as a *leave me alone to talk some sense into my sister* adventure.

I lifted my glass. "Come back soon."

Dario waited until they were both out of earshot. "Mom told you."

It wasn't a question, but I answered anyway. "Mom's told me many things. If you're referring to the bombshell she dropped this morning about my forthcoming marriage, yes, she told me." I finished the rest of the wine in my glass and began to fill it once more when Dario came closer and took the bottle from my grasp.

"I'd rather you be cognizant of this conversation."

"That makes one of us." I gripped the stem of my glass. "I want to forget it as soon as it's over."

"I never lied to you, Mia. I told you the day Rocco died that marriage was in your future."

"Don't you mean the day you killed him?"

My brother inhaled, his nostrils flaring. "Potayto-potahto."

"Tell me who my new husband will be, brother. It's pretty damn clear that I'm not a prize catch. I'm not a virgin and no longer the daughter of Kansas City's capo. Is this some old widower?" I turned and walked toward the windows, dodging the furniture along the way. With my attention on our conversation, I was oblivious to the natural beauty beyond the panes. My thoughts went to an old widower. There was a possibility in that scenario. "I hope he is." I spun back to Dario. "Maybe he's so old he won't be able to get it up. Raped on one wedding night is really my limit."

Dario's eyes darkened. "You should have told me."

"And what would you have done? I was Rocco's wife."

"I would have done what I did, just ten years earlier."

Maybe it was the few glasses of wine on my empty stomach but Dario's conviction made me laugh. "And I'm to believe you'll kill my next husband, too."

"Not all men rape their wives."

I lifted the glass, taking the last few drops of wine. Lowering the glass, I met my brother's stare. "I'm one for one. Forgive me for not appreciating the odds." When Dario didn't respond, I asked, "Who?"

"He's not old."

If that was supposed to make me feel better, it didn't. "Well, another wish smashed to smithereens."

"He's two years younger than you, and Mia, you are a prize catch. You're a Luciano. The ridiculous expectation of past generations requiring virginity is no longer as much of a standard."

A laugh bubbled from my throat. "Right. Mom and Aunt Francesca weren't thrilled to find blood on your wedding-night sheets."

"You've already bled for the famiglia. Now I'm asking you to cement the alliance."

"You're *asking* me?" My laugh grew louder. "You're not asking me, Capo. You're *ordering* me." I was probably playing with fire. If anyone else in this world was capo, I could expect a slap as a response to my insolence. Our father wouldn't have hesitated. As I looked around the room for the wine bottle, Dario's last words hit their target. My delayed reaction caused my humor to disappear and my forehead to furrow. "Alliance? No, Dario. I won't marry one of the cartel."

He nodded. "You will. And this won't be a wedding to a soldier but to the heir of the Roríguez cartel. This is the status you deserve."

"The heir?" My mind scrambled. Jorge was the drug lord. That meant this was one of his sons. "Aléjandro or Reinaldo?" I could barely recall the younger brother, but I had no trouble conjuring a picture in my mind of the elder one. Tall, muscular, handsome, arrogant, and an asshole. The memories of him after the wedding prickled my skin.

"Aléjandro," Dario confirmed.

"Wasn't he with Jasmine at the wedding?"

"Jasmine is in college. I won't allow her to marry until she graduates."

Shit.

Jasmine was in college—where I'd hoped to be.

This night just kept getting worse.

I found the prosecco bottle where Dario had set it down and refilled my glass. "Are you saying that Aléjandro wanted Jasmine and he's getting me?" I spun toward him. "Fuck you for making me a consolation prize."

Dario took two long strides toward me, taking the glass from my grasp. His words came from between clenched teeth. "Show some respect. I'm still your capo."

"Is he a murderer? A drug dealer? A criminal?"

"You know what we do. The cartel isn't that much different."

I shook my head. "Is Catalina still under Roríguez's rule?"

Dario's forehead furrowed.

"Is Catalina still under Jorge Roríguez's rule?" I asked again. "Or is she under yours?"

"Mine," he answered curtly.

"So, if I marry Aléjandro as you command, once I'm married, you're no longer my capo."

"You will always have the famiglia's protection."

"That's not what I asked. You can't sell me off to the cartel and expect to still make decisions for me. The cartel is no longer making Catalina's decisions. If you sell me off to someone in our famiglia, you will still be my capo. Even to another outfit, you'd lose your control of me."

"Fuck, Mia, this isn't about controlling you."

"Bullshit," I screamed. "It's all about control."

"You don't even know Aléjandro."

"You're right, Dario. I don't know him. I don't want to know him. I've met him and that's enough. Go ahead and marry me to some old limp-dick Italian. At least I understand the rules of that game."

The muscles on the side of Dario's face pulled taut. "You are a catch, Mia. Don't sell yourself short."

"I'm not selling me. You are."

"Aléjandro doesn't mind that you've been married. He requested you."

Does that matter to me?

"Why?" I asked.

"Because you're a Luciano. You're a valuable woman. Hell, I hated when Father gave you to Rocco. I was against the deal from the beginning, but you know how Father felt about Tommaso."

I nodded.

"You deserve more than a common soldier. Aléjandro is more."

I let out a long breath. "I hope he knows he's not getting an obedient, submissive virgin."

For the first time since our conversation started, Dario grinned. "He knows."

There was no way—short of running away and entering a protection program—that I would be able to stop this marriage. I had no more chance than I could have stopped Rocco's and mine a decade ago. God knew I'd pushed Dario further than he would have allowed by most. And yet, my brother and my capo had no intention of letting me out of the agreement he'd already brokered.

"When?" I asked.

"Your mourning will be over before the beginning of April. Your wedding will be small, as it's your second. Aléjandro has recently been assigned to California. The Ruizes are doing well, growing the cartel's US network. Jorge wants Aléjandro to stay within the States full-time to handle any challenges that arise. You'll wed at the Ruiz home near San Diego the first weekend of May."

I shook my head. "The Ruiz home—you mean Catalina's family?"

"Her parents. Their home is on a cliff overlooking the Pacific Ocean."

Turning away, I swallowed the bile bubbling in my throat. Dario was describing a destination wedding as if he were a travel agent. I wasn't interested in a house on a cliff, an ocean, or a marriage. I turned back. "And if I say no?"

"You won't."

I hated the confidence in Dario's voice. "I won't say no," I acquiesced. "But I can and will tell you that I hate you for doing this to me."

Dario nodded.

"I mean it, Dario. I'll hate you until the day you die, just like Father."

"That's your choice. You're my sister. I'll never hate you."

Exhaling, I sagged my shoulders. "I will never love anyone from the cartel. This will be a marriage bound by hate."

"Your emotions are your choice. From experience, I have to tell you, I never expected to love a cartel member. I was wrong."

I lifted my chin. "I'm not."

THREE

Aléjandro

Emiliano Ruiz drove us through the night along deserted roads in the Tijuana River Valley. The roads weren't completely deserted. A mile back we'd passed a truck, empty of merchandise with two of our men, killed. Bullet holes in the back of their heads.

"Fucking bratva," Em said, his grip of the steering wheel loosening for the first time since we'd come across the carnage.

"We'll find them. They can't be too far ahead of us." I sent a text message to another of our drivers, telling him to watch for and report any signs of trouble. "There's a shack about a half mile down that dirt road." I pointed to the right. "If I were the assholes who intercepted our drivers, I'd try to hide out there until we moved on."

"If you knew we were coming. Nothing says they know."

"Two million in product. They fucking know."

Em nodded.

"Cut the lights."

He turned off the headlights and slowed. The sliver of moon and thousands of stars overhead did little to light the way. My blood grew warm in anticipation, the way it did whenever I was on the verge of a fight. Some men may take that sensation as a cue to run. Not me. My hands itched for my guns and knives. I wanted to find the motherfuckers who dared to mess with us and make them pay.

Maybe we'd let one go—with his dick in his pocket —to take a message to his fellow Russians. Don't fuck with the Roríguez cartel. If you do, you'll never fuck again.

Em slowed the car even more. "Look out there on the road."

"Looks like fresh tire tracks."

He turned my way with a grin. "Ready to fuck up some Russians?"

"Si, amigo."

The two of us worked well together. We'd known one another most of our lives. The Ruiz men were some of *mi padre's* best soldiers. Upon *Padre's* demand for me to spend more time in the States, it made sense that I'd be stationed near one of our highest-producing operations.

We drove the next mile in silence, our windows down. Our vision and hearing were on high alert. Bugs and reptiles filled the air with sounds as our eyes adjusted to the darkness. This was why *mi padre* wanted me in the States. Emiliano was a fucking good soldier. So was his cousin Nick. *Mi padre* trusted the Ruizes to do their jobs. Emiliano's *padre*, Andrés, had spent his life making our organization wealthy.

That was the problem.

The more we made, the stronger we became, and the more of a target we were. It wasn't only the Russians who were fucking with us. It was also the Taiwanese. Truth be told, we weren't one hundred percent certain of who we'd find when we located our stolen merchandise.

Em cut the engine. About five hundred yards away were lights—bright lights. In the middle of fucking nowhere, they had to have a generator to produce that kind of electricity. There were only a few reasons why anyone would need that much light way out here. One was that they were counting the bales of cocaine. The second was one that caused me to remove my gun from my holster—a human-trafficking drop.

Quietly, we both got out of the car, crouching low to the ground.

With a nod to one another, we moved slowly and

steadily through the underbrush at the side of the road, going toward the fucking lights. There was little chance that they'd be able to see us in the darkness. Their damn lights could illuminate a fucking baseball stadium.

I reached out, stopping Em's progress at the sound of muffled crying.

Fuck.

His gaze met mine as we both pulled a second firearm from our arsenal.

The sickening feeling I'd had was right. This wasn't only a place to count their bounty of drugs. This close to the border, these assholes also had women and probably children. It was too easy for the coyotes to seduce immigrants forced to stay in encampment sites in *México* with promises of the land of the free and all the other bullshit. Only freedom wasn't the destiny of these people. It was servitude.

The Roríguez cartel made our fortune in drugs. We weren't boy scouts by any stretch of the imagination. That said, we didn't traffic humans. Shit like what we were seeing would be blamed on us, and that had to stop.

Depending upon the age and physical characteristics of the smuggled people, they would be sold either as sex slaves, prostitutes, or domestic help. If they didn't speak English, there was an even better chance they'd never get away with their lives.

Em and I lifted our faces, counting our adversaries.

He held up four fingers. I did another scan. Four was all I could count. Four men. The other people were sitting tied together on the ground with gags in their mouths. I wasn't sure how many hostages were present. Currently, they weren't our concern.

Once we killed the motherfucking smugglers and thieves, we'd worry about the cargo.

The four men were speaking in Russian, laughing, and busy counting the bales—*our* bales. No doubt that they had money signs dancing in their heads. It would be the last fucking thing they had in their heads, well, other than our bullets.

We nodded to one another, our heads bobbing in rhythm. On the count of three, we both stood. From about fifty feet out we were both scarily accurate with our shots. The women screamed as the four men systematically fell to the hard-packed ground.

Em and I hurried forward, our guns still out and ready.

A collective whimper came from the smuggled people. The women were dressed only in their bras and underwear. The few men or boys were wearing only boxers. Despite the earlier heat, the night had brought dropping temperatures. They were shivering. Of course, the blood spatter from their kidnappers dotting their exposed skin could also be a cause of their trembling. Wide eyes looked up at us as Em and I checked the pulses of the four men. One of mine had a weak pulse, nothing another bullet couldn't fix.

The blast echoed through the dark expanse of desert-like terrain.

"How many?" Em asked the bound people. He asked again in Spanish. *Cuantos hombres?*

It was a thin woman to the side who answered. *"Cinco."*

Fuck.

That meant there was one more.

The woman tilted her head toward the darkness. Not far from where we were was the shack I'd mentioned.

"Quédense callados," Em said, telling them to stay quiet.

The bound people feverishly nodded as Em and I went toward the shack. There was no way the fifth man hadn't heard the gunshots. Creeping low to the ground, Em went toward the door, and I went along the back, looking for another escape.

There was a window opening. The fresh scuff near the window let me know someone had recently jumped from the opening. I heard Em kick in the door. The absence of gunshots told me I was right. Our fifth man was out here in the darkness.

"Over here," I called as I scanned the terrain. I needed the fucking lights to find anyone in the dark of the night.

"Do you think he'll come back for the cocaine?" Em asked.

"Not if he wants to live."

"They were definitely bratva."

I nodded. "We need to get our product and call for backup. Someone needs to get those people."

"Nicolas would champ at the bit for a few of those girls at Wanderland."

The small hairs on the back of my neck stood at attention. "If it's their choice and if we can get them papers. Otherwise, they're going back to DHS. We don't need problems at the club because of a pretty pussy."

Em laughed. "My uncle isn't usually as kind."

"Well, he will be now, or I'll find someone else to do his job. I'm not saying we're out of the prostitution business. I'm saying we're out of the sex-slave business." I stood taller. "I'll be glad to talk to Nicolas myself if he questions me."

Em shook his head. "I'm easier to convince. Old men are stuck in their ways."

"Call for backup."

Em nodded. "We need to turn down the wattage on those damn lights. I'm surprised they haven't already summoned fucking border patrol."

Two hours later, we had all our product accounted for, two of our men dead, four of theirs dead, and one of theirs still missing. If he was smart, he'd eat a fucking bullet. His other choices were to tell his captain he'd lost both the product and the people, surrender to us, or give himself up to the US government. The bullet was probably the most appealing.

My brother Reinaldo and a soldier named Julian loaded all eleven women and two men into two large vans. They would take them to a halfway house we had hidden in the outskirts of San Diego. I was glad Reinaldo was involved. Since Padre had sent the two of us to oversee the workings of this operation of the cartel, we'd had more than a little pushback on some of our policies. Reinaldo would make certain that the thirteen people received a shower, food, and a bed for tonight. Tomorrow they would decide their own fates.

Back at Em's parents' home, after a shower, I kicked back on the pool deck with a glass of tequila. For the last two months, Reinaldo and I had been living in the Ruizes' pool house. It was a temporary situation, but it wasn't bad digs. Em's little sister was as pretty and pure as her older sister before her marriage. While Camila was a bit of a tease with the way she dressed by the pool, she was also off-limits. I'd never had the yearning to marry a timid child. Submissive was only appealing in the bedroom. When it came to sharing my life, if I was forced to do it, I wanted a woman with fire.

I didn't even care if she didn't like me.

Like and love weren't a part of my future.

Imagine my intrigue when a woman who fit that bill became available.

"When are you getting your own place?" Em asked as he appeared, hair wet, in a t-shirt, and nylon shorts.

"You can't kick me out."

Em laughed. "I'm kind of getting used to having you around. I've lived my life surrounded by sisters. You and Reinaldo have been a nice change."

"*Padre* isn't sure about his plans for Rei. He might be headed back to *México*. There's still shit happening with Herrera."

Elizondro Herrera started out as part of the Roríguez cartel. Over time, he found himself too enamored with wealth and power. He broke out on his own with a fair number of our men. The split was amicable until it wasn't. Nearly six months ago, he tried to double-cross us, enlisting the help of our newly acquired ally, the KC Mafia.

Em settled into a lounge chair at my side. Instead of tequila, he was a bourbon man. After the night we'd had, he had the bottle and a glass with him. The house and sky were dark. Our only light came from the colorful display under the water within the swimming pool.

"You're not going to cram your new wife into that pool house, are you?"

"New wife." I exhaled, laying my head back and looking upward at the stars. I'd lived twenty-seven years without a woman at my side. *Mi padre* decided that was too long. After the blip our alliance went through, he decided it would be best to form another bond with the Italians.

Cue my upcoming wedding.

"You're not changing your mind," Em said. "The

Mafia offered up their princess." He laughed. "Of course, she's not as pure as that redhead."

"The redhead," I said, speaking of Jasmine, "is too young. Too docile."

Em laughed again. "I didn't get to meet Mia during Cat's wedding. Never imagined she'd be up for another wedding. That husband of hers was a prick."

A smile curled my lips. "I hear the same about her next husband."

"Oh fuck yeah." Em laughed.

I never fathomed that Mia Luciano would be available to marry. If I'd known, I would have been happy to accelerate her late husband's demise. Thinking about Mia at the wedding, the way she acted...when we were alone in that dark hallway—the slap. I was seconds away from kissing her smart and sassy lips when her husband and brother appeared.

Yeah, the memory of that fire did something to my dick every time. However, I also remembered her asshole husband talking about Mia on their wedding night. He'd said something about how much she bled. The fucking kicker was that he made that comment in front of Vincent Luciano, her father, as well as Dario, her brother and now the new capo, and Dante, her other brother.

I didn't have a sister, and I was far from having a daughter, but if I had either one, and anyone spoke that way about her, I'd slit his throat first and demand his respect, second.

"It doesn't bother you that she's been married?"

"Who did you fuck last night?" I asked.

Em shook his head. "You want a name? I'm not sure I got a name."

"Did you give a fuck that she wasn't a virgin?"

Laughter filled the air. "I prefer my whores with experience."

"Mia isn't a whore." Why I had the urge to stand up for her was beyond me. I went on, "The experience doesn't bother me. Too much fucking responsibility to be the first. I've popped my share of cherries. If I'm going to settle down, I don't want a scared virgin."

"Does she know yet?"

I inhaled and exhaled as my cheeks rose with my widening grin. "The capo dei capi said she'd be informed this week. I'm flying to Kansas City next weekend for the engagement." I looked to my friend. "Come with me. You can see Cat."

"I'm still not sure I won't ruin the alliance and slit Dario's throat."

It was my turn to laugh. "You could have done that the night of the attempted coup, and no one would have known it was you."

"I thought about it." Em poured more bourbon into his glass. "*El Patrón* would have been pissed."

"And Cat would have been heartbroken."

Em sent me a disgusted look. The night of the attempted coup in Kansas City, the cartel learned that Dario Luciano was a man of his word. That didn't mean that Em was any more thrilled that he was also his brother-in-law.

"I'll go with you," Em said before downing the bourbon. "I'm headed to bed. Morning is coming early."

Staring up at the star-filled sky, I thought about what Em said. I needed to start looking for a place of my own. One thought led to another as I began thinking about Mia Luciano. I'd revisited the vision of her at Cat's wedding a hundred times since making the marriage deal with her brother. I saw her in the long silver dress that accentuated her tits. Her slender shoulders and suntanned skin. She stood out the way Jasmine stood out. Their hair. While Jasmine's was fiery red, Mia's was paler than most, a light brown with hues of caramel and even lighter strands of blond. The night of the wedding she had it all twisted in some fancy hairdo. I also remembered the way it looked while she was lying by the pool, piled on her head with rogue strands dropping in curls around her face.

Her pouty lips.

Her hazel stare.

Her stinging slap.

I sighed.

There was part of me who knew I wanted Mia the first time I saw her. I was thinking about a quick fuck, not a lifetime commitment. No matter my goal, it was no secret she didn't share that attraction—which was not what I was used to. Getting women to spread their legs was not usually a problem. And once they did, they were guaranteed to come back for more.

Mia's reaction was different. That's probably why it stood out.

The morning at the pool, the Mafia princess scanned *Padre*, Reinaldo, and me like she'd stepped on better things. When I learned she was married to that asshole Rocco, I felt sorry for her. She was supposed to be a princess, and if I was going to go with fairy-tale analogies, she'd ended up with a frog.

The night Dario took Rocco's life, many of us shared the satisfaction of watching him suffer. It had been Dario to do the honors of killing the rat. I remembered thinking—after Dario and Dante's interrogation as Rocco bled out in that basement—now it's your turn, motherfucker.

Bleed.

CHAPTER
FOUR

Mia

Mother put as much effort into the sham of an engagement party as she had for Dario's wedding. It was the news of the baby. No matter how she felt about the cartel entering her home, she would play the gracious host to keep Catalina happy. Mom wanted to be involved in the baby's life. If she had to grovel and cater to the cartel to do it, then so be it.

I didn't feel the same.

Not about the baby. I'd make a kick-ass aunt. I didn't feel the same about catering to the cartel.

When the evening of my engagement drew near, I was contemplating any and all possible means for disruption. Maybe if I caused enough of a scene, Aléjandro would change his mind and decide I wasn't worth the trouble.

The roadblock to my plan was being held in place by both my mother and brother. After allowing me to verbalize my displeasure, Dario made it clear that I would proceed with his plans, reminding me of my duty to the famiglia. He even allowed Mother and me to travel into the city, a scandalous thing to do while in mourning, to shop for a nonblack dress for tonight's dinner.

Now, wearing the sage-green Mac Duggal sheath dress with the beaded floral appliqué, I stood before the mirror in my bedroom. It hadn't gone unnoticed by Mom that this dress was a size larger than what I'd worn during Dario's wedding. Despite having all the exercise machines that money could buy in the workout room on the lower level, I'd let my solitude, mixed with freedom of choice, change both my eating and exercise routine. The mountains weren't a conducive place to hike in below-freezing temperatures with snow and sleet falling.

Now that spring had arrived in the Ozarks, I knew my schedule should change. Truth was, I hoped the extra pounds and curves would be another reason why Aléjandro may change his mind.

Nevertheless, my plan for disobedience didn't come in the form of my attire. I was ecstatic to not be wearing black.

The thigh-high nylons added shape and a silky appearance to my legs. The dress had an open seam in the back that would show the tops of my hose. I'd also opted for a pair of Louboutin blush pointed-toe pumps with a four-inch heel. Rocco didn't want me wearing too high a heel due to his height. If my memory served me well, even with the added heels, I wouldn't come close to Aléjandro's height. My hair was pulled back on the sides and curled to hang down my back.

As I was about to leave the bedroom, I remembered my wedding rings.

Why am I still wearing them?

I wasn't sure of the answer. Habit maybe. I sure as hell wasn't still wearing them out of some sentimental attachment. Looking down at the set, I wondered what I would do with them. Maybe I could pawn them. It could be Rocco's final gift, some cash in my pocket that didn't come from the famiglia or cartel.

Sliding the pair of rings off the fourth finger of my left hand, I stared at the setting. I always assumed that Rocco's mother had a hand in choosing the rings. It seemed like the only engagement ring I'd ever have a say in would be that of a son's if children were in my future.

Leaving the rings on my dresser, I headed toward the staircase. Dante, Dario, and Catalina were already present. Not only had I heard their arrival, but Catalina's bodyguard was again stationed near the front door. As I turned the corner into the front parlor, I chose to try my plan.

Four sets of eyes turned my way.

Dario and Dante were holding crystal tumblers with bourbon, and Mom had a glass of prosecco. Catalina's hands were empty.

Unlike the night of Dario's announcement, tonight I was greeted with approving expressions. If I could surmise my stoic brother's millisecond of expression, he was even relieved I'd not chosen my attire as a means of rebellion.

"Mia," Dante said, coming toward me and kissing my cheek. His infectious smile curled as his dark eyes shone. "I'm pleased to be the one brother you don't hate."

My gaze quickly went to Dario and back to Dante. "Don't be so sure. I doubt you went to the mat for me on this."

"Oh, but I did." He motioned toward Catalina. "She had to pull us apart. We were wrestling in the penthouse living room. It was awful."

Catalina's smile and the slight shake of her head told me what I already knew—Dante was full of shit. I rarely thought about the fact that he was also a stone-cold killer like Dario. Their personalities couldn't be further from one another.

"I tell you what," I said, looking at Dante. "If you unsheathe one of the knives you're currently wearing and take Aléjandro out, I might decide not to hate you."

"I'm sure she's joking," Dario said.

"Don't be so confident." I looked around for the bottle of prosecco.

"I had Rosa take it away," Dario said with a hint of a smile. "You will be on your best behavior."

"Oh hell no. I'm here, I'm dressed, and I'm not armed. Take your wins, brother." I raised my voice. "Rosa?"

Dario came closer, towering over me. "Mia, as your capo, I'm warning you."

"You think you can threaten me? With what, Dario? Death? I'll take that over the life sentence you're giving me."

The muscles in the side of his face pulled tight as he clenched his jaw.

"Mia, may we go for a walk?" Catalina asked.

I hid my relief. This had been my plan. I believed if Catalina sensed Dario was becoming angry, she'd step in to try to help. Now I had to assess if she would actually help. "I'm headed to the kitchen to find Rosa."

Catalina came toward me. "I'll go with you." She shot Dario one last glance as we walked from the parlor. She waved off her bodyguard, Armando, as our high heels clicked on the shiny marble floor. Mother had the house staff working around the clock to make a positive impression on the cartel.

I looked toward my sister-in-law. In the two weeks

since their last visit, she might have grown a small baby bump. That didn't mean she didn't look as lovely as always.

"I've known Aléjandro for most of my life."

Taking a breath, I stopped walking. We were out of earshot of the others yet not near the kitchen. "Catalina, I don't want this. I don't like him." Could I say I hated him? Not yet, but I was confident I would in time.

"You only barely met him."

"Did you hear about the night of the wedding, after you and Dario went upstairs?"

She nodded. "Aléjandro and Dante got into a disagreement."

"Do you know why?"

"No."

"I came across Aléjandro with Jasmine in one of the servants' hallways. I was trying to avoid people on my way upstairs."

Catalina's eyes were wide.

"I sent Jasmine away. Dante and Rocco found Aléjandro and me alone." I quickly added, "Nothing had happened except tense words. And...oh, yeah, I slapped him."

Catalina's cheeks rose in a smile. "I'm sure he deserved it."

I looked at my sister-in-law pleadingly. "Is there any way for you to talk to Dario? He won't listen to reason."

Her lips came together. "This wasn't a hasty decision. Dario and Patrón have been in talks for months."

"But Aléjandro would rather marry Jasmine."

"That's not true," she replied. "Aléjandro knew that bringing Jasmine to the wedding would upset Dario." She shrugged. "That's just who he is. He pushes boundaries, ignores rules, all in an effort to find others' limits."

"And you think I should marry him?"

"I married a man who does the same thing. If you haven't noticed, Dario has done his share of rule breaking."

I shook my head. "Now he makes the rules."

"And so will Aléjandro one day. The cartel is strong, especially with this alliance. I admit that Aléjandro and I haven't always seen eye to eye, but that doesn't mean he isn't a good soldier and a force for the cartel and now the famiglia. My brother likes him, and I trust his opinion."

"You won't help me."

"I'm trying to help you," she said. "You never deserved to be Rocco's wife. I didn't know him well, but he always gave me a bad feeling."

She wasn't wrong. Rocco detested the alliance and thus her.

"And," she went on a bit more sheepishly, "Dario shared with me what you said about your wedding night."

I looked down.

Inhaling, I looked back up and squared my shoulders. "I don't want your or anyone's sympathy or pity."

"I'm not giving you either. I'm giving you respect, Mia. You survived a horrible marriage with a man who never deserved to marry the capo's daughter. Aléjandro is a lot of things." She smiled. "Arrogant comes to mind."

That made me smile.

"He is also first in line to assume control over the Roríguez cartel. He never wanted to marry Jasmine. Neither Dario nor Jorge would allow that anyway." When I started to talk, she went on. "Because as much as Dario loves Jasmine, and I do too, she isn't part of the famiglia. Jorge didn't see her as worthy for his son. He saw you as worthy."

"Oh God. You're not going to help me stop this."

Catalina shook her head.

"Then at least help me find the wine."

Catalina hooked her arm with mine. "I can do that."

"Even though your husband told me not to drink?"

"I think you know what's expected of you tonight. I see nothing wrong with a glass of wine to take the edge off. You can even have one for me." She smiled. "Maybe you'll even decide this marriage won't be too bad."

"Don't get your hopes up."

A few minutes later, Catalina and I returned to the

parlor. I had my full glass of wine. Out of respect for my capo, I left the bottle in the kitchen. "Cheers," I said as we entered.

Dario didn't say a word about my wine. Instead, he looked down at his phone and announced that two cars of the cartel have passed the front gate.

"Dario?" It was my last plea.

His face was emotionless. "Mia, I know you'll make the famiglia proud tonight and throughout your marriage."

I sucked in a breath. "Is it easier to deal with the whores at Emerald Club or to make your sister into a whore?"

"Mia," Mom chastised. "You're an adult. Start acting like one."

"And spread my legs?"

"You're not a whore," Dario said. He'd said the same thing the night he gave me the news. "And without question, you're more trouble than all the whores at the club."

I'd take the small victories where I could.

I lifted my glass to my lips, hiding my smile.

"Jorge," Dario went on, "wasn't able to make it tonight. He and his wife will be at the wedding. Catalina's parents and brother have accompanied Aléjandro and his brother Reinaldo."

By the smile on Catalina's face, she was already aware of her parents' arrival.

"Do they know about the baby?" Mom asked.

"My parents do," Catalina said. "Em doesn't nor do the Roríguezes."

"That's the answer," I volunteered. "Let's forget the engagement part of this evening and spend our time celebrating my new nephew or niece."

"Tonight is about you," Catalina said.

On that note, I finished the rest of my wine.

Mother went to the front doors, ready to greet our guests. While Dario and Catalina went with her, I stayed back in the parlor, regretting that I didn't bring the wine bottle with me from the kitchen.

"Dario wouldn't have agreed to this," Dante said, "if he didn't know you could handle Aléjandro."

"I don't hate you."

Dante wrapped his arm around my shoulders and squeezed. "I'm too personable to hate."

I gave my brother a sideways grin. "I'm certain the enemies you interrogate feel otherwise."

Dante shrugged. "Can't win 'em all." He reached for my shoulders and turned us face-to-face. "You look very pretty. It's nice to see you not wearing black."

"Thank you."

"Six months ago, I would have gone to the mat with Dario on this."

"But not now?" I asked.

Dante shook his head. "Maybe it's Catalina. I don't know. I just know that deep down, we aren't that different. When I first met Aléjandro at Dario's wedding, I was ready to take him down a few pegs. I did." Dante flashed his grin. "Time has passed, and he's proven himself in our alliance. I believe if Catalina can melt the heart of a man like Dario, there is probably hope for all of us."

"When are you signing up to marry one of the cartel women?"

He opened his eyes wide. "Single for life."

"Or until Dario decides otherwise?"

Dante released my shoulders as we both turned at the sound of voices. I sucked in a breath at the sight of the man in the foyer. I'd picked him out of the crowd during Dario's wedding. And tonight he was here to choose me.

First, Dario shook hands with Andrés Ruiz, Catalina's father, and then with Aléjandro, who was only slightly shorter than my brother. I tried to look at Aléjandro without my prior prejudices. There was no denying he was a handsome man. He carried himself in a way that said he had confidence. His complexion was the color of the desert sand, the same as his brother and lighter than his father. Probably it was more than his looks although he was kind on the eyes. Tonight, he wore black pants covering his long legs, coupled with a white button-down shirt. No tie or suitcoat like Dario was wearing. His shirt was crisp and bright, contrasting his tawny skin. His hair was dark and wavy, and his brown eyes were round as his gaze found mine. His self-assuredness no doubt had to do with what Dante and Catalina said about him being a good soldier for the cartel.

I knew from experience, confident made men had an air about them.

As if sensing our awkward stare-down, Dario patted Aléjandro on the shoulder and spoke to him. They both smiled as they turned and came my direction. Aléjandro's gaze scanned me from head to toe in a way that made my stomach turn—as if he had won. Consolation prize or not, I was being handed to him on a silver platter.

Dario made the formal introductions, "Let me introduce my sister, Mia Luciano."

It was curious that in Dario's mind, I'd already given up my last name of Moretti.

"Mia."

My name rolled off Aléjandro's tongue with a hint of his accent as I caught a whiff of his sandalwood cologne, warm and woodsy with a hint of leather. I offered him my hand. Instead of shaking it, he turned it over in his grasp, bowed at the waist, and lightly brushed his lips over my knuckles.

The electricity surging through my circulation was inappropriately startling. While my mind was convinced that this marriage would never work, my body was a traitor to his obvious adoration.

How long had it been since Rocco had shown me even a fraction of this attention?

"Aléjandro," I said, retrieving my hand. "It's nice to formally meet you."

A lopsided smile grew. "Formally, yes. I remember meeting you here. The first time was by the pool. No?"

Warmth came to my cheeks at the memory. "And again at the wedding and afterward."

"*Qué demonios?*"

We all turned to Catalina's brother's remark, seconds before he and Catalina embraced.

"Any idea?" Aléjandro asked.

"I'd guess that she just told him she's expecting a baby."

Aléjandro's eyebrows shot upward. "They didn't waste time."

"Anything to cement the alliance."

His deep voice lowered an octave. "Without the alliance, I never would have seen your beauty at the pool or felt your flames after the wedding. For that, I'm thankful. Our future is about more than the alliance."

Our future.

My stomach twisted.

"*Voy a ser un tío.*" Emiliano announced, proclaiming he was about to be an uncle and saving me from thinking about the future.

"Dinner will be in a half hour," Mom said to everyone. "Why don't we go back to the living room and let Aléjandro and Mia spend some time together?"

When Rocco proposed, both our fathers were

present. It was deemed inappropriate for the two of us to be unsupervised. Ten years and the loss of my virginity created different guidelines as the room around us emptied, Dario closed the French doors, and we were left alone.

Dario wouldn't help me.

Catalina wouldn't help me.

That left one person.

As Aléjandro pulled a velvet box from his pocket, I blurted out the truth. "I don't want to marry you."

He took a step back, his grin still in place as he tilted his head. "I wasn't expecting you to say the quiet part out loud."

"Shouldn't we be honest with one another?"

"*Sí.*"

I let out a breath. "It's nothing against you."

Aléjandro scoffed. "That's code for it is."

I shook my head. He was right. I didn't want to marry him. I also didn't want to marry—period. "It's that I've been married since I was eighteen."

"To a prick."

My neck straightened. "You can't say that."

"Then you should. I only had the displeasure of meeting him a few times. I doubt more interaction would have changed my mind. The rat was a prick."

I nodded. "You're right. Can you see now why I don't want to be married again?"

"Yet, your brother—"

"My brother and your father want to build on the

alliance. You didn't want to marry me. You were at the wedding with Jasmine."

"Had I known killing your husband was an option, I would have done that in order to take you to the wedding."

I couldn't come up with a response.

Aléjandro reached for my hand. "Mia, I'm not Moretti. The capo will marry you to someone. I want that someone to be me."

My speechlessness continued as Aléjandro fell to one knee and opened the velvet box, revealing a solitaire diamond ring that was easily twice the size of the engagement ring upstairs.

His large brown eyes stared up at me. "I will make you a promise. I promise if you say yes, you won't regret being my wife."

Tears prickled the back of my eyes. "You're asking me even after what I said?"

He nodded. "The only answer that matters is yours, not your brother's nor *mi padre's*."

My hands began to tremble. "I regretted my first marriage from the moment he put the ring on my finger."

Aléjandro stayed poised on one knee.

"I'm not a virgin."

He laughed. "Neither am I. And if you were, your first husband would have been more than a prick. He would have been insane." He lifted the ring from the box. "Will you wear this?"

I was desperate to make him understand. "I don't like sex."

Aléjandro's eyebrows went up. "Because you were with the wrong man."

Arrogant asshole. "Do you have an answer for everything?"

He nodded. "Give me the rest of our lives to prove that to you."

I wiped a rogue tear from my cheek. "Till death do us part?"

"I'm not planning on dying anytime soon."

Finally, I nodded. "I'll wear the ring as long as you understand I don't want this. I'm being forced to agree."

Sliding the ring over my knuckle, Aléjandro smiled. "I've wanted you since the night of the wedding. That desire is enough for both of us."

He stood, capturing my cheeks between his large palms and bringing his lips down on mine.

Unnerved by his advance, I should have backed away. I should have slapped him as I did months ago. This never would have happened with my first engagement. A woman raised in my world was supposed to have her first kiss during her wedding, not at the engagement. Those thoughts came and evaporated as I lingered in the fruity-sweet and earthy taste of Aléjandro.

His confidence caught me off guard. There was no hesitation, his approach was no doubt well practiced on many women, and yet my hands slid to the front of his shirt, feeling the beat of his heart, and my body leaned into him. Nerve endings that I was sure had dried up and died were resurrected. My flesh tingled as I pressed against his hard, muscular body, feeling his solid torso and even his weapon beneath his shirt. His hands didn't move from my cheeks, and I found myself wishing they would.

My nipples grew hard as I imagined what it would feel like to have his strong hands on my body, to move lower, and wander over my skin.

I stifled a moan as his tongue slid past mine, bringing more sweet flavors. By the time our kiss ended, I was uncomfortably aware of the dampness between my legs.

Aléjandro grinned. "You won't regret this."

I was pretty sure I already did.

CHAPTER

FIVE

Giorgia stood back and smiled. "You're a beautiful bride...again."

We were in the bedroom we'd been assigned in the Ruiz home. While the house wasn't as large as Mom's place, it was beautiful in its own right: Spanish architecture and as Dario had promised, beautifully situated on a cliff overlooking the Pacific Ocean.

I turned to the full-length mirror. My cream-colored lace dress was formfitting with a hem that came to above my ankles. My hair was styled in an updo. I wore rhinestone-studded four-inch-heeled sandals and beneath my dress was a lace bra and panties. "At least Aléjandro won't be cutting this off of me." My attempt at levity wasn't appreciated by my cousin.

"I'm sorry you have to do this."

Bending my knees, I sank onto the side of the bed. "I think I've come to terms with it." I had yet to admit the way Aléjandro's kiss set my body ablaze. "Dario isn't going to let me change my mind. If he wouldn't let me change my mind last month, the day of the wedding is a definite no."

Giorgia sat at my side and covered my hand with hers. "You told him you don't like sex."

I nodded.

"I'm glad you were honest with him." She widened her eyes. "And he took it well. Think what Rocco would have said."

I shook my head. "Rocco would have been furious because it was sex with him I hated."

"Do you think Aléjandro's going to expect it anyway?"

"My world of experience is Rocco. With that as my guide, I'd say yes, he'll expect it."

"It could be better with him," she encouraged. "I mean, he seems fitter than Rocco."

The memory of Aléjandro's solid body beneath his shirt the night he proposed warmed my circulation. I sighed. "I feel like I'm going to be comparing the two for the rest of my life."

"That's normal," she said. "I mean, it seems normal."

Standing, I let my hands fall, slapping my thighs. "At least I knew Rocco when we married. I'd known him for as long as I can remember. I don't know much of anything about Aléjandro."

"Maybe that's better," Giorgia said. "You two can learn about one another. He proposed. That's a point for him."

"It is. Rocco never really asked me. The deal was done."

"Aléjandro knows he's not marrying a scared virgin."

My stomach twisted. "No, he's marrying a terrified nonvirgin." Walking to the windows that overlooked the ocean side of their house, I glanced down at the terrace, seeing the guests taking their seats. If only I could concentrate on the scene below and block out how awful sex had become. I'd come to dread it. Not only was I never sure when Rocco would demand it, but I had long since stopped being attracted to him, making the act itself painful even when he wasn't in an abusive mood.

Something caught my eye. "Oh my God, there is a mariachi band down there."

Giorgia stood and walked to the window. "Oh, if only Uncle Vincent could see this." Her navy-blue dress was a darker version of mine. Dario had said the wedding would be small. Even so, he agreed to let Giorgia stand up with me. I'd been told Reinaldo would stand with Aléjandro. Giorgia was the closest person I had to a sister. I supposed I could have requested Catalina, but we only knew one another slightly better than I knew my future husband.

"I should have asked Catalina more about a traditional Mexican ceremony." My stomach twisted. "It can't be that different, can it?"

Giorgia's eyes were big. "I don't know. I will say, your future father-in-law is a little scary."

Jorge Roríguez.

El Patrón.

Drug lord.

"Every man here is, and I don't mean only on the cartel side. At least I'm not as concerned about a famiglia-slash-cartel war as I was at Dario's wedding."

The bedroom door opened, and Mom entered. She looked radiant in a dark blue dress. Apparently, a daughter's wedding was an acceptable excuse for forgoing black attire. Her exemption was on a time clock: black was only spared for last night and today. Mom was enjoying her reprieve. In some ways she looked younger and happier as a widow than she ever had married to my father.

"Are you ready?" Mom asked, before stopping, scanning me from my head to my toes, and smiling. "You're beautiful, Mia. Aléjandro is a lucky man." She came closer and wrapped her arms around me. "I'm going to miss having you at home."

"I'm going to miss you, too," I said honestly. As much as I didn't want to move to the mountains after Rocco's death, sharing our mourning with one another was comforting. I'd originally moved away when I was young and starry-eyed. Coming back as a woman put Mom's and my relationship into new perspective.

I looked at my cousin. "I'm going to miss Kansas City." It wasn't enough that I'd agreed to marry a stranger; I also had to leave the only place I'd ever known, a place with all my friends and family.

Mom pulled back, straightening her shoulders. "Dario is ready."

Of course, my brother was walking me down the aisle—what aisle there was on the Ruiz terrace. "I was thinking," I said, feigning excitement. "I made six thousand dollars by selling my old wedding rings. Maybe instead of walking down the aisle, I could call a cab and head to the airport."

Mom's lips pursed. "Mia, stop that."

I shrugged. "It was a plan."

"Aléjandro would hunt you down," Giorgia said.

"Not because he loves me. If I ran, his pride would be hurt, and men can't stand for that to happen."

"There is more to marriage than love," Mom replied. "You knew that the first time."

"Don't remind me."

Mom reached for Giorgia's hand. "Come on. The wedding is about to start." She opened the door.

My brother stood there, filling the doorframe, wearing a dark blue suit similar to the ones worn by the other men in the wedding party. After Mom and

Giorgia walked past him, he smiled. "You're lovely, Mia."

"Compliments won't make me stop hating you."

He shrugged his shoulder. "I'm only saying the truth. You are beautiful." He bent his left arm at his side. "Shall we go downstairs?"

I had a nasty retort on the tip of my tongue, but even I realized it was too late to run and baiting our famiglia's capo wasn't in my best interest. Instead, I stepped closer to my brother and placed my hand in the crook of his arm.

"Thank you for not making another scene," he said. "I hope you know I want you to be happy."

I pressed my lips together.

"I should have killed Rocco a long time ago."

"Stop before you make me cry with all this sweet talk."

Dario scoffed, cutting a bit of the tension. "I don't know if you were expecting it, but there is a mariachi band playing for the ceremony."

"I wasn't expecting it. Do you know any other traditions I might have tried to learn before now?"

Dario shook his head. "Catalina's and my wedding was more what I'm used to." He lowered his voice. "I think it is good that we kept this small."

Inhaling, I walked at Dario's side through the hallway, down the staircase, and through the house toward the back terrace. This was a lovely home, but it wasn't where Aléjandro and I were to live. All I'd been told was he recently purchased an oceanfront home. Dario already had many of my things shipped.

As we approached the oceanside terrace, I saw the rows of chairs filled with people. A small wedding meant there were less than fifty guests, a fraction of the number of people who attended Dario and Catalina's wedding. Nevertheless, Aléjandro was the heir to the Roríguez cartel, and I was the only daughter of Vincent Luciano. This union warranted the attendance of some top brass in both organizations.

By the time we made it to the glass doors, Giorgia, the priest, Aléjandro, and Reinaldo were all standing in front of a flower-covered arch. Beyond the terrace, an azure blue sky met with the aqua hue of the ocean. The faint scent of sea filled my senses as the sun shone down, and music came from the band to the side of the terrace.

This wasn't the grand production of my first wedding, but it was by no means a lesser substitute. As Dario and I stepped out, the sun kissed my cheeks as the ocean breeze tingled my skin.

My gaze met Aléjandro's. With his hands clasped behind him, his wide shoulders filled out his custom suit coat, creating a V with his trim torso. A knowing arrogance shone in his eyes combined with the victory of his win as he too scanned me as I'd done him, and his wavy black hair blew gently in the soft wind.

"Who gives this woman...?"

My body stiffened as Dario replied, "I do."

His answer was painfully accurate. I wouldn't be standing here in a home owned by a top lieutenant of the Roríguez cartel if it wasn't for my brother. However, *give* was probably not the right word.

Sell.

Bargain.

Negotiate.

The priest wouldn't use those words, but as Dario placed my hand in Aléjandro's, I heard the words in my head. They were words that confirmed my sentiments from over ten years ago, that of being no more than a commodity.

That was what I was—a product to be bought and sold.

The Morettis bought me with the hopes of joining their family with my father's. By this time Rocco and I were to have a house full of children sharing our DNA. With Rocco's death, Dario bought me back, returning me into our family fold. And now here I was being sold again, this time to the heir to the Roríguez cartel.

Defining the transaction in my head chilled my flesh. I opened my eyes as the warmth of Aléjandro's fingers encased mine. Without trepidation, but not without regret, I looked up at the man who was about to own me. As much as I wanted my marriage to work, I couldn't see past my loathing for Aléjandro and all he represented.

My freedom only lasted six months.

His grasp of my hand was the completion of the deal.

The priest spoke, "Mia Luciano Moretti and Aléjandro Roríguez, have you come here to enter into marriage without coercion, freely and whole-heartedly?"

It was too late to answer truthfully.

Our only escape from this marriage would be the one that had saved me from my first.

Death.

Aléjandro waited for me to respond.

As our wedding progressed, it seemed the obedient Italian girl wasn't fully gone. At every turn, I responded appropriately, even reciting our vows as instructed. My hand was steady as Aléjandro slid the wedding band onto my finger. And I didn't tremble as I slid the white gold band onto his. In some ways I felt detached from the ceremony itself, as if I were watching, not participating.

Perhaps I was back upstairs, peering through the window. It wasn't me who was committing until death to a man she didn't know and was pretty sure she didn't like. No, I was safe upon the second floor watching someone else.

From that view, it was a beautiful wedding.

My out-of-body experience ended when, after our vows and the exchange of rings, the priest instructed us to kneel. It was then that Reinaldo handed the priest a long rosary, resembling a lasso. I stiffened as the beads were wound over and around us in a figure eight, and the priest again began to pray.

Aléjandro no doubt sensed my unease. A squeeze of his hand and a sly smile reassured me that this was a normal part of the wedding.

Tying us in front of the guests?

If this was normal, I'd never seen it before.

The priest lifted his hand and explained, "The lasso is a symbol of Aléjandro and Mia's mutual support for each other in carrying out their duties and responsibilities as a couple."

At the sound of the priest's words, I looked up at Aléjandro.

Mutual support.

Me for him.

Him for me.

It was as foreign to me as the lasso itself.

Once we stood, the priest removed the lasso.

The next was the presentation of wedding coins—apparently, another tradition I'd never experienced. I stood in silence as the priest blessed thirteen coins. Next, he handed the ornate box of coins to Aléjandro, who presented them to me.

"The coins," the priest said, "remind Aléjandro and Mia that their treasure is now one, and they will share in all that they have together. At the same time, it reminds them to help those who have less than they do."

A lump formed in my throat. I had a hard time

believing the heir to a drug cartel was also philanthropic. Everything was outside my sphere of
knowledge. Catalina's sister said our traditions were
savage. I was beginning to see the difference.

Lastly, Aléjandro was given permission to kiss his
bride. When we turned to one another, his lips curled
in a knowing smile. This wasn't our first kiss. His
strong lips came to mine, lingering a bit longer than
expected, and sending a bolt of energy to my core.

Thankfully, with the lack of formality, we didn't
have a receiving line following the ceremony. There
would be plenty of time for us to interact with the
guests during the reception. Nevertheless, we were
instructed to wait for our parents. My mother was the
first one to greet us as husband and wife. She'd truly
perfected her ability to sound sincere, despite my
natural doubt that she wasn't. Mom's only motivation
was staying in Dario's good graces.

Josefina Roríguez was stunning with her dark eyes
glistening with tears as she hugged me. I had no way
to assess her sincerity as she welcomed me as her new
daughter. While her accent made her more difficult to
understand, I believed the tears in her eyes as she
called me *mi hija*. If nothing else, the scene made
Aléjandro happy. Jorge Roríguez was next. I recalled
seeing him for the first time at my mother's pool. As
opposed to his gruff persona I witnessed on that day,
today he was boisterously joyous, wrapping me in
another hug.

After they moved away, Aléjandro took my hand and led me into the house. My pulse quickened as he separated us from our guests.

"Where are we going?"

"With as hot as you look, I don't think the Ruizes will mind if we use the master bedroom suite to consummate our marriage."

"What?" I asked, stopping my steps as a wave of panic flooded my system.

CHAPTER
SIX

"You're not serious," I said, mortified.

Aléjandro's hand gently cupped my cheek. "You look as if you're about to faint."

"I wasn't. I was doing okay, but..." I looked around.

"Breathe, Mia. I was joking. My family, the cartel, they can be overwhelming. It seemed that no one prepared you for the marriage-unity lasso."

That was what it was called.

Haven't they ever heard of a unity candle?

I shook my head. "No one mentioned it or the coins." My expression softened. "I think they were meaningful."

"I'm glad. I would have told you. It didn't occur to me that you wouldn't know what was happening." Aléjandro laughed. "I thought we'd sneak away to get a break. I imagine it's a bit overwhelming. After the

71

unfamiliar wedding traditions, my father's hugs can be crushing."

I tilted my head. "I've grown up and lived in the Italian Mafia. Our families will need to compete for which is the most overwhelming."

His gaze focused on my lips. "I want to kiss you. Not like we did out there. Like we did the night of our engagement...like I wanted to after Cat's wedding."

My mouth felt suddenly dry.

I enjoyed the kiss on the night of our engagement, but I didn't want Aléjandro to get the wrong idea. I'd made up my mind. Kissing was as far as I was going in this marriage. I lifted my hand to his chest. "We can kiss, but that's all we're going to do." I shook my head. "I don't know you well enough—"

The brown of his orbs darkened. "You're my wife. You're mine."

I nodded. "I am."

"You would refuse me what is mine?"

Refuse him access to my body.

My body was mine. For too long I'd let someone else rule it.

Swallowing, I looked into his eyes. "Rocco raped me the night of our wedding."

Aléjandro's jaw clenched, black swirled within his dark orbs, and his nostrils flared. "He deserved to die. That said, we're married. I won't spend the rest of my life living under his shadow."

"Then show me you're different."

There seemed to be a war raging in my new husband's gaze. Finally, his eyes again focused on my lips. "I still want that kiss."

As I'd done the night of our engagement, I leaned into him as our lips met. The woodsy scent of his cologne tingled my nose while the taste of tequila captured my tastebuds. This time, his hands didn't stay on my cheeks, but wandered down my back, wrapping me in his strong arms and pulling me closer. Through his suit coat, I again felt the hardness of a weapon.

"Hey, you two."

We turned to Emiliano, Catalina's brother.

"People are starting to speculate about where you went."

Warmth filled my cheeks.

Aléjandro ran his thumb over my lips and winked. "Let them wonder. Let them think I'm ravishing my wife."

I looked up and met his stare. "Are you mad at me?"

"Not on our wedding day."

"And you're okay with what I said?"

"I don't consider this conversation complete. I have an entire reception to woo my wife. Don't underestimate my abilities in this department."

Catalina was right. Aléjandro was arrogant.

He was also smiling even after my bombshell.

Just maybe it was a start.

With my hand in his, we made our way down one level to the reception on the pool deck. The guests clapped when we appeared. Normal pool furniture was gone, replaced with a rectangular table for the four members of the wedding party and multiple round tables for the guests.

As at Dario and Catalina's wedding, we were met with periodic cheers for kisses from both families.

"*Bacio. Bacio.*"

"*Beso. Beso.*"

Our kisses came easier with each try.

Dario gave the first toast in place of our father. Jorge Roríguez also gave a toast, followed by a few words from Reinaldo and Giorgia. By the time the priest asked for the blessing for our meal, I'd made peace with the reality that the man at my side was my husband.

Legally, we were bound.

I just hoped he realized that was as far as this relationship would go. There wasn't time to worry; once the food was served, it kept coming and coming.

There were delicious spicy meat stews, savory tamales, chiles rellenos, chiles en nogada, and seafood stews. There was also seasoned rice, stewed tomatoes, salsa, refried beans, and corn and flour tortillas. I was relatively certain I wouldn't need to worry about my wedding night; soon, I'd fall into a food-induced coma.

Through course after course, I kept thinking about my cousin's comment regarding my father. I couldn't imagine him participating in the choice of menu, much less the band and drinks that seemed to be flowing freely.

When it came time to dance, Aléjandro offered me his hand and escorted me to the makeshift dance floor near the deep end of the pool. The sun was nearing the horizon, casting orange and red beams across the sparkling ocean.

Wrapping his arm around my waist, Aléjandro pulled me close as the band began a slow and faintly familiar waltz. I was pleasantly surprised by my new husband's dancing ability. Rocco mostly stood and swayed. I found myself smiling as Aléjandro glided me over the pavers.

"Your smile is stunning," he said softly in his deep voice.

"I don't think I've ever danced like this."

His smile grew as he took a step back and lifted my arm, causing me to pirouette, before pulling me back against his solid chest. My giggles floated away with the romantic music and setting sun.

He leaned closer, whispering in my ear, "I told you; your choice of partner makes all the difference."

Pressing my lips together, I tried to scowl, but I suspected that the surprise and merriment in my eyes couldn't be hidden. I wasn't fooling him or myself. Truthfully, I was shocked that I was having fun. The night went on with the usual dances. After Aléjandro, Jorge was the next to ask me to the floor. Then I danced with Dario followed by Dante. By the time I'd danced with many in Aléjandro's family, I decided the four-inch heels were a poor choice of shoe.

Unlike the formality of Dario and Catalina's wedding, this celebration was festive. The only people not seeming to have a good time were my uncles. While I hadn't been told, I could guess that their presence was at the order of their capo. Moving from Father to Dario was a more difficult transition for those of Father's generation.

I also suspected that when it came to the cartel, the older generation harbored the same prejudices my father would have. As my uncles Salvatore and Carmine stood near one of the bars talking under their breath, my aunts Aurora and Giulia sat with Mom. At least the women were smiling.

Everyone seemed excited to talk to Catalina. Her growing midsection was more evidence of our working alliance.

"Who are those people?" I asked Aléjandro when we had a rare chance to sit and rest.

He followed my line of sight. "Members of the Ruiz family. I don't know much more. Why?"

"The girl looks as if she could cry at any moment."

Aléjandro looked around and waved to Emiliano, Catalina's brother. He came our direction.

"Mia," Emiliano said with a nod. "Congratulations. Welcome to the family."

That would be the greater cartel family. The Roríguezes and Ruizes weren't actually related—to my knowledge. Unless Dario marrying a Ruiz and my marrying a Roríguez...it was getting complicated.

"Your family knows how to throw a party," I said with a smile.

"*Qué pasa* with the couple over there?" Aléjandro asked, getting right to the subject of my question. "Did they miss the part on the invitation that this was to be a celebration? They don't seem to be having a good time."

Emiliano sighed. "That's my Uncle Gerardo and his new wife, Liliana. Our aunt passed away about a year ago."

Another arranged marriage.

"She isn't happy," I said, stating the obvious.

Emiliano didn't try to sugarcoat it. "She's not. See the girl next to her?"

I nodded.

"She's our cousin Sofia. Liliana, our new aunt, and Sofia have been best friends most of their lives."

The food in my stomach churned. "And Liliana married your uncle? She's now her best friend's step-mother? Why would they make her marry someone so much older?"

"Uncle Gerardo is important to the cartel. He needed a wife."

I turned to Aléjandro. "Did you approve of their marriage?"

He shook his head. "That would be *mi padre.*"

"She's a child."

"She's eighteen," Emiliano replied. "Gerardo is a lieutenant who has proven his worth. He got who he asked for."

Maybe he should have considered Liliana's or his daughter's needs in the process.

Emiliano walked away.

Aléjandro reached for my hand. "It's the way it is in my world."

"Mine too," I said, looking up at my husband's handsome features, his prominent brow, high cheekbones, and full lips. Was I imagining it or did Aléjandro appear as if he actually cared? "It still isn't right. The woman should have some say."

"You had your say."

I scoffed. I had told anyone who would listen that I didn't want this marriage. "I did, but no one listened to me."

Aléjandro lifted the hand he was holding to his lips. "I'm not defending the ways of our worlds, but at the same time, I'm happy that those rules brought you to me."

Watching Liliana affected me deeply. I'd been her but had hidden the reality from others, refusing to let anyone see my private pain. Liliana couldn't even do that. Was her pain so acute that even at a wedding, she couldn't bring herself out of its depths? I wanted to help her, to go to her and tell her that I understood. No, I wanted to do more than that. I wanted to drag her away from the man at her side, the one who had essentially secured a young wife for his own pleasure, not for hers. I turned to my new husband. "One day, will it be you who makes the decisions about marriages in the cartel?"

Aléjandro nodded.

"I hope you can see things differently when that time comes."

As he turned toward Gerardo and Liliana, his smile dimmed. "Up until now, my preparation for taking *mi padre's* place has concentrated on business." He again lifted my hand to his lips. "I never saw the need for a wife."

His candidness surprised me.

He went on, "But in only a few hours, you're showing me things that I never took the time to see or consider." His dark orbs settled on me. "There's wisdom to the idea that it takes a wife to complete a man." He reached for his glass of tequila and drank what remained before standing. "More dancing?"

"My feet," I protested.

"Take off your shoes."

My eyes opened in shock. Being barefoot at my own reception would be a scandal in the making. "I can't."

"You're my wife. That elevates your status among

the cartel women to second only to *mi madre*. Do as you please. Being comfortable is more important than what others think."

His comment reminded me of my argument with Dario. Once I was wed to the cartel, I was no longer under the famiglia's control—Dario's or even my mother's.

A smile teased my lips as I reached down and unbuckled the strap to each sandal. When I stood, the top of my head barely surpassed my husband's shoulder. Wiggling my toes, I relished the easing ache in my feet. Looking up, I whispered, "I feel like a rebel."

"I've been known to be one, too." Aléjandro ran the pad of his thumb over my lower lip. "It's why we fit well together."

I didn't want to think about how well we fit together. I wanted to convince myself that I already regretted my decision, and that arranged marriages were a horrible injustice to women everywhere. However, as Aléjandro wrapped his arm around my waist, pulling me close and pressing my breasts against his solid chest, I inclined my hips toward his, and the tingling and twisting in my core told me that my argument was quickly losing relevance.

The music slowed, followed by Aléjandro's steps. Instinctively, I laid my cheek against his muscular shoulder, taking in the woodsy and leather scent of his cologne as his hands lowered, resting just above my butt. Before I closed my eyes, I spotted my brother on the dance floor with Catalina in his arms. It was a good thing that she announced her pregnancy before today because there would have been little chance that people wouldn't have suspected. Her midsection was growing.

Dante had said Catalina melted Dario's hardened heart. After Josie's death, Dario had shut down, striving only to become capo. Watching the two of them dance, chat, and smile gave me hope. Not all arranged marriages were hell. Dario and Catalina were an example of that. As I looked up at my new husband, he turned toward me, and without the cheers of the guests, he craned his neck until his strong lips brushed over mine.

"The rest of your dances belong to me," he said, his deep voice stirring something within me.

I nodded. For a millisecond, my life felt right.

What occurred today was not a marriage my father would have ever accepted. I'd heard negative things about the cartel for most of my life. Rocco was the man Father approved. In Father's eyes, being beaten and raped was more acceptable than marrying outside the famiglia. Perhaps, these were other reasons for me to give Aléjandro a chance.

Time would tell.

The clock approached midnight, and yet the party was still going strong. Emiliano and Reinaldo carried two chairs to the center of the dance floor. I turned to Aléjandro who was again smiling.

"La Vibora de La Mar," he said.

I shook my head.

"The sea snake dance."

"Oh no. I'm not dancing with snakes."

Laughing, he took my hand and led me to the chairs.

"Am I supposed to sit?" I asked.

"No, stand." He offered his hand.

I was glad my shoes were under the head table as I stood on top of the chair in bare feet. Aléjandro gracefully stepped onto the other. Taking my hand, he lifted it. The guests cheered as the music began. One by one, the guests took one another's hands, and danced, passing under the arch of our arms. With each stanza, the beat quickened. Faster and faster the guests danced. Their line swayed and our guests roared with glee, trying to keep their chain from breaking as Aléjandro's and my hands stayed united.

Finally, the band stopped and once again the guests cheered.

Aléjandro jumped down and with his hands to my waist, lifted me from the chair to the floor as if I hadn't gained a size but weighed nothing. As my feet contacted the pavers, the chants resumed.

"Bacio. Bacio."

"Beso. Beso."

With a grin, I leaned into his kiss. The men cheered as the kiss lasted longer than the ones earlier in the night.

"It's time for us to go," Aléjandro said.

The merriment of the wedding celebration faded as I nodded in agreement. I wanted to ask him if he remembered what I'd told him, about expectations for tonight. However, as we walked hand in hand toward the house, I decided not to spoil the mood.

No doubt, it would be spoiled soon enough.

SEVEN

S eeing our new home would wait for tomorrow. We would spend the first night of our married union here at the Ruiz home, as was another tradition. As Aléjandro walked me into the house and up the stairs, he explained that Mexican weddings were a two-day affair. Tomorrow, the family and guests would come back together for brunch where we would open our gifts.

"There won't be sheets for your mother to see."

Aléjandro lifted his chin. "That's a barbaric tradition beneath our standards. We believe that a wife is precious, a jewel, and the matriarch of her family. Discussing her bleeding is degrading."

It was the first thing Aléjandro had said that I agreed with.

As we ascended the staircase, my body moved beyond the festive celebration to an agitated feeling of terror. I wasn't a frightened eighteen-year-old girl. No. I had experience, which made this worse.

With each step, I grew more confident that I wasn't willing to give in to the man holding my hand, not without a fight. Common sense told me that fighting would only encourage a man like Aléjandro, but as we approached the primary suite, our destination for the night, I knew Dante wouldn't save me as he had months ago.

I was running out of options.

The double doors were slightly ajar. Aléjandro opened one wider, bidding me entrance. By the time I crossed the threshold, my hands were trembling and the excessive amount of food I'd consumed was threatening to make a second appearance.

Aléjandro closed and locked the door. The French doors leading to a balcony were open. The sounds of the ocean as well as the continued celebration from below filled the room. With my feet still bare, I stepped out onto the cement balcony. Walking to the railing, I peered down at the pool, seeing the party progressing without us. Though I couldn't see the ocean, the massive dark hole below the star-filled sky, as well as the swoosh of the waves, confirmed its presence.

Crossing my arms and covering my breasts, I turned back toward the bedroom.

Biting my lip, I watched as Aléjandro removed his suit coat. His tie from earlier was loose and hanging around his neck, and the first button of his shirt was opened. Removing the cuff links, he rolled the sleeves of his shirt to his elbows, revealing muscular forearms. Last, he removed the holster containing a gun from his chest.

He moved to the open doorway, his dark gaze on me. "I chose you, Mia. Don't ever doubt that."

"I've been honest with you. I didn't want...*don't* want this marriage."

With his chiseled jaw clenched, he stepped outside. The look in his eyes made me want to run, but there was nowhere to go. With the cool banister against my lower back, I contemplated screaming. If I did, would the guests hear me above the continued sound of the band?

Refusing to submit, I lifted my chin, maintaining our stare-down.

He came closer, pinning me between his muscular body and a two-story fall. Wrapping his arms around my waist, he pulled my hips against him. Even at eighteen, I'd recognized the feeling of an erection against my body.

"Aléjandro."

"You're mine." He cupped my cheeks as he had the night of our engagement. "You're beautiful." He nestled his lips near my neck. "You smell of sweet, wet arousal, even sweeter than the night in that hallway." His warm breath sent chills over my flesh. "You can try to deny it, but your body is speaking louder than your words."

My nipples beaded beneath my dress and my core grew damp, yet I refused to give in so easily. I moved my palms to his wide chest and with all my might, I pushed him away. "No."

He lifted his gaze to mine with a look of confusion. "You were smiling during the celebration."

"Because I had fun." I hated to admit it, but it was the truth.

"Dancing?"

"You're a good dancer." I pushed my way around him and back into the bedroom. Aléjandro was merely a step behind me. I turned, facing him. "I don't want to have sex with you." When his orbs grew darker, I asked, "Are you not used to women telling you no?"

His lips twitched. "Women, no. Men, as I'm about to kill them, *sí*, they say it often."

If that was meant to scare me, he chose a woman from the wrong famiglia. Men killed, it was what I was used to and despite a hope for better, it was what I would always know.

He reached for my shoulders and slowly walked me backward. I was unsure where I was trying to flee or where I would be safe, but I kept moving my feet until my shoulders collided with the wall.

"Kiss me." His tone didn't suggest a request.

My breasts heaved as I took a ragged breath. "If

you force me, I'll hate you forever, just as I hated Rocco."

Aléjandro's stare turned darker as his finger came to my lips. "I don't want to hear that name when I'm about to fuck my wife. I'm not him. Don't expect me to live in a shadow of his mistakes."

He had said something similar the first time I mentioned my limits.

"You are him" —I threw his vulgar words back at him— "if you're going to *fuck* me after I told you no."

I gasped as Aléjandro snatched my wrists with one hand and lifted them over my head. He pulled me to my tiptoes with his iron grip as I struggled to get free.

"You can scream, Mia. I'm certain the band will be playing until dawn. My family likes to party. You'll be hoarse by the time anyone could hear you, and I could have fucked each one of your holes until my heart is content."

Despite my best attempts to stay strong, warm tears filled my eyes. I flinched as he lifted his other hand.

Instead of striking me, Aléjandro left a ghostly touch down the length of my raised arm from my wrist down to my shoulder, to my neck and behind my ear. With a satisfied grin, he looked down, scanning my body. "Your tears tell me one story. Your hard nipples and the way you shift your legs tell another."

"Fuck you." My curse held less zeal than it had before.

His lips came to the spot behind my ear, kissing and nipping the sensitive skin. I wanted to kick and push him away, but he was right about my hardened nipples. They were almost painful against the bodice of my dress. And as for my core, I couldn't remember ever being wound this tight or so wet. None of that correlated with his horrible, vulgar threats.

My wrists ached, yet my body trembled with something between hatred and need. I couldn't think fast enough to stop the moan from my lips.

Aléjandro leaned back, his erection still hard against my stomach. "Kisses. You told me earlier we could kiss."

I quickly nodded. "Kisses. No more."

"I won't fuck you, Mia. Not tonight. When I do, you'll be begging me for it."

"When hell freezes over."

He grinned. Releasing my wrists, he kept my body pinned between him and the wall. "The forecast is for ice." He ran his finger over my cheek and down my neck to the V on the front of my neckline. "I was wrong."

It was hard for me to follow his train of thought. "About?"

"The famiglia women being cold as ice." Roughly capturing my chin, he brought his lips down hard and possessively on mine. I pushed back, not fighting but adding to the ongoing give-and-take. He stole my breath as he swallowed my complaints.

Kisses.

I'd said yes to kisses.

I didn't back away, opening my mouth as his tongue made entrance. His hips rocked against me as our kiss deepened. Although I had the urge to lift my hands to his shirt, I kept them at my sides, trying to appear unaffected.

Aléjandro pulled back and ran his thumb over my swollen lips. "You're the opposite of ice, Mia. You're fire. I'm going to learn what you like and when I do, hell will be frozen over for eternity."

Arrogant.

His eyes were black holes, sucking me into their void and the timbre of his accented deep voice ricocheted through my nervous system, warming my circulation while simultaneously scaring me that he could be right. "You will welcome my cock and writhe beneath the pleasure it brings you. I know you're not a virgin, but that doesn't mean you're experienced. I don't think you've ever enjoyed what a man can do to you. I'm not talking about a prick who's weak enough to hurt a woman. I'm talking about a real man who knows how to use pleasure and pain to bring you ecstasy like you've never known."

My tears broke through, streaming down my cheeks as I concentrated on the first part of his speech. He wasn't going to fuck me.

I didn't want to think about what else he'd said.

I couldn't.

My mind couldn't comprehend that I'd ever find pleasure with sex. Pain, yes, there could be pain but not any that brought me ecstasy.

I swallowed and stared into his eyes still simmering beneath his protruding brow. "I'm not right for you. You would be a lot happier if you chose someone else. You should have listened."

Aléjandro shook his head. "You were made for me. My only regret is that you had to live with someone else first. Like I said, I won't live in the shadow of his mistakes, but one by one, I'll show you that he was wrong." The tendons in his neck pulled tight. "No one will make me happier than you will, and one day, you'll say the same about me."

My thoughts went back to the ceremony.

Until death do us part.

Death saved me once; maybe it will save me again.

I looked beyond his broad shoulders at the luxurious bedroom around us. "There's only one bed."

"I'm sleeping beside my wife." He tilted his head. "No fucking. You have my word. It won't be easy." His lips quirked to a grin. "Your brother warned me that you could be difficult. I told him that I'm up for the challenge."

He took a step back and by the sight of the massive bulge in his pants, he was up for what wasn't going to happen.

Aléjandro went on, "The maids should have your things in the bathroom. After you change, I'll shower and come to bed. Maybe you should already be asleep."

Taking his cue to walk away, I made my way to the bathroom and closed the door. I contemplated turning the lock in the handle but decided against it. I'd felt his strength as he captured my wrists. A simple handle lock wouldn't keep Aléjandro out if he wanted in.

I didn't know what to think of the woman in my reflection. Was I brave? Strong? Weak? A terrible person? A challenge and difficult—to quote Dario?

To Aléjandro's credit, he had been nothing but kind during our wedding celebration, even trying to make me more comfortable with traditions I knew nothing about. Maybe he believed he could woo me into changing my mind.

Of course he did.

Aléjandro was an egotistical, arrogant male who thought every woman should fall prostrate at his feet. His words came back to me. 'I won't fuck you, Mia. Not tonight. When I do, you'll be begging me for it.'

If this marriage was a contest of willpower, Aléjandro would learn I wouldn't be easily dissuaded. If I'd learned anything over the last ten years, it was to stay strong in my resolve.

As I plucked hairpins from my hair, I recalled the way my new husband held me as we danced, as well as his ability to make me smile. He was right that I wasn't frightened during our reception. I'd spent the lead-up to our wedding being scared. No, I'd spent the last ten years minus the months since Rocco's death terrified.

Aléjandro wasn't Rocco.

Intellectually, I knew that.

Apparently, it was more than my mind that knew it. The physical reaction my body had to Aléjandro was ten, twenty, no... one hundred times more than I'd had for Rocco in years or ever.

Shaking my head, I promised myself I wouldn't back down.

Maybe one day.

First, Aléjandro needed to prove that he wasn't like my first husband. It wasn't fair. He wasn't the one who hurt me. Life wasn't fair. If it was, I wouldn't be remarried. I'd warned him.

Wearing a white satin and lace nightgown and the lace panties from my wedding outfit, I opened the bathroom door.

Aléjandro was sitting out on the balcony. Slowly I moved closer. The music from below was still going strong. There was a glass with amber liquid in his grip and an open bottle of tequila on the table.

"I'm done," I said, standing in the doorway.

He scanned me up and down. "You could have chosen something less sexy if you were planning on me keeping my word."

I crossed my arms over my breasts. "Classic blame-the-victim."

Aléjandro scoffed as he stood. "Don't worry, Mia. I am a man of my word."

The idea of reaching out and experiencing another kiss was on my mind as he entered the bedroom. I couldn't deny that despite his arrogant attitude, I found him attractive. He brushed by me, leaving the scent of sandalwood and tequila in his wake.

Turning, I watched Aléjandro remove his shirt, pulling it over his wide shoulders. Beneath the shirt, his tanned skin was littered with scars, and yet his chest was solid, and his abdomen defined. Dark hair matching the color on his head filled a patch upon hard pecs. Another line of dark hair trailed from below his belly button to beneath his boxer briefs. Aléjandro removed a second holster from his back and a third from his ankle.

Now that his shoes, socks, and pants were missing, the erection I'd felt against my stomach was even more pronounced beneath the silk boxers. Wearing only those boxer shorts, he lifted the glass he'd taken from the balcony and drained the remaining tequila. His orbs met mine. "Don't wait up."

With that, he disappeared into the bathroom.

As I climbed into the bed, my thoughts went to the man behind the closed door.

What is he doing in the shower?

Why am I curious?

Switching off the light on my bedside stand, I turned away from the bathroom door, pulled my arms and legs to my stomach, and tried to calm my nerves. It had been a long day. Sleep didn't come easily. I wanted to believe Aléjandro, but how many times had I been lied to? Each time Rocco hurt me, he swore it was the last.

I wasn't sure how much time passed before I heard the bathroom door opening. The room around me went dark, yet I refused to move from the edge of the bed. The clean scent of bodywash filled my senses. When it seemed safe that Aléjandro wasn't going to go back on his word, my tense muscles began to relax. Listening to the music from our celebration, I drifted off to sleep.

CHAPTER
EIGHT

Aléjandro

Blinking, I woke to something tickling my face. My nose twitched as I made sense of the world around me. Mia was sleeping on her side, her long hair fanned out near my face, and I had my arm draped over her trim waist.

My dick was at nearly full mast as her tight ass lay only centimeters away. You'd think the whacking I'd done last night in the shower would have been enough to keep the bad boy at bay. Apparently, waking next to a beautiful woman was not the formula for keeping my dick down.

Sighing, I rolled to my back, flopped my arm over

my forehead, and stared up at the ceiling. Who doesn't get pussy on their wedding night?

The answer would be me.

Fuck, before Mia's declaration after the ceremony, I was counting the minutes until I would get her alone. I'd been half-serious about leaving the reception, burying my dick in her warm pussy, and then coming back for the party.

Obviously, things didn't go as planned.

The soft sounds of her sleeping breaths gave me a jolt of reality. I was married.

I'd been concerned about sleeping unarmed beside someone. Despite never having done it before, I slept better than I would have predicted. Oh, I'd bedded plenty of women. There were those who made a living at it and others who were just in it for the fun. The first had a place of business and sleeping overnight wasn't an option. With the latter, I tended to follow an invitation to their place, not extend one to mine.

It's not like my parents would give two shits if Rei or I brought a woman home, but *mi padre's casa* was well guarded. Most women looking for a one-night stand or even an on-and-off-again relationship weren't thrilled about entering the equivalent to Fort Knox. Sure, his house was giant. Nevertheless, I wasn't a fan of introducing a woman I barely knew to *mi madre* at breakfast.

The thought made me smile.

I barely knew the woman still sleeping beside me.

I barely knew my own wife.

As much as I wanted to be upset about what happened, or more accurately, what didn't happen on our wedding night, I wasn't. I was challenged and in some fucking weird turn of events, totally in this for the long haul. I meant what I'd said: one day Mia would beg me to fuck her and when that day came, I'd make it so fucking good, she'd forget all her bad memories of the asshole before me.

Last night, by the time I'd finally made it to bed, Mia was pretending to sleep. I was relatively certain she wasn't actually asleep, but I wasn't willing to find out. Despite taking care of business in the cool shower, my fortitude was tested to its max. Maybe she wanted to be sure I wouldn't rape her in her sleep or that I hadn't changed my mind.

My mind was uncertain, but I wasn't about to take from her what she didn't want to give. I wasn't the piece-of-shit husband she had before. The smile she'd shown during the wedding celebration was my encouragement. Mia had fun—she even admitted it.

She may think she hates me, and I may have mentioned her name to *Padre* because I knew she felt that way, but at the end of the day, we were now married. We needed to learn to do more than co-exist. We needed to be partners, such as the priest said with the presentation of the coins.

I was excited to show Mia our new home. It was a one-in-a-million find. The day I contacted the real estate agent, the house had just gone on the market. It was everything I wanted. Working on a limited time schedule due to my own procrastination and things being busy with the cartel, I made an offer—fifty thousand over asking and a promise to pay all the closing costs.

The sellers took the money.

Now the only thing standing between us and this new home was being sure Mia was happy with it too.

Rolling onto my side toward Mia, I lifted my head onto my fist held up by my elbow and watched her sleep. Even without the makeup from the wedding, in this relaxed state she was stunning. I reached for the silkiness of her long hair, running a soft strand through my fingertips. My mind started to conjure images of what she would look like finding her bliss, allowing me to touch her, to wind her up and hold her as she fell into an orgasmic stupor.

The images weren't helping my dick relax.

I slipped from the bed.

We'd left the doors open to the balcony. The pool area was quiet. I wasn't sure who else would be awake at this hour. The music was part of my dreams throughout the night. Hell, the rest of the wedding guests may not have gone to bed until the sun came up.

I looked around for a coffee pot.

This wasn't a hotel. It was the Ruizes' primary bedroom. Coffee could wait. My first concern was taking care of business so I wouldn't be walking around all day with a fucking hard-on.

Closing the door to the bathroom, I again turned on the shower.

If Mia continued to refuse sex, I could be the cleanest man on the West Coast.

The warm spray created a cloud of humidity within the glass enclosure. Dropping my boxer shorts on the floor, I stepped in, lifted my face to the spray, ran my hands over my head, wetting my hair, and turned to the shower wall. It seemed backward. Rarely before my wedding had I jerked off. This was my second session in less than eight hours.

As a married man, pussy should be at my fingertips.

That was the fucking problem: it was at my fingertips, just unobtainable.

I tilted my forehead against the tile and gripped my length, running my hand up and down my hardening dick. Closing my eyes, I pictured Mia, the way she looked at me when I had her pinned against the wall. The fear in her eyes shouldn't turn me on, but I'd never claimed I was a good man.

Faster and faster, I moved my grip, increasing my pressure as my dick turned to steel. Squeezing harder, spots appeared behind my eyelids and my balls drew closer. The pain was real and so was the pleasure. My lips opened, yet I couldn't stop.

Hunching my shoulders, I closed my eyes tighter.

With the rush of endorphins drowning out the world, I pumped faster and faster. My orgasm came like a fucking barreling freight engine. The rumble of the train and the clicking of the wheels. Like that train, I was out of control, speeding through a dark tunnel when I gasped for air.

The tunnel ended in blinding light.

I exploded, my body shuddering more violently than it had the night before. Instead of stopping, I kept stroking myself, draining every drop so I could fucking walk without blowing a wad.

"Aléjandro?"

Fuck.

I spun around, facing my wife, her lips open and eyes wide.

I reached for the shower door and slid it to the side. "Join me, Mia."

She took a step back.

Her hair was down and mussed. Her satin nightgown covered her body to her mid-thighs. The spaghetti straps hung from her slender shoulders, and the material was tented from her hardened nipples. She was a sight of beauty.

How long has she been watching me?

Water droplets dripped from my body as I stepped from the shower onto the soft bath mat, my nudity on full display. "I know this isn't the first time you've seen a naked man."

Mia's face paled. "You're..." She peeled her eyes

away from my dick and brought them up to mine. "It's the first time I've seen you."

Leaving a trail of water on the floor, I stepped closer to her and brushed one strap of her nightgown off her shoulder and then the other. Mia stiffened. It only took a little more encouragement for the gown to slip from her body. I sucked in a breath as I took in her luscious curves. "Take off your panties."

Her wide hazel orbs stared up at me.

"No sex, Mia. I want to see my wife. All of her."

She nibbled on her lower lip as she snagged the waistband with her fingers and pushed the panties lower. The lace fell to the floor, lost in the puddle of her nightgown.

"You're fucking gorgeous."

Mia's eyes looked down. "I've gained weight—"

I laid a finger on her lips, and her eyes came back up to mine. "You're gorgeous. That's the end of that discussion." I lowered my hand to hers, feeling the way it trembled. "Come into the shower with me."

"I...I..."

"No sex."

Mia nodded.

Once we were both inside, I closed the glass. Thank the Lord I'd been hard on myself only minutes earlier. Otherwise, this proximity would be impossible. Blocking the spray with my back and shoulders, I reached for Mia's chin and lifted it until her lips were at the perfect height to kiss. Unlike last night, I moved slower.

This was uncharted territory for me. My first sex was at fourteen. My uncle hired a prostitute, against *mi madre's* wishes. He said it was time for me to be a man—*hacerte un hombre*. After that time, I never worked to get a woman to spread her legs. If she didn't accept the challenge, I moved on. The next one would say yes. Hard and fast was my speed. Mostly, a quest for self-gratification.

Mia was testing my patience, and I found the challenge sexy as fuck.

After a moment, she leaned in, sandwiching my penis between us. Immediately, she jumped away.

"My dick won't bite you."

Her neck and cheeks pinkened, and I fucking loved that she blushed.

"I want to wash you."

"Wash me?"

I peppered her neck and shoulders with kisses. "No sex. Only bodywash."

It took a few seconds, but finally, Mia nodded.

"Turn around."

I poured the liquid soap onto a washcloth and slowly ran it over her shoulders and back, down both arms. This was the first time I'd touched her all over. I took my time, running my touch over her soft skin. Mia moaned as I ran the washcloth over her round ass.

Crouching down, I made sure that each leg and foot was sudsy.

"Turn around."

Mia obeyed; her expression morphed seeing me still on my haunches. Her pink pussy was right in front of me. With a grin, I said, "I need to work my way back up."

Instead of using the washcloth, I slowly and methodically kissed her calves, knees, and thighs. It took all my willpower to jump over her bald pussy. Sometime I would tell her to give me a fucking landing strip or something. If I were to guess, her late husband was a wuss when it came to hair. I preferred a sign that my wife wasn't a child.

I thought she may protest. Instead, Mia leaned her shoulders against the tile and closed her eyes as my lips moved over her stomach and up to her tits. They were perfect and round. Not huge but not small. By the time I made it to her lips, Mia opened her mouth, willingly accepting my tongue while giving me hers.

"Fuck," I growled.

"What?"

"My dick won't stay limp around you."

She swallowed as her eyes looked down. "Do you want help with that?"

"More than you fucking know."

When her knees bent, I stopped her. "No, Mia. I made you a promise. Kisses only." Her eyes grew wide. "Do I want your lips on my dick? Yes. But not until you're ready." I took a deep breath. "Turn around and I'll wash your hair."

Under the spray, her hair appeared darker. I liked the array of colors it had when dry. For a moment I thought about our home and the pool, wondering if the sun would help bring out those lighter shades.

By the time I turned off the water and wrapped my wife in a plush towel, we were both clean. None of our sexual tension had been expelled, but I hoped that just maybe a bit of her fear was.

I'd touched her body without mauling her.

The looks she was giving me said she still believed we were on thin ice. If sex was coming when hell froze over, I had high hopes for the ice growing more solid.

"Are you going to tell the other men we had sex?" Mia asked as she combed her long hair.

"I'm going to avoid the conversation. If pressed, I'll lie. Some would see it as weak on my part. I won't lie to Rei. I trust him with my life."

Mia nodded. "I can lie too."

"Why would you do that?"

"I don't know." She shook her head and spun toward me, her arms crossing over her towel-covered tits. "You didn't force yourself on me. I don't understand how rape is a macho thing, but to some it is. Sex is too. Dario didn't force Catalina, yet everyone was thrilled they'd had sex. I guess I don't want them to think less of us."

"Us?"

"You for being kind or me for not doing what I was supposed to do."

I cupped her soft cheek. "What you're supposed to do is be honest with me. The rest, what anyone else thinks, is bullshit."

"I'm surprised you're being this understanding."

A smile curled my lips. "Not as surprised as I am. I had my mind set on fucking you last night."

"Thank you."

I inhaled. "I wasn't sure what I'd say if I was asked, but if you want the lie, we'll lie together."

"Giorgia, my cousin—I guess she's to me what Reinaldo is to you. I never had a sister, and Dario and Dante aren't exactly the sharing type. She's been my confidant through everything. I probably won't lie to her."

"Do you trust her?"

I nodded. "Without question. Even Antonio won't know the truth."

My cheeks rose. "Then it's set. We fucked like rabbits all night long."

Mia's smile was perfect.

And then she surprised me. Pushing up on her tiptoes, she kissed my cheek. "Thank you, Aléjandro. I was terrified."

"I'll never hurt you more than you want."

"I can't imagine wanting it at all."

"First, you need to learn that I can be trusted."

"Can you?" She looked down. "Sorry, it's just that the man whose name you don't want me to say didn't think highly of the cartel."

"I hope he's fucking rolling over in his grave at the thought of you in my bed. By the time you're begging for my dick, he'll be wanting to claw his way out." I shrugged. "Kind of difficult after what your brother did to him—well, both your brothers."

Mia's cheeks rose. "Let's not talk about that."

"We have family waiting downstairs."

"We've been busy...rabbits."

The tension from last night seemed to evaporate as we both dressed for the day. While I put on blue jeans and a black t-shirt, Mia dressed in a long blue dress that had ties on both shoulders. I imagined untying those bows and getting another good look at her perfect tits.

She dried her hair, bringing back the multicolored highlights, and pulled it back in a low ponytail. I reached for her hand and lifted it, leaving a kiss near her wedding rings. "You won't regret this."

Mia's smile seemed sadder than it should be. "I don't yet. It's a start."

Together, we left the room and made our way downstairs to the sea of voices. Unlike the fucking production that the famiglia made the morning after Dario and Cat's wedding, by the time Mia and I made it to the first floor, the men and women were sitting and standing in clusters around the kitchen and dining room, eating and talking. Roríguez guards were stationed around the property.

Civilized people.

Mia

Giorgia cornered me as Aléjandro left my side to find us both coffee. Her eyes were huge, and she looked as if she hadn't slept. "Are you okay?"

"Are you?"

"I couldn't sleep with the music and for worrying about you."

I looked around, making sure we weren't overheard. "I'm good."

"Did he force you?"

Shaking my head, I smiled. "I was afraid, but he didn't." I lowered my voice even more. "But if Antonio or anyone asks, we fucked like rabbits."

Giorgia giggled. "Is that your agreed-upon cover story?"

"Yes."

She took my hand and squeezed it. "This is going to be better, Mia. I know it."

Wrapping my arms around my cousin, I whispered in her ear, "I miss having you around already."

"Me too."

Sex may have been a subject with the men, but other than some well-meaning questions as to my wellness, the women didn't ask for specifics. Flashbacks of the morning after my first wedding reiterated the savage nature of some of the famiglia's traditions.

Aléjandro was across the room speaking with his brother and friends. I had a new appreciation for the way his biceps bulged beneath the sleeve of his t-shirt. My gaze moved lower, remembering the way he looked stepping from the shower.

The shower had been unplanned. Ten years married and I'd never watched a man jerk off. When I first entered the bathroom, I was unsure what my husband was doing. Once it was clear, I found the vision beautiful, the way his muscles in his back and shoulders contracted and the change in his expression...I was mesmerized, unable to turn away. I probably should have snuck back out, not getting caught with my voyeurism. The more I watched, the more I was trapped, like a deer in the headlights.

When he stepped out of the shower, I was hardly

able to look away from his penis. Aléjandro was right I'd seen a naked man before but not one proportioned like my new husband. To say he was blessed would be an understatement.

My fears returned, worried if I would be able to handle his size. I may have even been trembling when he removed my nightgown. My mind was trying to compute, and I didn't know what I was doing. I could blame my acceptance to enter the shower with him on the guilt of my ogling or maybe it was simply curiosity. Whatever the cause, as he held my hand, I willingly chose to accept his invitation.

Never in a million years could I have predicted the gentle and reverent way he cleansed and caressed my body. When I saw him crouched down, I longed for his lips to go to the one place they didn't—the place I'd deemed off-limits. If he had searched between my folds, I wouldn't have been able to hide my arousal.

As I ate a bagel, I spotted the girl from the wedding reception—the one who looked miserable. Emiliano had said she was his new aunt. That would be hilarious since she's younger than him if it weren't so sad.

She was standing on the terrace, staring out at the ocean. I waited to see if her husband was about take his place at her side, but he didn't. Looking around the crowd, I spotted him speaking with Catalina's father. I can't explain the pull I had to go to her. Taking a blueberry muffin from the counter of foods, I walked toward her.

"Hi, Liliana, I'm Mia."

She looked up at me with huge eyes. "Yes. I know. You married Aléjandro."

"Oh, I guess that's true." I handed her the muffin. "I brought you this."

"Gracias." As she reached for it, the sleeve of her sweater moved up, revealing the brown and green of a bruise on her wrist. I didn't think she realized I saw it, and I knew from experience, if I mentioned it, she would make an excuse. I'd used them all myself.

Slowly she peeled away the muffin paper.

"I think Aléjandro told me you were recently married."

Her face paled as she nodded. "Aléjandro, Patrón's son, knows about my marriage?"

"I heard your husband is a trusted lieutenant."

"Sí. Gerardo works hard."

"You probably know this," I said, "but I'm new to the area, and I really don't know anyone. Since we're both newlyweds, I wondered if maybe we could get together? Coffee? Lunch?"

Liliana looked around. "We live in Northern California. I don't know anyone there either."

"Where in Northern California?"

"Qué pasa aquí?"

Liliana and I both jumped at the booming deep voice of her husband.

"Nada," Liliana said quickly, lifting what was left of the muffin. *"Señora* Roríguez brought me a muffin."

Clenching my teeth, I steadied my shoulders as Gerardo Ruiz turned to me. At Liliana's use of my new last name, his menacing expression changed. Her husband couldn't complain that she was speaking with *el Patrón's* daughter-in-law.

"*Señora*," he said with enough sugar to put me in a diabetic coma. "*Felicidades* on your wedding."

"*Gracias.* I was just talking to your lovely wife about being newly married and not knowing many people." Although I saw the way Liliana was cowering, I went on. "She tells me you live north."

"*Sí.*"

"It would be lovely if Aléjandro and I could visit sometime."

He stood taller. "We would be honored."

"I'll speak to him." I turned to Liliana. "I hope you enjoy the muffin. Thank you both for coming to our wedding."

When I started to walk away, I saw Aléjandro looking my direction with a puzzled expression. Smiling at other guests, I went to him and reached for his arm. My smile stayed in place, and I spoke in a whisper. "She has bruises on her wrists."

He turned his gaze on me. "Mia, he's her husband. Maybe it's kink, not abuse."

I shook my head. "I offered for us to visit them sometime."

His lips were pressed together.

"The possibility of a visit from you could save her a lot of pain."

"And you know this how?"

"I know it."

Aléjandro exhaled. "We can plan a visit."

"No. Tell him you'll let him know the next time you're in the area. Keep him wondering. I promise it will be better for her."

Aléjandro wrapped his arm around my back and squeezed me to him. "Day one and you're causing problems with one of our lieutenants."

My cheeks rose in a smile. "Dario warned you."

"He did."

After brunch, both families gathered around as Aléjandro and I opened the few presents we received. It was more about the thought because we truly didn't need anything. From what Dario had told me, there wasn't anything Aléjandro couldn't afford. Like he said, this was a marriage better suited for the daughter of a capo.

Once my family began to leave, it was also time for Aléjandro and me to go. We both thanked Andrés and Valentina for their hospitality. I gathered my belongings. Next, my husband led me to a Porsche 911 Turbo with a sleek silver exterior and a deep red and black leather interior.

I settled into the soft leather seat as Aléjandro put our bags under the front hood and got behind the wheel. After all the noise and activity of the morning wedding continuation, the quietness within the car was sensory deprivation. There were millions of questions in my head, each one eager to be voiced. Yet as he started the car, and drove down the lane toward the gate, I remained silent.

My thoughts were too random. I was having trouble reconciling the man last night who was unhappy about my demand with the one who this morning carefully and gently caressed my body and washed my hair...and even turned down a blow job.

Soon, the scenes beyond the windows captivated me, being so different than what I was used to in Missouri. The streets were lined with palm trees and flowering bushes. The sky high above was a vibrant blue. He drove us down a road that wound high along the cliffs above the ocean beaches far below. The sea was alive with waves sparkling like the diamonds in my wedding band.

Finally, we came to another gate similar to the one at the Ruiz home. Aléjandro entered a code and the gate slid back, allowing us entry.

"Do we have guards?" It was the first question I allowed myself to voice.

"*Sí*," he turned to me and back to the road. "You will stay protected, Mia."

"I grew up with bodyguards. Rocco kept a guard outside the house."

"Not inside?" he asked.

I shook my head, realizing I'd said my late

husband's name. Perhaps it wasn't an issue if we weren't in an intimate state. I explained, "He wasn't so much a bodyguard as a jail keeper."

Aléjandro reached over and covered my knee with the warmth of his hand. "You're no longer in jail. I have chosen a bodyguard for you, a real bodyguard. You're free to come and go as you please as long as he's at your side." He pressed his lips together. "I had to have someone I trust without question to keep you safe and never act inappropriately. He's due to arrive tomorrow. In the meantime, we have plenty of guards on the property."

"Arrive?"

Before Aléjandro could explain, he stopped the car on the wide brick driveway. The building before us was ultra-modern with two large garage doors and a gated front entrance.

I looked up through the window. "Is this all ours?"

"I recently bought it. If you don't like it, tell me now, and we can look at others."

"If I don't like it?" I repeated, surprised my opinion mattered. From what I could see, this was so much more than the townhouse I'd shared with Rocco, and that was without seeing inside. "Aléjandro, it looks massive for just the two of us."

His smile returned. "Come, let me show you inside."

Leaving the car on the driveway, Aléjandro opened

my door and took my hand. "If you like it, we'll have a new security system installed."

That was the second time he'd mentioned my opinion. "You care if I like it?"

"It will be your home. Of course I care."

I stared for a minute, wondering where the asshole Aléjandro had gone. Maybe my new husband suffered from dissociative identity disorder.

As I pondered, he opened the front gate. The ground between the gate and house was covered in large pavers and rocks. Smaller sandstone rocks decorated the exterior of the lower level. There was also a trellis covered in vines that covered what appeared to be a small patio. I could barely take it all in as Aléjandro put his hand in the small of my back and led me through the door. "Welcome home, *Señora* Roríguez."

That was my name.

My father was officially rolling over in his grave.

I pushed that thought away as the interior came into view.

The room we entered was large, reminding me of one of my mother's rear living rooms. At one end was a stone fireplace with built-in bookcases on each side. The kitchen and dining areas were the other direction. The floor was a lovely natural wood, and there were three massive sets of glass doors.

Aléjandro led me toward the middle one. It opened like an accordion, the wall of glass moving, revealing a beautiful outdoor oasis. Pavers covered the large expanse around an inground pool. Beyond the grass, the Pacific Ocean glistened beneath the sunshine.

"This view reminded me of the Ruiz home."

"It's beautiful." I stifled a laugh as I looked around. "There's no furniture."

"There's some. There are stools for the kitchen counter, and two of the bedrooms have furniture. I'm not attached to any of it. I asked the sellers to leave it." Before I could speak, he went on, "I thought you might want to decorate."

"Me?" I spun around, looking up at the two stories. "I get to decorate?"

"Whatever you like, Mia. I don't know anything about furniture or décor. Fuck, I've been living in the Ruiz pool house for the last two or three months and been content. I have the name of a decorator, but I wanted..." He took a breath. "You don't have to, but I thought...maybe you could take over the responsibility."

"Yes. I'd love that." I couldn't contain my smile if I tried. "Do I have a budget?"

He laughed. "No. Whatever you want."

Whatever I want?

He took my hand. "Come, there's more." He walked me through the over four thousand square feet of home. There was a primary suite on the first floor and one upstairs. They both had beds, bedside stands, and dressers.

"Do we each have our own room?" I asked as we entered the second-floor suite. Both suites also had sitting areas. The upstairs one had a balcony that looked over the pool and ocean. The first-floor suite had the patio with the trellis I'd seen from outside.

"No." His smile grew. "I may have to take ten showers a day, but I'm sleeping next to my wife."

I caught my lower lip between my teeth, stifling a smile. It wasn't right for me to enjoy his discomfort. "The other bedroom?"

"I started telling you about your new bodyguard. His name is Silas. I trust him because he's worked for my parents for over twenty years. He's also married to one of the best cooks in the world, Viviana. I asked them to consider moving here with us."

"Your family won't miss them?"

"I'm sure they will. Silas and Viviana accepted my offer. They wanted to move to the States for a while. This was a good reason. Currently, they have a work visa, but your brother promised to pull a few strings and get their paperwork fast-tracked." He grinned. "The famiglia has connections the cartel appreciates."

It was interesting to hear the alliance from the other side.

Aléjandro went on. "The first-floor suite will be theirs. Silas will be available to you at all times." His smile faded. "I'm afraid in this house we aren't as isolated as your mother's home. The cartel has done well, and that success has made us a target. I trust

Silas with protecting you. And because he's happily married, I trust him not to overstep with what is mine."

With me.

Warmth filled my cheeks. "I look forward to meeting them. But for the record, I'm used to cooking and cleaning."

"You shouldn't be."

I pressed my lips together.

Aléjandro went on, "Once they're here, you and Viviana can work out whatever you want. Silas will also be overseeing the other guards assigned to our home. I won't take any chances. Oh, warning, there may be a bit of a language barrier."

I opened my eyes wide. "Tell me they speak English."

"*Un poco* but primarily Spanish."

I shrugged. "I wanted to go to school. Learning a new language can be my first lesson."

"You wanted to go to school? And what would you study?"

Swallowing, I shook my head. "It doesn't matter anymore."

"*Hola*," a deep voice called from somewhere in the house.

Aléjandro shook his head. "Rei. We're up here," he called.

Stepping away, I went out on the balcony as Aléjandro walked toward his brother's voice. Lifting my face to the sea breeze, I held tight to the railing and closed my eyes. I'd almost asked my husband if I could attend college. That realization made me sick to my stomach and as if the walls were closing in on me at the same time.

For the second time in my life, I was trapped in a marriage that I feared would end up like my first. Soon, I would be thirty years old, and I was supposed to behave as I did when I was twelve—asking permission for things that should be my own choice.

Staring out at the glistening water, I felt the prickle of tears. It was stupid. I should be happy. Most women would be ecstatic about this house and a blank check to decorate. Tomorrow, a bodyguard and cook would arrive.

Aléjandro hadn't asked why I cooked and cleaned. Rocco and I couldn't afford to hire a full-time cook or housekeeper. Once I moved back in with my mother, I fell into her lifestyle with maids, cooks, gardeners. Name it, she had it.

The life Aléjandro was offering me was what I thought I'd always wanted, but with it staring me in the face, I wasn't happy. My chin fell forward as I let a few of the tears escape.

"Mia."

Quickly, I wiped my cheeks with the back of my hand and turned toward the bedroom. Aléjandro and Reinaldo were both standing in the open door. I feigned a smile. "Welcome to our empty house."

"Maybe I'll move in here and out of the Ruiz pool house."

"The more the merrier," I replied.

Aléjandro quickly answered, "Camila would miss you hanging around their pool." He laughed. "My brother, breaking eighteen-year-old hearts in two countries."

"Eighteen is legal," Reinaldo said with a smirk. "Of course, Andrés would probably kill me if I so much as touched her hand. And since I'm living and sleeping there, I have remained hands off."

"I'd be more concerned about Em," my husband said. "He was still contemplating killing the capo until he found out about the baby."

"Should I warn my brother?" I asked.

"I think he's safe," Aléjandro replied.

TEN

Aléjandro and Rei went downstairs to talk business, leaving me alone in our bedroom. Wrapping my arms around my midsection, I spun a slow circle, thankful we had some furniture. The furnishings weren't bad, a bed, dressers, and bedside stands. The sitting area was empty. For a moment, I imagined what could fill the void while trying to get excited about buying whatever I wanted.

I didn't want to hate my life.

There were moments I forgot that I hated it.

I walked toward the closets I'd only peeked in before. Looking at the stacked boxes containing everything I called mine from Missouri, I remembered again: this wasn't the life I wanted. I recalled that I'd been uprooted and discarded by the famiglia. At least that was the way it felt. As bad as my first marriage had been, I was surrounded by family and friends.

Dario and Catalina were on their way back to Kansas City and so were Giorgia and Dante. Mom was on her way to her big house in the Ozarks. Other women from the famiglia would be gathering for wine and movies as their husbands worked the streets and clubs.

The life I'd known was gone.

Now that my wedding was over and my marriage was official, the people who used to be special to me could move on. After all, I was now cartel, and I knew how they felt about Catalina. She had the one advantage of being married to the capo. I'd been shipped away.

Maybe it was time for me to move on.

Sliding down the doorjamb, I sat on the soft carpet, pulled my knees to my chest, and wrapped my arms around my legs. The mountain of boxes embodied nearly thirty years of life, a sad representation of how little I'd accomplished.

They were filled with things.

Objects.

Clothes.

Jewelry.

All replaceable.

My friends and family were across the country.

I didn't have an education or children.

All I had was a new husband.

As my temples began to pound, my gaze went over to the large bed. Tonight, my husband would expect to sleep together—would he expect more?

My stomach twisted.

I had to trust him to keep his word about sex because as sad as it was, Aléjandro's word was the one hope I was pinning my future on. A man I didn't even like before yesterday. I wasn't sure I liked him now. Given my vast choices of people in my current life—I could acquiesce to *liking* him.

Laying my forehead on my knees, my eyes burned with the return of tears. This time I didn't try to stop them. I wasn't sharing my grief. It was all mine, and if I had to bear it, I needed to let a little out when I could.

I wasn't certain how long I sat crying before I forced myself to stop. It was more that the tears were no longer flowing, and my head was aching.

No one could understand my sadness from the outside. My life appeared better than it had in years past. While Rocco raped me on our wedding night and sex was always at his demand, his routine abuse took years to surface. One successful night with Aléjandro didn't exactly mean I was out of the woods. I knew from experience that dispositions can easily change.

How long will he put up with my refusal of sex?

Splashing my face with cool water in the bathroom, I stared into my reflection. Self-pity wasn't the answer. I needed to stay busy. Opening a cabinet to the bare interior, I decided I'd start my unpacking in the bathroom. After all, I'd need my cosmetics. They were all in the suitcase we brought from the Ruiz home. Walking back into the bedroom, I realized we hadn't gotten our bags out of Aléjandro's Porsche.

As I neared the front staircase, I heard the raised voices from down below.

There seemed to be more than two voices. Quietly, I made my way down the staircase. In the foyer, I turned to the left, and with each step the voices grew louder. Stopping a few feet from the door to the room Aléjandro claimed as his office, I pressed myself against the wall and listened.

They said immersion was a good way to learn another language. If I wanted to learn what was happening, I'd need to pick up on the Spanish language sooner rather than later. My eavesdropping wasn't doing me any good.

Steeling my shoulders, I made my way to the doorway. Aléjandro, Rei, Emiliano, and another man were all standing and speaking fast to one another. Of course, they were standing, their only other choice would be to sit on the floor. I made a mental note to furnish Aléjandro's office soon.

I waited, but their conversation was obviously intense enough that no one paid any attention to my intrusion. "Hi," I said, knocking on the doorjamb.

All four men turned my direction.

If this wasn't my house and my husband wasn't one of the dark sets of eyes, I might be frightened. It appeared my famiglia didn't dominate the market on intimidating-looking men.

"Mia," Aléjandro said, stepping away from the others as his expression softened. "*Lo siento*—I'm sorry if we were loud."

"Loud is fine. I'm sure whatever you're discussing is important." I feigned a smile and spoke to the one man I didn't know. He seemed familiar. I assumed he was at the wedding. "I'm sorry" —I offered my hand — "I don't recall your name."

The man took a step forward. He was a bit shorter than my husband and Rei, but taller than Emiliano. And while I got the feeling, he was trying to be polite, I also sensed that he wasn't happy about the interruption. "*Mi nombre es* Nick, *Señora* Roríguez."

"Nick, nice to formally meet you. Mia, please." I turned to Aléjandro. "I came down to get the suitcase from the car." I tilted my head. "Do you have the keys?"

Aléjandro sent a look to Rei that meant more than I could glean. "I'm going to help her. You three work this out by the time I'm back."

Rei answered affirmatively aloud while Emiliano and Nick merely nodded.

My husband laid his hand in the small of my back and walked me away from the office. "I moved the car into the garage. I should have remembered our bags."

"It seems you're busy."

Aléjandro scoffed. "It's bullshit you don't need to worry about."

We were now in the kitchen near the door that led

to the garages. Coming to a stop, I looked up at him and lowered my voice in case anyone else could hear us. "I've spent my entire life around angry men. I'm used to being in the dark. I've had the 'you don't need to worry about it' lecture more times than I can count. I won't ask you for details. I only ask that if it involves my safety, my family's, or yours, you'll warn me."

Aléjandro took my hand in his. "It's not really about the famiglia."

"Not really?" I pulled my hand back.

"Nick's father is one of *mi padre's* top lieutenants. He runs one of our clubs, Wanderland. It's supposed to be higher end."

"A strip club?"

"A private club," Aléjandro corrected with a grin.

"So, there are also prostitutes." When he didn't reply, I added, "I'm familiar. Rocco oversaw the workers at a famiglia club called Emerald Club."

"Your brother—"

"Dario?" I asked.

"Dante. He made a comment or two to Nicolas, Nick's father, about Wanderland. Let's just say he wasn't complimentary and now Nicolas is pissed off." Aléjandro shook his head. "The thing is, I agree with your brother."

"You do?"

Aléjandro inhaled, his nostrils flaring. "Nicolas has been in charge of Wanderland and a few other casinos for years. I come in here and see shit that needs to change. As *mi padre's* son, it's within my right. To Nicolas I'm a hot-headed kid who hasn't done his time."

A smile came to my lips as I took in the over six feet, four inches of solid man before me. "I'd say you're more than a kid."

He nodded. "Dante should have spoken to me. There's more than a little ill will within the cartel about the famiglia—about the alliance in general. Stirring up shit was stupid."

I inhaled. "First, thank you for talking to me and not treating me as if I'm too dense to understand."

Aléjandro nodded.

I went on, "Dante is behind the alliance. He told me that when I found out about our wedding. He even said at first, he was skeptical. If he said something to the lieutenant, my guess is that whatever it was that he mentioned bothers him. The famiglia has concerns too. Both organizations reflect on the other. Dante probably doesn't want whatever he mentioned to reflect poorly on the famiglia. The alliance needs to work for both sides."

As Aléjandro opened the door to the garage, he seemed to let my words sink in. "Let me get the suitcases. Rei will stay here at the house until I get back. We have guards outside, but I'm not willing to have any of them in here with you until Silas arrives."

My forehead furrowed. "Where are you going?"

"To Wanderland. I need to deal with Nicolas

face-to-face. *Mi padre* is still near, but if Nicolas is going to respect me, I should be the one to handle this."

"Is it safe?"

Aléjandro's lips twitched. "Too early to be a widow again?"

"Please don't say that." I stepped down into the garage seeing not only the Porsche, but also a black Mercedes and a large black SUV. Over to the side, I also saw a Ducati motorcycle. "No furniture, but plenty of vehicles."

Aléjandro went to the Porsche and hit a key fob button. The hood opened.

"That's odd, being in front," I said.

"The engine takes up the rear half of the car. You'll appreciate the speed if you decide to drive."

"I don't know how to drive." When Aléjandro's eyes opened wider and his forehead furrowed, I added, "My father didn't think it was necessary and Rocco agreed."

Lifting the suitcases out of the car, my husband shook his head. When his gaze met mine there was a gleam in his eyes. "I can teach you more than to like sex. I'll teach you how to drive."

Ignoring the comment about sex. I concentrated on the second part of his statement. "You will?" I asked incredulously. "What about Silas?"

"I don't want you off by yourself, but it seems unsafe not to know how. There may be a time when you might need to jump in one of these and drive away."

Turning back to the Ducati, I asked, "Will you teach me to drive that?"

Aléjandro's laugh echoed through the garage. "Let's start with four wheels." He wheeled both suitcases back into the kitchen.

"I can take them both upstairs." Reaching for the handles, I stopped. "Are you sure you shouldn't take Rei with you? I'll be fine in the house."

"I trust Em and Nick to be with me. Rei won't bother you. I'll tell him to stay downstairs."

I looked around at the empty rooms. "And do what?"

"Wi-Fi is up and running. He can stay busy."

"Stay safe."

Aléjandro splayed his fingers on each side of my waist and leaned close. Our noses were almost touching. "Kisses. I get those."

I nodded before shutting my eyes and leaning in, closing the gap. There was nothing to hate about Aléjandro's kisses. They could even become addicting. When we pulled away, we both had smiles. "Please let me know you're all right."

"I entered my number in your phone last night. Call me if you need anything." He looked at the suitcases. "I can take them upstairs."

"I'm good."

As I carried the two small pieces of luggage up the

stairs, I wondered if I was as I'd just said—good. Just maybe I was. Soon, I was lost in the job of unpacking. There were things I hadn't seen since I'd packed them away after Rocco's death. As I hung up and put away my clothes, I thought about Aléjandro's offer to decorate. If he was okay with my buying large items, maybe he wouldn't mind if I did an upgrade to my wardrobe. SoCal was a bit trendier than Missouri. Or at least, I imagined it was.

I hadn't even noticed the time or the movement of the sun toward the horizon until the thunder of pounding footsteps caused me to turn toward the open door to our bedroom. In the dimming sunlight, Rei appeared in the doorway. His face was flushed as if he'd raced up the staircase.

"Mia," he panted, holding tight to the doorframe. "We have to go."

CHAPTER

ELEVEN

I stood up, befuddled at my brother-in-law's demand. "Why? Where is Aléjandro?" My palms grew clammy. "Is he okay?" As Rei appeared to be measuring his words, I asked again, "What's happening?"

Before he could answer, my phone rang, Aléjandro's name appeared on the screen. I let out the breath I was holding. "This is Aléjandro."

"No, Mia. It's not." Rei came closer. "Give me the phone."

I turned away, hitting the green button. "This means you're okay."

"*Señora* Roríguez?" An unfamiliar voice came from the phone.

Rei was now inches away, his voice a low growl coming from over my shoulder. "Disconnect the call."

I looked down at the phone in my hands and

turned back to my brother-in-law. Before I could decide, he ripped the phone from my grip and hit the disconnect button.

The small hairs on the back of my neck were standing to attention. "What the hell?"

"Have you had any other calls?" he asked as he hit the button to turn off the phone and slid it into his pocket.

"Give me that back." I clenched my teeth.

"Any other calls?"

"No." I let my hands drop, slapping my thighs. "I've been unpacking." I looked around the bedroom. "Tell me why you took my phone and disconnected that call." I recalled the unfamiliar voice. Looking up, I asked, "Is Aléjandro okay?"

"*Sí*, he will be. Come with me."

With my circulation thumping in my ears, I turned a circle, taking in our bedroom. Once I was again facing Rei, I said, "He told me to stay here."

Rei offered his hand. "Come with me. Something happened after his meeting at Wanderland. Aléjandro trusts me to take you to him."

"Take me where? Is he hurt? Who was calling?" My questions were coming faster than answers. I didn't take Rei's hand, but I did nod. "I'll go with you."

"We should hurry."

That didn't help my nerves. My quick assessment of myself was that I needed to change clothes. I'd been unpacking all afternoon, and I looked haggard.

Instead, I ran my hand over my hair, slipped my feet into a pair of sandals, and grabbed my purse. We quickly made our way downstairs and out the front door. As we stepped out into the evening air, I realized I didn't have a key to the house.

Rei pushed buttons on the keypad and the lock clicked with its activation.

"I should know that."

Rei nodded. "I believe the plan was to put in a new system if you liked the house."

If I liked it.

Aléjandro said the same thing.

Rei's car was still parked on the driveway. After locking the gate with another series of numbers, Rei opened the passenger door. Instead of opening out, the car door went up.

I looked up before getting inside. "That's..."

He grinned. "Too bad they quit making these. It's a hell of a lot nicer than Jano's Porsche."

Now didn't seem like the time to be comparing sports cars. "Where are we going?"

"To one of the cartel hideouts."

"And that's safe?" I asked.

"Aléjandro wouldn't ask me to take you there if it wasn't."

There were too many alarms sounding in my head to make sense of what was safe and what wasn't. A cartel hideout. That didn't sound safe. Settling into the front seat of Rei's Audi R8, I tried to settle my nerves.

I watched as the driver door opened upward, the same as the passenger door. If they were both open at the same time, they'd look like wings.

Once Rei was behind the steering wheel, I started my list of questions. "What happened? And why didn't you want me to speak to that caller?"

Rei's dark brown eyes looked at me, purposely scrutinizing me—or that was how it felt.

"I'm his wife."

Rei nodded. "And I'm his brother. Aléjandro trusts you. Sorry, Mia, but I don't know you." Turning away from my stare, Rei pulled the car up toward the gate.

Know me.

I didn't know my own husband.

To hell with this.

I wasn't going to some unknown place with a person who couldn't be honest with me. As the car came to a stop, I reached for the door handle. The car door popped open.

Rei reached out and seized my arm. "*Qué diablos?*"

While I didn't understand what he'd said, I recognized the tone. I pulled my arm from his grasp. "If you can't trust me, I can't trust you. I'm staying here where Aléjandro said to stay."

Rei exhaled. "Close the damn door."

Pushing on the door, it began to rise.

"*Mierda.*" Rei exhaled. "Jano wasn't lying when he said you're stubborn." When I didn't respond or move, he went on, his tone softening, "Close the door, *por favor.*"

Slowly, I reached for the handle and pulled it toward me. The car took over from there and the door closed. I turned back to Rei. "Tell me what's happening."

"Will you stay in the car, or do I need to worry about you jumping out when I'm driving?"

I gestured toward my seatbelt I'd rebuckled. "I'm belted in."

Rei nodded as he put the car into drive and pulled out of the gate. "What did he tell you before he left?"

Laying my head against the seat, I remembered. "He said Dante said some things that upset a lieutenant named Nicolas, and he was going to Wanderland to set things straight. He said Emiliano and Nick would be with him."

We were now on roads with more cars.

Rei nodded. "Nicolas is Andrés Ruiz's brother."

The family that hosted our wedding.

"He's worked for our father for as long as we've been alive. You can see why he's not too happy about taking orders from us."

My thoughts went to my uncles. "Yeah, Dario has some of the same issues, especially with our uncles." As soon as the words left my tongue, I wondered if I shouldn't be sharing things about the famiglia. I quickly added, "He has them under control."

Rei smiled. "*Sí*, I saw how happy they were at the wedding."

"What happened at Wanderland?"

"Nicolas listened, according to Jano. With our *padre* still near, he didn't have much of a choice. Nicolas agreed to investigate changes with the whores at the club." He turned my direction, as his grip of the steering wheel tightened. "As Jano, Em, and Nick were leaving Wanderland, there was a drive-by."

"A shooting?" I asked, my heart rate accelerating.

Rei nodded.

"Are they...is anyone dead?"

"The fucking Russians. Nick was shot. Jano and Em took chase. They got into Em's car and followed the bratva car to a storage facility. When the bratva car stopped, Jano jumped out of their car and pulled one of them from the car. Em followed. The good news is there's two less Russians to worry about, but in the fight, Jano was stabbed."

Aléjandro was stabbed.

My stomach twisted with the news.

I sucked in a breath. "He was stabbed. Is he in the hospital?"

Rei shook his head. "We have our own doctors. Hospitals ask too many questions and keep records."

The famiglia did the same thing. Sometimes, the hospital was the better option, such as with my father. Although, there's no way to know if the hospital could have saved him. More importantly, there's the question of whether or not anyone wanted him saved.

"Did they get Aléjandro help?" 'Did they want to save him' was what I wanted to ask.

"They did."

"And Nick?"

"He's being patched up, too."

"What about the call?" I asked.

"Jano's phone is missing. Our men should have it turned off soon. They fucked up, not realizing it was missing sooner. Jano's concerned that the person who found it would try to call you, and it seems he was right."

"It was his number. Could the call have been from the bratva?"

"It depends when he lost it. The bratva or the police. Neither is good. If it was the bratva, they could triangulate the call to find your house. Jano bought it under a shell company. It's too dangerous to have his name on the deed." We came to a stop at a red light as Rei checked all directions. "Until Silas arrives and the new security system is set up, it's not safe for you to be there."

"Where will we stay?"

"Our *padre* made a request."

Jorge made a request?

"What does that mean?"

"It means you need to talk to Jano."

Based on the setting sun to our right, Rei was

driving south. The view outside our windows changed from the palm trees, flowering bushes, and gated homes to cracked streets, concrete walls, and graffiti. Streetlights were beginning to illuminate sidewalks littered with trash and weeds coming through the cracks.

Rei pulled up to a gate. Appearing above the fence under a dusk sky, I saw multiple large buildings and a ship, its paint chipped and sails down. After entering a code, Rei drove us through the gate. I turned, watching it close behind us. Rei continued through a large garage door and into one of the buildings. Through the darkness, he drove us to the far end where there were probably ten to fifteen other vehicles of all different makes and varying ages.

"Stay by me," he said before turning off the car.

That was an order I had no problem following.

Before my door was opened, two men rushed toward the car from the shadows.

"Lock the doors," Rei said, jumping from his seat and slamming his door.

Hurriedly, I did as he said, frantically searching and finally finding the button. The click of the lock echoed. The car muffled the men's voices. It didn't matter. I couldn't have understood them even if they were distinct. I sucked in a breath and pushed back against the seat as with a kick to his chest, Rei sent one of the men flying. Less than a second later, he had the second man pinned over the hood of his car with a long blade against his neck.

My entire body trembled as my eyes opened wide at the scene playing out before me.

Rei was asking questions and the man with his face near the windshield was trying desperately to shake his head. Suddenly, Rei took a step back and the man slowly stood with both hands raised.

Rei yelled at both men.

My heartbeat echoed in my ears.

What would happen to me if Rei was hurt?

I held my breath as Rei walked away, toward the direction we'd entered the building. My gaze scanned the dashboard, wondering if I could drive this car if necessary or if Rei had left the keys. Given my lack of experience with driving, I couldn't guarantee that attempting to drive an Audi R8 was any safer than encountering the men outside.

Lost in my thoughts, Rei pounding on the window caused me to jump.

He motioned for me to come out.

For longer than a moment, I sat, trying to collect my breath and thoughts. A salty tear slid down my cheek as I longed for Kansas City and people I knew and trusted. My gaze went back through the window, seeing Rei's impatient stare.

Nodding, I opened the car door. The chill of the evening sea breeze combined with the darkness caused my flesh to pebble with goose bumps. "Are we safe?"

"Mistaken identity is all. Nothing to worry about." He gave me one last look over his shoulder. "You might want to stay with me."

Good idea.

Doing as he said, I stayed at Rei's side as we climbed a long case of metal stairs. Our steps reverberated noisily through the large building. My legs were complaining by the time we made it to the landing. Looking down, I saw we were easily two or three stories in the air. The door we reached had a small panel within. After Rei knocked, a man opened the small panel. The setup reminded me of an old speakeasy. The man within scrutinized us, his gaze lingering on me.

"*Señora* Roríguez," Rei said.

The window shut and after a series of clicks, the door opened. With a full view of the man, I sucked in a breath. He was tall and beefy, with the perfect bouncer physique. As we stepped inside, my nose scrunched at the multitude of odors permeating the air. The volume of voices rose with cat calls, whistles, and comments about my ethnicity as thirty or more sets of eyes turned in our direction.

Rei removed the same blade from wherever he kept it hidden. "*Señora* Roríguez," he said loudly.

All the eyes turned away and the remarks ended. The low din of conversations resumed.

The giant room we'd entered was filled with long picnic tables, enough to seat probably a hundred or more people. Scanning the people within, I saw I was obviously the only woman. The men sat scattered around in small groupings. Electronics and weapons of all types were on the tables.

Rei tilted his head toward one end of the room. I stayed at his side as we walked between the tables toward another door. As we progressed, the men pretended to ignore us, instead concentrating on their task at hand. They were cleaning guns, sharpening knives, working on computers, or eating from takeout containers.

An armed man stood beside the door Rei led me to. The guard didn't question us. He nodded and opened the door. This room had an overwhelming odor: the distinct combination of perspiration and disinfectant.

As I tried not to inhale too deeply, my focus zeroed in on the man sitting up on a cot—my husband. He wasn't wearing a shirt, and his left arm was wrapped with bandages. His dark stare went from Rei to me.

"Aléjandro," I said softly as a lump came to my throat. I hurried to him. "Are you...? Can I touch you?"

His lips quirked as he lifted his right hand. "Always."

Aléjandro looked up at the men standing near us. Seeing his brother's knife, he asked, "*Que pasó?*"

Rei responded, knowing I couldn't understand what they were saying.

From the sound of it, my husband wasn't happy about our downstairs welcoming crew. Finally, Aléjandro cocked his chin to the side, and Rei as well as the other few men stepped away, leaving us as alone as possible.

I waited until their discussion ended.

Taking his hand, I scanned from his messy hair down his handsome face that had a dark shadow of whiskers. My gaze continued down his bare chest, his sculptured abs, and finally, to his trim waist where his blue jeans began. Once I was certain the only bandages were on his arm, I sat at his side and ran my fingers over his chest before looking up into his gaze. "If you're trying to scare me, you're doing a good job."

With a grimace, he lifted both hands to my cheeks and pulled me toward him until our lips touched. "You're trembling," he said as our kiss ended. "Are you scared?"

Swallowing, I nodded. "Of everything. But" —I hesitated to say anything— "I got the feeling I'm not exactly welcome here."

"You are and I'll kill anyone who makes you feel that way."

I feigned a smile. "I think you're outnumbered."

"Rei and I are Roríguez." He grinned. "You are too. We receive respect. If not, we take care of the problem."

His words were laced with a permeating scent of testosterone, a predatory odor that filled the air, daring others to give him a reason to demonstrate his dominance. The scent was almost as frightening as the conviction in my husband's expression.

"Once Rei told them who I was, they seemed" —I lifted my brows— "better."

"Then they'll all live to see tomorrow."

"You went after the shooters? You purposely put yourself in danger."

He nodded. "Danger is what we do." His expression soured. "The bratva is a fucking cancer in our city. It's up to us to remove them any way necessary, one by one."

It was then I recalled something Rei said. "Is Nick all right?" I widened my eyes. "Rei said he was shot."

Aléjandro tilted his head toward a curtain I hadn't noticed before. "They have him medicated. The bullet is out. He'll be good soon."

"Is anyone with him?"

He shook his head. "His *padre* has been here, but he's left. Nicolas needs to be at Wanderland in case the Russians return."

"You could have been shot." I lifted my hand to his scruffy cheek. "Please don't make me a widow again."

Aléjandro took my hand in his. "It's nice to hear concern even if it's not one hundred percent sincere."

"It is."

He tilted his head. "You're not going to make me believe that you haven't thought about my death.

145

Death saved you once. It would make sense you would consider it the second time."

I had thought of Aléjandro's death. I wasn't proud of that, especially now.

"We're just getting started," I said, forcing a smile. "I don't know what I want. But I know that on the way here, I feared losing you."

"That's a start." He grimaced. "Doc said the cut is deep. Said it missed the tendon, mostly muscular damage. I won't be lifting weights for a while, but it will heal."

"I guess that's good news." I scooted closer. "Can we go home, or do we need to stay here?"

Aléjandro's jaw clenched. "We've received an invitation...one we can't refuse."

This was probably what Rei meant. "From your father?"

"*Sí.*"

"Does he want us to go to Mexico?"

TWELVE

I wasn't sure how I felt about going to Mexico.

"No," Aléjandro said. "He wants us to stay with him and *mi madre* until Silas can be certain our home is safe."

"Stay with him where? Are they staying in a hotel?"

Aléjandro shook his head. "When he's in the States, if possible, he prefers to stay on his yacht."

I tilted my head. "Your parents are on a boat?"

"A big boat," he said with a scoff. "He keeps it in international waters. That way he's not subject to the US laws."

"How far away is that?"

"Over twenty-four miles from shore." He shrugged. "About a half-hour boat ride or less than fifteen minutes by helicopter."

My eyes grew wide. "I've never been on a boat that travels that far that fast. I've been on a helicopter. My father had one to get to and from the mansion in the mountains. My mom hated it. When he died, it was one of the first things she got rid of."

He reached for my hand and slowly turned it over in his. After his Adam's apple bobbed, he met my gaze. "I don't know which mode of transportation we'll take. It will depend on who's available to transport us and weather conditions."

"How big is this yacht? I've been on a few yachts in the Ozarks, but they wouldn't be safe in international waters."

"Trust me, it's big. *Mi padre* was rather insistent with his invitation. Jorge Roríguez doesn't believe in coincidences or random acts of aggression when they're aimed at him or his family. He wants us close." Aléjandro lowered his voice. "You know that your first husband was in cahoots with your father and Elizondro Herrera to take down the current alliance."

"Dario didn't tell me everything. He said he'd keep the details secret for my reputation. I pieced some of it together."

"Your reputation isn't based on the asshole you married."

It seemed that my identity was continually linked to my husband—or make that husbands.

Aléjandro went on, "*Mi padre* believes since Herrera's plan failed, he's trying other avenues. *Padre* wouldn't put it past Herrera to make a deal with the

Russians. And next is the question, how did they know we were at Wanderland?"

"You think you were being targeted?"

"*Mi padre* wants to be certain, especially if there's an alliance between Herrera and the Russians."

I shook my head. "No one deals with the bratva."

Aléjandro's lips curled. "Before this, no one would imagine the cartel and the Italian Mafia being allies."

"I guess that's true. So, your dad thinks the attack on the three of you involves Herrera?"

His handsome face contorted into a grimace as he shrugged. "He wants to rule it out. There's also the idea that people aren't happy with our alliance. There has been rumbling in the ranks. No one thought Cat would stay with your brother. Now, there's us. Rei said your phone was called while you were in our home." There was a sharp edge to his chiseled jaw. "Before we can live there, we need to up the security." He lifted my hand to his lips and looked at me through long lashes. "Killing you would send a message to both our cartel and your famiglia."

My empty stomach twisted. "Me? I'm a target?"

"Not if you can't be found. Few people will know where we've gone. It will appear as if we're on a honeymoon."

I nodded.

"What about our things? Is it safe for us to stop by the house and get clothes?" I remembered something. "And Rei has my phone."

"You can't have your phone." He looked around.

It was the first time I noticed Rei was gone.

Aléjandro went on. "Our men probably have it by now. We have some fucking great hackers. They've been trying to determine where the call from my phone originated. Your phone will help them."

"But my phone is how I contact my family and friends."

Aléjandro squeezed my hand. "You'll get a new phone. We'll go by the house and get our things."

We both turned to see Rei entering the room and coming toward us. "*Padre* is sending the chopper."

Night had fallen since Rei had brought me into the hideout. Since Rei's Audi only had two seats, I rode back to the house with him while Aléjandro rode with two trusted cartel soldiers.

Once we were at the house, the soldiers did a sweep inside as we waited on the pavers within the front gate. With the outside lights illuminating the area, my attention went to the shadows. I had the unwelcome feeling of being watched. The soldiers were only in the house for less than a minute when they came out. I couldn't understand what they were saying, but I heard the agitation in their voices and saw my husband's reaction. Rei took off running around the back of the house.

"What is it?" I asked, reaching for Aléjandro's arm.

The muscles pulled tight on the side of his face and the tendons in his neck came to life as he removed his gun from the holster strapped to his back. "Someone broke in. The glass doors to the pool were jimmied open."

"Someone broke into our home?" I felt my body temperature rise and my temples throb as I stared at the gun in my husband's grip. Weapons had been an everyday occurrence throughout my life. That didn't mean that I wasn't alarmed that the person or persons could still be on the property. "I was here most of the day."

Aléjandro said something to his soldiers. He turned back to me. "Rei was with you. This happened after you left." His nostrils flared. "I don't like this. Diego and Felipe are making sure the house is safe. Then we'll go in and grab our things."

"I thought there were other guards."

Rei came from around the back of the house. "I think whoever was here came by sea. In the dark, I can't see the beach, but there's broken grass and sand on the pool deck that wasn't there before."

"Fuck," Aléjandro growled. "That's how they avoided the guards." He cursed under his breath. "Word is out I bought this house."

What does that mean?

Will we need to move?

Diego and Felipe returned to the courtyard.

"No one is inside," the taller one said. He turned to me. "*Señora*, your bedroom. It's in shambles."

"They went through my things?" I turned to Aléjandro. "Why would they do that?"

"We'll fucking find out." After holstering his weapon, he took my hand. "I'm staying with you. Let's go inside."

I clung tightly to him as we went inside.

What hours ago had been pleasant surroundings now felt violated. We went up the staircase and straight back to our bedroom. I gasped at the mess within. The drawers to the dressers were opened and the contents strewn over the floor. Stepping into my closet, I saw my clothes pulled from their hangers.

"Is anything missing?" my husband asked.

Tears slid from my eyes. "I don't know. I just unpacked all these things."

Aléjandro wrapped his arms around me. "I promise we'll get to the bottom of this."

Swallowing back my emotions, I nodded against his shoulder, relishing the strength in his hold. I spoke into his shirt, "I need to throw some things into a suitcase." I lifted my head and met his gaze. "How long will we be gone?"

"You won't need more than a few dresses and bathing suits. The staff will help with laundry."

"Staff?"

"About fourteen usually. And *Padre* has guards. We will be protected."

"I wasn't sure about spending time with your

parents. I don't know them, but now" —I looked around— "I'm glad your father offered."

Aléjandro's lips quirked. "It was more of a summons, but I agree."

"What about your things?" I asked.

"Most of my clothes are still back at the Ruiz pool house. I was going to get them after my meeting at Wanderland. Rei is headed over there to get things for both of us. He'll meet us at the pickup point."

It didn't take long for me to fill a small suitcase. I hated leaving our room in such disarray, but Aléjandro kept reminding me to hurry and promised that Viviana would take care of everything once she and Silas arrived.

"If there's anything that's sentimental, bring it."

I stood for a moment thinking of all the things I'd unpacked. When I'd originally packed everything in the townhouse, I'd purged many items from my first marriage that could be considered sentimental.

There was something. I recalled a ring my grandmother, Gia, had given me. I went to the closet, searching for my jewelry box. I pulled the drawers farther open and looked under the piles of clothes on the floor. I distinctly remembered placing my jewelry box in the back of the third drawer. "My jewelry box is missing."

Aléjandro appeared at the doorway to the closet. "Fuck, Mia. I'll buy you new jewelry."

It was one more straw piled on the straws weighing me down.

Sniffling, I wrapped my arms around my midsection and unsuccessfully held back tears. "Honestly, there was only one thing I wanted. My grandmother's ruby ring—my mother's mother. She gave it to me when I was a child."

Aléjandro's jaw clenched, a sign of his returning rage. The violent emotion swirled in his brown orbs, darkening the color to match that of his growing pupil. "I'm sorry."

The sense of loss knotted in my chest combined with everything that had happened in the last few hours. "Me too." The chance of recovering the stolen ring was slim to none. "Why would they take my jewelry box?"

"My guess is to make it look like a robbery."

"That's what it was."

Aléjandro shook his head. "No, it was an expedition. Someone wanted to confirm that we live here. Your jewelry box will provide the evidence."

"To whom?"

"Whoever sent them. The frightening monsters in my world rarely do their own crimes."

My thoughts went to my grandmother's ring. I rarely wore it because the band size was too small. It fit on my pinky finger and that felt odd. I remembered the high prongs and the yellow-gold band and the large vibrant ruby. It was simple and elegant. I should have had it made larger, but I never did.

As we were leaving, Aléjandro and I went out to the backyard. The vast darkness beyond our lighting made the small hairs on my arms stand to attention. Again, Aléjandro removed his gun from his holster and went to the far side of the pool. He crouched down, investigating the sand and broken grass before peering over the cliff into the darkness.

My heart pounded in my ears. I was certain every crash of waves below or rustling of grass was a threat hidden by the shadows. "How did they get up here?" I asked.

"Climbed, I suppose."

Because I hadn't explored earlier in the day, I had no idea how high up the cliff we were or if there was even a pathway down to the beach. As my thoughts raced on, I wrapped my arms around my midsection, fearful that someone could still be there, watching us from the pitch-black darkness, guns aimed at one or both of us. "May we leave?"

Aléjandro nodded.

"Will Silas be able to stop people from coming up the cliff?"

Without sheathing his weapon, Aléjandro put his hand in the small of my back. His touch and words were strong and confident. "When I bring you back here, our home and grounds will be completely safe. You have my word."

I wanted to believe him.

Is cartel life more dangerous than the famiglia?

It wasn't a question I wanted to ponder.

Felipe, the taller soldier, drove Aléjandro and me to the pickup point Rei had mentioned. I expected to be driven to an airport or public heliport. Instead, we arrived at another gated home. Felipe must not have known the code. He spoke into a speaker. The only part I recognized was our last name.

The gate opened.

"This is Nicolas Ruiz's house," Aléjandro offered.

"The man you spoke to at Wanderland earlier today."

Pressing his lips together, Aléjandro nodded. "He has a helipad. Even if he's not thrilled with me, he wouldn't deny *mi padre's* request."

Rei's car was parked on their driveway under overhead lights. As our car came closer, the front door to the house opened, and Rei came out with a woman.

"I know her," I said softly. "From the wedding."

"She is Em's cousin, Mireya."

"Are she and Rei dating?"

"No." Aléjandro laughed. "She lives here."

I appreciated the reminder of the woman's name as Mireya and Rei came to our vehicle.

"Mia, hello again." Mireya was petite and pretty with long dark hair and round brown eyes. I guessed her age to be somewhere in her early twenties. She spoke as we got out of the vehicle. "You're headed out to the yacht. Is this a honeymoon?"

"*Sí*," Aléjandro answered. "Every woman's dream is to honeymoon with her in-laws."

Her smile grew. "Oh, the yacht is so big, I'm sure you can find time for yourselves." She looked at me. "You're going to love it." Leading us into the house, Mireya continued talking as Felipe followed with our luggage. "Papá called. The helicopter should be here in a few minutes. He said to be sure to invite you in."

"That's very kind," I replied, taking in the grandeur of the house.

Their home was large and stately. Mireya led us back to glass doors that went out to a pool. The surrounding area was lit up like a resort. It appeared Nicolas's home was bigger than Andrés's, but I'd take the latter for the ocean view.

Mireya made small talk as Aléjandro and Rei kept their eagle-eyed stares on the shadows beyond our bubble. It wasn't long before the thrumming of a helicopter could be felt as well as heard. Peering into the dark sky, I wrapped my arms around my midsection and squinted as a blinding spotlight shone down, finally settling on the helipad beyond the pool. As the helicopter landed, the skirt of my dress, the grass, and the flowers swayed in the whirling wind from the propellers.

"Tell your papá thank you," Rei said, making his voice louder.

Mireya waved.

As the rotors continued to spin, Felipe opened a door on the side of the helicopter. With my hand in Aléjandro's, he led us forward. There weren't steps but a high footboard. Soon, the three of us and the pilot were aboard with our luggage. I was seated next to my husband, and Rei was sitting in the copilot's seat. Our seatbelts were nothing special, resembling those in a car. Aléjandro handed me a pair of headphones motioning to me to cover my ears.

This wasn't my first helicopter ride. Nevertheless, I held my breath as we were lifted off the ground. The pilot's voice came through the earphones. Once he stopped talking, I looked to my husband for a translation.

"He said we should arrive in less than twenty minutes to the Bella."

"Bella?"

"The name of the yacht. She was named after *mi mama's madre.*"

I had more questions to ask, but I didn't know this pilot. Aléjandro said he worked for Jorge. That would make him cartel. And while he would respect Aléjandro and Rei, he could have issues with me as some of the famiglia had issues with Catalina.

I decided my questions could wait until Aléjandro and I were alone.

Alone.

My thought was an epiphany. I wanted to be alone

with my husband. That realization was amusing considering that as recently as this afternoon, I was dreading our time alone. Looking down at my hand in his, I was conscious of how things had changed in a relatively short period of time.

No longer did I have my family or friends. My choice was to face my new life alone or at the side of my husband. In the eye of this current storm, Aléjandro was my anchor, keeping me grounded as we flew above the city lights.

Once beyond the coast, we were enveloped by darkness. An eerie green glow from the dashboard illuminated the interior. Outside, a million stars peppered the sky while below us, the Pacific Ocean faded into nothingness.

And then in the distance I saw our destination. I sucked in a breath as the Bella came into view. In a sea of blackness, the yacht's LED lighting glowed like a blue beacon. As we flew closer, I got a better idea of what Aléjandro called a yacht. This was more than that—a superyacht. I counted at least four levels, the second to the top containing a swimming pool and hot tub, both glowing with underwater lights. The Mexico flag was flying from the rear deck.

THIRTEEN

My temples pounded with the thumping of the ever-present whirling as I tried to come to terms with my situation. I was approaching the huge superyacht of an infamous drug lord. Oh, and he was also my new father-in-law. My husband had been injured, and I'd watched my brother-in-law pull a knife on a man. It was a lot.

Suddenly, I became self-conscious. Looking down, I registered the fact that I was still wearing the long blue sundress from this morning. "I should have changed clothes." At the moment it was probably an irrational concern, but for some reason, my presentation spiked in importance.

Aléjandro laughed, confirming the nonissue. "I killed two Russians and was stabbed today." He made a face as he sniffed. "I'm in need of a shower. *Mi esposa*, you're stunning."

"But this boat is" —I wasn't sure I had words— "really nice..." I held my breath as the pilot lowered us to the helipad near the stern of the yacht. Once the landing skids touched down, I said, "We should be better dressed for your parents."

"My parents are happy we're here and safe. They don't care about what clothes we're wearing." Again, Aléjandro translated the pilot's instructions, telling me that we were to remain seated until the rotors came to a complete stop.

During the time it took for them to stop, a line of people in white uniforms appeared, all standing with their hands clasped behind their backs. I glanced down at my watch. It was nearly nine at night, and it appeared that we had an entire staff at our beck and call.

My ears echoed with the residual whirling of the propellers as one man came forward and opened the door. He offered his hand. I took it, the leverage helping me step down. The skirt of my dress blew, and my hair tousled in the sea breeze as my sandals contacted the helipad. From the outside, an opening where there could be a window showcased a brilliantly lit, luxurious living and dining area. Above us, the dark sky twinkled with an abundance of stars.

As I waited for my husband to disembark, I couldn't believe my eyes. This boat was crazy, reminding me of a story I'd seen about a Bezos superyacht. I was certain I was unsuccessful at hiding my awe. By the time all three of us were out of the heli-copter, Jorge Roríguez stood near the staff. He too was dressed in white. A short-sleeved linen shirt and long linen pants. Despite his grin, I couldn't help but see him for the intimidating and dangerous man he was. His smile broadened as Aléjandro guided me with a touch to the small of my back, and we walked toward him.

"Mia," he greeted, again wrapping me in a hug. The combined scents of spice and cigars tickled my senses. While his accent was thick, I had no difficulty understanding his English. "We're so happy to have you stay with us for a few days. We can get to know one another."

"Thank you for having us."

He spoke in Spanish to Aléjandro and Rei. What-ever he said to them sounded more serious than his greeting to me.

"You can get comfortable," Jorge said. "We'll have dinner at ten."

Dinner.

At the sound of the word, my stomach grumbled. I'd forgotten that I was hungry. The first pang seemed like days ago, not hours.

"*Sí,*" Aléjandro and Rei replied.

I couldn't look in every direction fast enough to take in the opulence surrounding me. My father wouldn't be happy that I'd married into the cartel. Despite his willingness for an alliance, it was obvious he considered himself above them. I smirked, knowing that if he saw me now, he'd be green with envy at the sight of this superyacht. It was quite literally a floating castle.

"I'll show you around after I shower," Aléjandro said. "We're headed to our suite."

The breeze disappeared as my husband led me down a staircase and through a hallway. I wondered if I would need a trail of breadcrumbs to find my way back out. When he opened the door to our cabin, I couldn't contain my awe.

"Is this always your room?" I asked, spinning a circle as a man laid both of our suitcases on the bed and left with a bow, closing our door behind him. Not only did we have a king-sized bed, but there was a deck with chairs and a table as well as a sitting area inside. One wall was lined with cabinetry, closets, and drawers. "This is magnificent. It is a honeymoon."

"I'd like to tell you it is, but it's not. Being here is all about safety."

His tone took away a bit of my excitement. "How long will we be here?"

Aléjandro frowned. "As long as necessary." He stalked my direction and possessively reached for my hips.

I sucked in a breath.

Holding his hand or him putting his hand on my back were becoming more comfortable. The way he held me against him was different—intimate. I could feel his erection hardening against me. "Aléjandro..."

He didn't loosen his hold as conviction saturated his proclamation. "You were in danger today. I won't allow that to happen again."

Trying to ignore his arousal, I lifted my hand to his left arm and gently touched his short-sleeve and the bandage peeking out from beneath. "You were in danger." I shook my head. "I wonder what I got myself into with our marriage." I scoffed. "Or what Dario got me into."

He lifted his hand to my cheek, staring intently into my eyes. I concentrated on the swirling shades of brown until his hand dropped, his eyes closed, and he leaned his forehead to mine. His words came out in a long breath. "I said you wouldn't regret this marriage."

"I don't."

Aléjandro's eyes opened. "You don't?"

I shook my head.

"I'm not an easy man, Mia. Neither is my father. Some would say I come by it naturally. This war with the bratva is" —he inhaled— "it's a war we must win. I won't allow you to be a casualty."

"Because my death would harm the alliance?"

"That's true. The real reason is that when I asked for you, I thought I was ready to marry. *Mi padre* warned me about a wife."

I took a step back. "He warned you about *me*?"

"No, about taking a wife. He told me that a wife is a weakness."

My mind was spiraling. "Does Jorge think I'm responsible for your injury or the shooting?"

Aléjandro exhaled. "I'm not saying this right." He ran his hand over his messy hair. "You, Mia, are important to me."

He didn't say he loved me, but I wasn't expecting that.

He went on, "And anyone who is important to me is a weakness. That was abundantly clear tonight when Rei told me about the men who ambushed his car." The muscles in his arms tightened as he balled his fingers into fists. "So, when *Padre* said to bring you here, I didn't hesitate. Until we figure out who is responsible for breaking into our home, and Silas is overseeing security, you—my weakness—will be where you are safe."

"Does my brother know where I am?"

"Only cartel know, and only a limited number of us. If Herrera is trying to take us down, we can't be sure who to trust." His expression softened. "Not many people are welcomed onto Bella. You're an honored guest. And more importantly you're *familia*."

"This yacht is like something out of the movies."

"It's strategic. You saw the flag?"

I nodded.

"In international waters, a ship or yacht is governed by the flag they fly. *Mi padre* is close enough

165

to handle matters in California, yet not staying in the States, therefore not subject to their laws."

He grimaced as he tugged the black t-shirt over his head, revealing his toned abdomen while simultaneously reminding me of his injury.

"Does it hurt?"

"Like a motherfucker. The doctor gave me pain meds, but I prefer to be mostly clear when dealing with *mi padre*."

"Mostly?"

Aléjandro opened a cupboard and pulled out a crystal decanter filled with a light amber liquid. "Tequila." He lifted two glasses. "Would you like a drink?"

I looked down at myself and back up. "I need a shower."

"Coincidence, so do I."

Pressing my lips together, I narrowed my eyes.

He pointed to his arm. "I'm injured. I thought you could reciprocate our earlier shower and wash me. I'd hate to rip the stitches."

Aléjandro was doing what I'd thought a day ago to be impossible: making me more comfortable around him. Perhaps it was by isolation. While I didn't really know my husband, I knew him better than I knew anyone else around us.

"I can do that."

He poured a few fingers of liquor into one of the glasses. "Did you decide on the drink?"

Inhaling, I walked closer. "Let's see, I was married yesterday. Today, I was shown my new home, taken to a cartel hideout where I was ambushed—your description. And where my husband was recovering from a stabbing. I learned I might be a target and then discovered someone had broken into our new home and ransacked our bedroom. Oh, and then we flew in a helicopter to a superyacht strategically floating outside of US waters."

His dark gaze shone with amusement. "That about sums it up."

"Yes on the drink. Make it a double."

Aléjandro handed me the glass he'd already poured. Next, he poured his own and lifted the glass.

I lifted mine to his.

The two crystal tumblers clinked.

"May you never grow bored with our life."

I scoffed and took a drink, before coughing.

"Take it easy," he said. "I don't plan to lose you to tequila."

The alcohol warmed my circulation. "That's a lot for two days. I'm thinking a little more boring would be all right."

Carrying my drink, I walked into the attached bathroom, taking in the huge glass shower and the sunken bathtub. When I turned, Aléjandro was standing in the doorway with his drink in hand.

"What are we going to do about keeping your bandage dry?" I asked.

Together, we wrapped Aléjandro's bandage with a plastic bag we found in one of the cabinets. It was surprisingly easier to step fully naked into the shower with him than it was this morning. This time I was on a mission. I wetted the washcloth and added body-wash. To keep his bandage dry, he needed to keep his arm raised. While he held onto the top of the shower door, I washed his hair, weaving my fingers through his dark mane. It was as I brought the washcloth close to his partially erect cock that I grinned. "Are you sure it won't bite?"

"No biting until you ask for it." Aléjandro pistoned his hips. "Keep going and let me know if you like what you feel."

Asshole.

Biting my lip, I ran the cloth up and down his penis. His length and girth grew harder under my touch. He was considerably larger than Rocco—my only comparison. And yet, despite his obvious arousal, I detected restraint. Aléjandro was letting me touch him at my own speed.

Maybe I was becoming comfortable. Maybe it was our near-death experiences. I wasn't exactly sure of the cause, but as my core clenched and my nipples drew tight, I sensed a change in my feelings for my new husband. After all, I wasn't frigid. I'd heard and read the stories about sex being pleasurable. Perhaps Giorgia was right. It could be better with Aléjandro.

With my lower lip between my teeth, my gaze met his. "Let's change things up a bit?"

He tilted his head, his dark stare swirling with emotions reflecting the intimacy of our position. "What do you want to change?"

"No intercourse. Not yet."

Aléjandro's lips pressed together in a straight line as he nodded.

An onset of nerves threatened the strength of my voice. "You see, I've been thinking that *sex* is a rather broad term."

"Okay." His voice was gravellier than it was a moment ago.

"We could start with oral."

His Adam's apple bobbed in his throat. "Just so I'm up to speed on these possible rule changes, are we talking about you sucking me or me getting to put my lips anywhere on that gorgeous body I want?"

Even under the hot water, my flesh covered in goose bumps as my core twisted. "Both."

CHAPTER
FOURTEEN

Aléjandro

Any pain in my arm was immediately forgotten as a wave of red pinkened Mia's otherwise pale skin, floating up her chest, to her neck, and coloring her cheeks. Waiting for my reply, she veiled her gorgeous eyes. Their usual hazel shade morphed with her declaration for a change in rules, darkening her orbs as they swirled with a deeper, richer green hue.

I wanted to reach for her and take what she just offered. There was no doubt that I'd enjoy every second of fucking her pouty lips. If my damn arm wasn't covered in plastic and bandages, I would.

Instead, being down one arm, I censored my usual desire for domination.

With Mia's nipples hard and her round tits heaving with anticipation, perhaps it was best to let this progress at her speed. With only the mention of her sucking me, my dick was three times the size it was a moment ago.

"I can be persuaded," I said.

Mia looked up, a smile curling her sensational lips. Dropping the washcloth to the floor, she kneeled, her soapy palms sliding down my legs lower and lower as she came face-to-face with my erection.

I'd never taken the time to consider the woman's thoughts as she fell to her knees before me until now.

What exactly is she thinking?

Her pink tongue darted to her lips as she rinsed her hands under the spray and reached for my heavy cock.

Fuck, does Mia have any idea how fucking gorgeous she is?

With her wet hair flowing down her back and her body glistening with water, she was a goddess come to life. Amphitrite, the Greek queen of the sea and the one chosen by Poseidon.

Fuck that. I wasn't sharing her with anyone, not even a Greek god of mythology.

This woman was mine.

Just as her name suggested, *Mia.*

She hadn't even brought her lips to me. Yet watching her expressive eyes as she tried to fist me, her fingers and thumb unable to meet, caused me to bite my tongue, careful not to blow my wad.

Time stood still as she slowly and painfully leaned forward. My grip of the shower door tightened and every nerve in my body exploded as she ran her tongue from the tip of my cock to the base.

The fucking door was in danger of breaking as she moved her lips back down and swirled her tongue, licking the slit. My muscles tensed when she opened her pink lips and took me in.

Fucking warm and wet.

The damn world turned black as I fought the heavenly sensation.

Originally, I mentioned Mia to *mi padre* not only because I was attracted but because she didn't reciprocate. It was a power move that I could probably only admit to Rei. In a little over twenty-four hours, my thoughts had shifted. Mia was doing something to me that I could never have predicted.

Not the blow job.

She was wedging her way into my thoughts.

This wasn't about a power play anymore. *Mi padre* had been right. A wife was a weakness but fuck if I didn't want to explore more with my new weakness—more of her body, mind, and soul. I wouldn't be satisfied until I possessed all of her, every thought in her head while being responsible for all her pleasure.

Bobbing her head, Mia tested her own resolve. Once in a while, gagging, she backed off. As I watched,

I marveled at the idea that I hadn't married a virgin. I hadn't wanted that. Of course, up until yesterday, I assumed her experience would mean wild and hot sex from the first night.

The woman before me was a dichotomy of sorts.

Confident.

Insecure.

Poised.

Uncertain.

My breathing stuttered as Mia used her hands, with one gripping my cock and the other teasing my balls. "Fuck yeah." I couldn't have stayed quiet if I tried. Every move she made felt too good.

With my free hand, I wove my fingers through her wet hair and resisted the desire to direct her movements. Damn, she had this more than covered.

The shower's spray continued to assault my back as my muscles tightened.

"Fuck, Mia."

Wrapping her arms around my thighs, she continued her head bobbing and the sounds of her mews and moans combined with the warm humidity of the shower. I released her head, conscious of scaring her.

Mia didn't stop, taking every drop as I came, over and over.

"Fucking better than jacking off," I said as I offered her my hand.

Her shy smile was stunning.

I cupped her cheek with my one good hand. "Do I need to get injured to earn your affection?"

Mia shook her head. "I'd rather you not be injured." She looked up at me with wide eyes. "I've never..." She shook her head again. "I know you don't want me to talk about...before."

I didn't. I wanted her fucking first husband to be obliterated from her mind. Yet, she looked so damn pleased, I had to encourage her. "You've never *what*?"

"Initiated...anything." Her smile blossomed. "I wanted to do that."

We were sailing in fully uncharted territory. And even without a fucking map, I wanted to explore everything about this woman, from her luscious curves to her flat plains and her deep valleys. However, as I stared at her smile, I wanted to go beyond the surface, to learn what she was thinking and feeling.

I tilted my forehead to hers. "Consider this an open invitation, *Señora* Roríguez. My cock is always available anytime" —I ran my thumb over her swollen lips — "you get the urge to suck." I lifted my eyebrows. "It's available for more than that."

Mia nodded.

"Now, it's my turn."

She stiffened. "Your parents are waiting for us for dinner."

"Does that mean that you're not turned on?" I tilted my head. "If I ran my tongue over your pussy, I wouldn't find it wet and your clit swollen?" I peered pointedly down at her tits. Her areolas were a deeper shade of red, and her nipples were hard as diamonds. "Your nipples are telling me something else."

Her stare softened. "I am turned on, and you'd find all you predict. I've just never been the guest of a drug lord before, and it seems to me that after giving us this amazing place to stay, punctuality isn't too much for him to ask."

"Just know, Mia, that when I look at you or reach for you during dinner, I'm thinking about the permission you've granted me. I'm thinking about my tongue claiming your pussy until you scream out my name. I'm imagining my face and chin drenched in your sweet juices."

The pink was back to her cheeks.

"I fucking love that you blush."

She lifted her palms to both sides of her face. "It's one of my least favorite traits. I try to hide my feelings, but it rarely works."

I stifled a laugh. She was right. Our first few interactions she did a piss-poor job of hiding her dislike for me. I'd take blushing and coming over that.

"Let me help you with your arm," Mia offered as I turned off the water.

Mia dressed in another long sundress. This one was white with small golden flowers. Saying that she didn't have time to dry her hair she plaited it into a single braid that she pulled over her shoulder.

If she was fishing for me to apologize for our

extended shower, she'd have a long wait. Although I didn't think she needed it, Mia added a small amount of makeup. The mascara made her beautiful eyes look even wider and the blush gave a rose hue to her cheeks. Her lips were still slightly swollen and so fucking kissable.

I pulled on a clean pair of blue jeans and Mia helped me with a button-up shirt, collar open, tails out, and sleeves rolled up. It was easier to get over my bandages and loose enough to cover my holster.

"I thought you said your father has guards," Mia said as she helped me button the front of the shirt.

"He does."

"Why do you need your gun?"

"I have a knife on my ankle too."

She tilted her head.

"No one can be fully trusted. Father's guards have shown their loyalty. Duty on the Bella is coveted." I inhaled. If I went on with my explanation, she might not be able to relax as I'd like her to do.

"Is there more?"

"Pirates are real. It's unlikely they could get close to the Bella without detection. It's better to be prepared."

"Should I?" Mia inhaled. "I've never carried a weapon, but Dante told me that Catalina does."

My eyes opened wider.

"A knife. Em taught her how to use it, and Dario continued her lessons."

That made me scoff. "Maybe Dario is a braver man than I gave him credit for." I saw Mia's expression. "Oh, I know he's the capo dei capi but to arm his wife... that's bravery."

"Maybe the secret is that he treats his wife in a way she doesn't want to stab him."

"Tell me, Mia. Do you want to stab me?"

She shook her head with a sexy-as-hell grin. "Not right now. Besides, someone beat me to it."

I was a bit concerned about *mi padre*. There was no question that he cared about family, but that never stopped him from putting the cartel first. My hope was that dinner would go well and nothing would come up to frighten Mia more than she already was.

With my hand in the small of her back, my wife and I arrived in the dining area at a minute before ten. *Mi padre* and *mi madre* were present, standing with drinks in their hands. *Mi padre* had tequila. Codigo 1530 XII Extra Anejo Tequila was one of his favorites. *Mi madre* had a glass of wine. I believed Andrés Ruiz made a point of gifting multiple cases from his wife's winery in SoCal.

Madre's smile grew as she came toward us. "I'm so happy you're all here and safe."

She was making a point of speaking English for Mia, and I appreciated it. Releasing my wife, I leaned closer and kissed *Madre's* cheek. *"Gracias."*

Rei entered, also looking freshly showered as *Madre* gestured toward the set table. "We don't always eat so late. When we learned you were coming, I was afraid you wouldn't have eaten."

"We've been a little busy killing Russians," Rei said.

I shot my brother a scowl. Before I could tell him to shut up, *Madre* waved him off.

"No talk of that here." Her gold bracelets jingled as she lifted her hand. A server appeared from the kitchen door.

"Señora?"

She spoke in Spanish. "Fill drinks for our children and now, it's time for us to eat."

I turned to Mia. "Would you like a drink with dinner? *Mi padre* has the best tequila money can buy."

"It was a gift," *mi padre* said with a grin.

Yes, in his line of work, he received many gifts.

"Wine with dinner," Mia said. "I've had my quota of tequila for one night."

"You're still standing," Rei said. "That means you haven't reached the limit."

"Vino," I said to the waiter, *"para mi esposa. Tequila para mí."*

As anxious as I was to get Mia back to our bedroom following the dinner, I held no illusion that our suite would be my next stop. As *Madre* asked Mia about the wedding and our new home, it was painfully clear that our *padre* wanted time with Rei and me alone to learn what the fuck was happening.

We all took seats around the table. *Padre* sat at the

head, *mi madre* to his left, me to his right, Mia beside me and across from Rei. One end of the room was open, looking out over the dark ocean. A warm breeze kept the temperature comfortable as the staff began serving our meal.

After the first course was taken away, I laid my hand on Mia's thigh. When she turned my direction, I lifted my eyebrows, hoping she remembered what I'd said and what would be on my mind. The pink hue filling her cheeks was the answer I was looking for.

Madre's warning kept our conversation light, at least the part that was spoken in English. Once we were all filled, *mi padre* told Rei and me to follow him to his office. I laid my hand in the small of Mia's back. "Rei and I need to talk to *Padre* about what happened today. Can you find your way back to the suite?"

Her body tensed beneath my touch.

"I'll be back as soon as I can."

She scanned from me to *Padre* and back with only her nervous eyes. "Okay. I'll wait up."

We remained quiet as *Padre*, Rei, and I walked out into the night and up the stairs to the next level. As far as home offices go, the one on Bella was smaller than his office at home. For safety reasons, the room was interior. The ceiling was high, yet without windows, it was as if we entered a golden box. Rei and I dutifully took the chairs across from *Padre's* desk as he sat in the large leather seat.

He leaned back, resting his elbows on the chair's

arms, and templed his fingers. "We have the Russians' phones."

My brother and I both sat forward. "Any connection to Herrera?" I asked.

He nodded. "It seems we are at war." He looked at me. "Not a good way for a marriage to begin."

CHAPTER

FIFTEEN

Mia

Leaving the dining room, I headed toward our suite. Walking around to the outside, I chose to follow the catwalk along the deck. I lifted my face, feeling the salty sea breeze. The black sky high above was filled with stars. Our peaceful bubble was a contrast to my thoughts.

"Mia."

I stopped and turned toward the voice. Josefina, Aléjandro and Rei's mother, was headed in my direction. Her orange outfit billowed around her slender body, and her gold jewelry reflected the lights within, a lovely contrast to her golden-brown complexion. In that second, I realized who she looked like to me— Salma Hayek. She was equally as beautiful and dressed as elegantly. Despite her youthful appearance, Josefina held herself in a welcoming, motherly way that also said she was in control. No doubt it took a strong woman to care for a dangerous husband and two equally dangerous sons.

Closing my eyes, I tried unsuccessfully to block out the vision of Rei holding the knife to the man's throat. 'Danger is what we do'—Aléjandro's words. Inhaling, I held on to the rail and waited as my mother-in-law approached. "Dinner was delicious, *Señora* Roríguez."

She smiled. "I didn't cook it. And in case you were wondering, my name is Josefina or *Mamá,* whichever makes you more comfortable."

I smiled.

"Do you have a few minutes to talk?" she asked.

With her heavily accented English, I wished I could speak back to her in her native language. "I don't know how long Aléjandro will be."

Josefina waved her hand. "The men. They can talk for hours. There's always a crisis."

My cheeks rose in a smile. "I'm used to it."

"Come." She led me toward the back of the yacht. Turning the corner, we were shielded from the wind. There was a lovely couch surrounding a firepit. As soon as we arrived, a man in white came forward and lit the firepit. "Would you like an after-dinner drink?" she asked me.

"No, thank you."

Josefina dismissed the man. I was taken with her willowy blouse as we sat on the couch near one another. This woman who was married to an infamous drug lord could easily be a model. Maybe she had been.

Her voice rolled gently through the air. "I'm sure this isn't easy for you."

I exhaled and feigned a smile. "It's been a lot for two days."

Clasping her hands on her lap, she leaned forward. "If you ever have questions or would like to talk, I'd like to be there to help where I can." Her eyes opened wide. "It's strange how sometimes marriage can be lonely."

Keeping my lips together, I nodded. The ache was real. During my first marriage, I had my friends and family.

Josefina went on, "I know you've been married before, but each marriage is its own unique entity. Roríguez men can be" —she hesitated— "a lot to handle." When I didn't respond, she continued, "They're passionate. I've heard the same about Italians." Her smile broadened. "I don't know about them firsthand. Our family. The men we trust. They're a different breed. My Jorge is a complicated man to those on the outside. Not to me."

A smile curled my lips. "It gives me hope that you love him."

"I didn't say that." She winked. "I do. Together we've built a world I'm proud to call ours. I know it's dangerous. That's why when Jorge told me about today's events, I insisted that the three of you join us. I know my sons. Given the choice, I know they would want to be back in San Diego, in the thick of the action."

It made me think of how Aléjandro had purposely gone after the Russians who shot at them.

I could blame it on the long day as a tear silently slid down my cheek. I wiped it with the back of my hand. "I think I became immune to the danger that the famiglia dealt with on a regular basis until that danger took my husband. Now, I'm extra-sensitive to the fear of losing another."

Josefina shook her head. "No. It won't happen. I won't bury a child."

"No mother should."

After pressing her lips together, she spoke, her voice reflecting sadness. "However, it does happen. It seems that death happens in both our worlds." She leaned closer and patted my hand, her more joyful cadence returning. "I wanted to tell you personally that I'm glad you're here. I mean *you*. My son chose well. You're a strong woman. I sense that."

"Thank you."

"Mia, we're now family and your safety and well-being are important to me. Please make yourself at home on the Bella. If I know my husband and sons, they will come and go over the next few days. I hope you're comfortable, knowing you are welcome to stay put."

I tugged on my lower lip. "I don't know what Aléjandro will want me to do."

"He will want you to stay safe. When my sons do what they do, they need to concentrate. Having you here, safe, is what's best for Jano until your new home can be made secure." She pursed her lips and sat taller. "I could be upset that Jano stole Silas and Viviana from me, but I won't be. I know in my heart that they will have your and Jano's best interest at heart. They've had a special place within our family." Her eyes opened wide. "Perhaps Jano didn't tell you, but Silas and Viviana have a daughter and two grandsons living in the States. The opportunity Jano offered with the assistance of your family's connections is an answer to their prayers."

"I didn't know that. It makes me feel better about their move. I was afraid they might not be happy here in California."

"Oh, child" —she gestured about— "here is *México*. Our home."

I turned to the flag on the flagpole. "Aléjandro told me how laws work in international waters."

She laughed. "And you didn't even need your passport."

Lifting my hand to my lips, I unsuccessfully tried to hide a yawn. "I'm sorry."

Josefina shook her head. "You have had a long day." She stood. "Go and get ready for sleep. I'm sure Jano will do his best to keep their meeting short. After all, he has his beautiful bride waiting."

I stood. "Thank you again, *Señora*" —I smiled— "Josefina. After our home was broken into, I would be too frightened to spend the night there."

"You are welcome as long as you want even if you go back to *México* with us."

"I'm here."

"*Sí*, you are. Do you need help finding your suite?"

I was tired, but my sense of direction was still strong. "I hope I'll be all right."

"Sleep as late as you want. Consider this your honeymoon." She grinned. "And when things quiet down, make Jano take you on another."

Make Jano.

Does anyone besides Jorge make Aléjandro do anything?

"Good night."

Going back the way I came, I found myself again taking the catwalk along the edge of the yacht. The blue lights I saw from the air illuminated the water around the Bella, making an eerie glow as if the boat was suspended on a blue cloud in the middle of black nothingness. Once down a deck below, I faltered as I came upon multiple doors. For a moment I stood staring and hoping the correct door would make itself known. Nibbling my lip, I looked up and down the hallway, wondering where all the people in white had gone. Surely, one of them could help me find my room.

Then it hit me.

Who would these rooms be used by except for Aléjandro and Rei?

And if they're both in their meeting with Jorge, the worst that could happen was that I opened the wrong door. The length of the day was getting to me as I reached for a doorknob with a trembling hand.

The door opened inward. The suite was exactly like ours, without our dirty clothes lying on the floor where we left them. It appeared unused. Next, I went to the door on the left. Once the door was opened, I let out a breath.

This was our suite.

Our dirty clothes were missing, and the bed was turned down, but I recognized my purse on a shelf and the decanter with tequila was still sitting where Aléjandro left it. I walked into the bathroom, seeing that it too had been tidied.

This was even better than living at my mother's.

It was then I noticed that our suitcases that we'd laid on the bed were also missing. I went to the closet and found many of our clothes hanging. Opening a few drawers I found other items, such as my lingerie and underclothes. It seemed that Josefina ran a full-service yacht.

After washing my face, I let my hair down, unbraiding it to a wavy mess. As I chose the night-gown for tonight, I marveled that I'd only been married for one full day. It didn't matter that the day lasted weeks and weeks long—it was still only a day. When I stepped from the bathroom, I was met with my husband's dark stare.

"How was your meeting?"

He shook his head. "I don't want to talk about it." My core clenched as he came closer, each step controlled with the grace and finesse of a predator with its eyes on his prey. "I have other things to do."

Desire burned within his eyes, melting his orbs from chestnut to pitch black. My nipples hardened, tenting the satin of my nightgown.

"Turn around."

I sucked my lip between my teeth. "Remember—"

His finger came to my lips. "Turn around."

Swallowing, I complied, turning a full circle. When our gazes again met, Aléjandro lifted a finger and spun it. Again, I turned, a ballerina moving to his command. After two complete turns, he captured my waist as I faced away.

His lips came to the nook in my neck as his warm breath skirted over my flesh. "I remember my promise, Mia."

Each word reverberated through me, prickling my skin with goose bumps.

"I won't fuck you."

My breathing stopped at his crass vocabulary. Despite my appearance of strength, there was a frightened eighteen-year-old buried deep inside me that was scared he would do what he said he wouldn't.

He gathered my hair, murmuring words. While I couldn't understand their meaning, their rhythm and timbre calmed me. I tilted my head, giving him access as his kisses cascaded from behind my ear down my neck and onto my shoulder.

"You're so fucking beautiful and brave. Having you like this makes me hard, painfully so. Having your lips around my cock earlier was heaven. Feeling how warm and wet your mouth was... I can only imagine how fucking great it would feel to be inside your warm, wet cunt. My cock is so damn ready, I'm not sure how many times it would take for it to stop being hard." He pressed his hips against my lower back, emphasizing his point with his probing erection. He grasped my ass through my nightgown. "What about this hole? Where does it fall in the definition of sex?"

I shook my head.

Aléjandro laughed. "I want you to remember last night and tonight. I want you to remember every damn time we're alone and I don't do what I want to do to you."

Garnering my strength, I spun until I was facing him.

"Stop."

Aléjandro lifted my chin. "These are only words, Mia." He nodded toward me. "I know what you're thinking. I feel your trembling. You're worried about what happened to you before. When I fuck you, I want every last thought of your asshole first husband out of your mind. I want you to be so feverish with desire that mine is the only name on your tongue." He held me tighter as I tried to push away. "No, you're my wife, and if I want to tell you all the things I can do to you, I will." His lips curled into a grin, and he lifted his chin, inhaling. "You don't hate this, Mia. I smell how turned on you are right now, and soon my tongue is going to delve between your swollen folds to discover how fucking sweet you taste. And you can bet that I won't stop until you've come apart, over and over."

My breathing grew ragged as his words zapped through me, igniting synapse after synapse. "Aléjandro. I'll remember."

He reached for the hem of my nightgown and lifted it, inch by inch revealing my only other clothing, a pair of lace panties. The front of his jeans strained with the pressure of his erection as he scanned me from my hair to my toes. "Push those down. Show me my dessert."

Latching my fingers under the waistband, I pushed the panties lower, until they fell to the floor. I stepped out of the lace.

I expected that tonight would be like it was earlier with the shower, but this was different. More intense. More palpable. I felt his gaze as his eyes traced my body, every dip, curve, and crevice. I fought the trembling his predatory gaze elicited.

"You know I want to fuck you?"

I swallowed and nodded. "I know." I knew without his declaration. The bulge in his blue jeans was testing the strength of the zipper.

"And I could."

He could.

I wasn't strong enough or big enough to stop him.

"You won't." My breasts heaved with a lethal combination of fear and desire.

"Because?" His question lingered in the air, floating on the sea breeze.

Because... My focus was set on his eyes. "Because you're not him." I worked up my bravery. "Before... Well, there's something you should know."

"Do you want to change the rules again?"

I shook my head. "Today, in the shower...I wanted to do that...what I did."

His lips quirked. "Suck my cock. You can say it. You were amazing."

Yes, that was what I did.

Heat creeped from my neck to my cheeks. "If you don't want to...reciprocate, it's okay. I rarely come with oral."

Aléjandro's eyebrows shot up. "Oh, Mia, challenge accepted."

"It wasn't a challenge. I just know men would rather receive, so if you're tired or—"

My husband's lips collided with mine, stopping the rest of my attempt to give him a reasonable excuse. When he pulled away, his gaze was on mine. "If that's what you think, you're ill-informed. Men love to eat pussy, the wetter and messier the better."

Pressing my lips together, I tilted my head.

"We're done talking." Aléjandro's lips curled as he scooped me from the floor and carried me to the bed.

"Your arm," I exclaimed.

"Fuck my arm." He laid me on top of the turned-down covers. "I'll keep my word."

I let out a breath as I looked up at him.

"You won't sleep tonight until you're too wrung out to dream."

I squirmed at his words. It wasn't only what he was saying and how he was saying it. My husband's expression was laser focused and intense. The concoction melted my resolve as his smoldering gaze caused my breathing to hitch.

Aléjandro took a step back and unbuttoned his shirt. While he wouldn't admit that his arm was still hurting, I picked out the grimaces he made every now and then as he undressed. I took my time devouring with my eyes the body I'd washed before dinner. My attention was drawn to the silver scars littering his golden flesh. From this distance they stood out even more than they had in the shower. While I didn't know how he'd gotten them, I knew in my world—and I imagined his—scars were viewed as badges of honor, times when he'd stared death in the face and come out victorious.

I didn't want to think about Aléjandro in conjunction with death. Instead, I let my gaze linger on his wide shoulders and down to his sculptured abdomen. When he turned, he had those dimples above his firm ass that did something to me. It wasn't until he wore only his black silk boxer shorts that he turned down the interior lights, filling our cabin with the blue hue from out on the balcony.

"Spread your legs for me."

I'd fought once before.

I didn't want to fight.

That meant I needed to trust him.

Aléjandro didn't repeat himself, giving me time to comply.

And comply I did.

A low growl filled the air and the mattress dipped as starting from the bottom, he crawled onto the bed. Knee, fist, knee, fist...he was back to being that predator, and soon I would be his prey.

Once Aléjandro reached my ankles, he pulled me down, causing me to gasp. The coarseness of his cheeks tingled my nerves. His affections began measured and controlled, yet the higher his kisses and nips came on my ankles, legs, and inner thighs, the faster and more unpredictable his movements became. The slow burn of his assault ignited fires throughout my circulation. With each kiss the temperature within me rose.

You're not him.

I didn't realize I needed to say the words, but having said them, I sensed a deeper connection to the man currently showing my body reverence. This was a man who accepted my limitations, heeded my lines, and still was finding a way to bring me pleasure.

My insides melted as Aléjandro brought his lips to my folds and his tongue delved within me. I reached for the sheets, clawing at the material as he pushed my legs apart, pressed my knees back, and buried his face in my core.

My God Almighty. I wasn't certain what he was doing, but I knew it was like nothing I'd ever experienced before. His tongue flicked faster, his fingers adding to my pleasure.

"You taste fucking sweet." His dark stare met mine. "From the night of the wedding when I smelled your arousal, I knew you would be."

That night I slapped him.

Now...

My head fell back as he again buried his face between my legs.

The noises filling my ears were raw, wet, slobbering, and uncivilized. A younger me would be humiliated that I was turned on by this savagery. Today's me knew there was no way to deny my reaction. What he was doing was something from a new level of sexual encounter. My muscles contracted and spasmed.

His arm cradled my hips as they began to buck, holding me in place. Oh God, it was almost painful how tight he wound my body. My orgasm hit with the strength of a tornado, my brain fried, and my nerves shredded, swirling into the funnel cloud of destruction.

"I came," I panted.

Aléjandro didn't slow, a man on a mission, licking and drawing out my body's reaction.

Shit.

He wasn't going to stop. It was a useless pursuit. Never had I come more than once and usually I didn't. Wriggling in his grasp, I wanted him to end this torture. "Please." Despite my brain's apprehension, my body reacted. Hard as diamond nipples. Twisted core. Even my scalp tingled. My plea changed. "Please... don't stop."

No longer was I debating the possibility of multiple orgasms.

My body wasn't trapped in a storm, but aboard an old-fashioned roller coaster, clicking up the steep hill, anticipating the free fall that was on the other side. This was like nothing I'd ever known.

The fall came with a jolt as my legs grew rigid, holding his head in the vise of my muscle spasm.

Cognitive thinking was beyond my ability, yet the name I called out was his—even in my raptured state, there was no mistaking Aléjandro for the man who came before him.

You aren't him.

Aléjandro trailed kisses along my thighs, hips, stomach, and up to my breasts. By the time his lips reached mine, I was hungry for him. Starved.

"See how good you taste?"

CHAPTER
SIXTEEN

Our mouths collided sharing the taste of me and stealing my breath. Aléjandro's tongue slid over mine, rekindling the heat of my last orgasm. We were a flurry of kisses, faces turning and noses bumping. It was as if neither of us had ever kissed before. My limbs were rubber, and my mind was mush. A hunger like I'd never felt burrowed deep within me.

With Aléjandro's weight over me, his hard-as-steel penis probed my thigh—a reminder of what was still to come. All the pleasure from moments before crashed down around me. The euphoria I'd experienced drained from my circulation, the endorphins replaced by adrenaline. With each passing second, my blood pressure increased, and my heart rate spiked.

My lungs refused to accept the abundance of oxygen readily available.

"Stop." Pushing against his shoulders, I panted for my next breath. "Don't." I pushed with all my strength against his unmoving stone chest.

Aléjandro stiffened, his entire body going rigid. Waves of tension vibrated through the air.

I clenched my teeth.

Oh God. I'd done it.

A chill ran down the length of my spine.

After all the restraint he'd shown, how did I respond? By making him mad.

My emotions were all over the place, swinging too drastically in too short a time. Scrunching my eyes shut, I fought the tears prickling my eyes, balled my fists, and protectively brought them to my chest. My stomach filled with dread as I waited for his outrage.

When Aléjandro lifted his weight, my sense of self-preservation kicked in. I rolled away from him, settling on my side and pulling my knees to my chest. I wanted to reach for the blankets. Maybe the warmth would stop my shaking, but I refused to move more than I needed to.

Still and small.

It was a ridiculous notion that after igniting someone else's anger, I could become small. As I swallowed back tears, I recognized that was my goal—to get small and disappear.

Lost in my litany of thoughts, I didn't notice the mattress move or feel Aléjandro leave the bed. My eyes stayed shut until I heard the sound of the bathroom door closing. Confused, I dared to peek beyond my cocoon. Lifting my head, I scanned the bedroom suite. Aléjandro was nowhere to be seen.

Where was his rage?

Josefina said that Roríguez men were passionate.

Wasn't wrath the emotional equivalent of passion?

Keeping an eye on the bathroom door, I unfolded my body and sat up, placing my feet on the floor. If I were thinking rationally, I would be ashamed by the excessive moisture between my thighs. I wasn't thinking sanely. Instead, I was contemplating avenues of escape. If I could dress before Aléjandro came out of the bathroom, I could go...

We were on a superyacht.

My options were limited.

Josefina.

If she was still awake...if I could find her...and tell her what?

Anna Moretti, Rocco's mother, cringed in fear whenever Tommaso raised his voice. I'd never tried to tell her about the way her son treated me. I'd figured he'd learned his behavior by example.

Using a tissue, I wiped the evidence of our encounter away from between my legs. Next, I located my panties and nightgown. The sound of a shower came from the bathroom. My chest ached as I worried about Aléjandro's arm. I could offer to help him again, but there was still the residual fear.

If he wasn't going to lash out at me, would he decide to punish me in other ways?

I tried not to think of Rocco's ability to be cruel. His punishments didn't always leave visible bruises. Sometimes the emotional torture was worse.

Pulling my nightgown over my head, I went to the closet and retrieved the long plush robe I'd seen earlier. This yacht was stocked like a five-star hotel except there was no monogram or label on the robe. I ran my fingers through my tangled hair.

Running away would get me nowhere. Besides the obvious fact that there were only so many places I could go on a yacht, Aléjandro would eventually find me. And making a scene could only fester his anger.

The decanter on the counter called my name. I poured two fingers of tequila into one of the clean tumblers.

The sound of the shower behind the bathroom door disappeared.

It wouldn't be long before the door would open.

With the tumbler in hand, I padded out onto our balcony. My bare feet met the coolness of the tile. The outside temperature had dropped, making me appreciate the warmth of the terrycloth robe. LED lights reflected blue upon the clear railing. Bringing the tumbler to my lips, I relished the burn as the alcohol made its way down my throat.

How long would it take to dim my senses?

At the opening of the bathroom door, I turned

away, staring out at the dark ocean and up to the heavens. When I was a little girl, the nuns at my school taught me that all answers could be found in prayer. As an adult, I learned that wasn't true. Solutions didn't come from above, but from whoever had control of your world. Whether it was my father, Rocco, or later Dario, I knew in the depth of my soul and marrow of my bone that God was out of the equation. If he wasn't, then he wasn't a merciful being but a vindictive one—if he truly existed at all.

With my body flush against the railing, I waited for what was to come. I was trapped in a gilded cage. Yes, my surroundings were more luxurious than before, but that made me no less a captive by the vows we'd spoken.

The fresh scent of bodywash infiltrated the sea air before the warmth of Aléjandro's body materialized behind me. My grasp of the tumbler tightened, threatening to crush the crystal as every muscle tensed.

I startled as his deep baritone voice cut through the stillness. His warm breath skirted across my neck. "Are you contemplating jumping?"

Jumping.

Death.

No.

My chin fell to my chest as new tears slid down my cheeks.

Aléjandro's arms wrapped around my waist, tugging me against his hard chest.

I remained still, fighting the urge to pull away. Out of the corner of my eye, I saw the bandage. "Did you get it wet?"

"No." He craned his neck and softly kissed my cheek. "You didn't answer. Are you considering a midnight swim?"

My mind couldn't compute.

I spun in his grasp.

"I wouldn't do that."

"Sometimes women feel it's their only option. You know—until death do us part."

I shook my head. "I couldn't do that to my mother. She lost my father, not her daughter too." But she had lost me, lost me to the cartel.

Aléjandro took the tumbler from my grasp and stepped back. I scanned his bare chest. As I dared to look down, I found that he was wearing pajama pants. Lifting the tumbler to his lips, he drained the contents and set the empty glass on the table. Then, once again, he wrapped his solid arms around me, resting his hands on my lower back. His dark stare settled on mine. While I couldn't read what he was thinking, I believed my emotions and thoughts were on full display.

He wiped a tear with his thumb. "That's good to hear. Don't jump."

Why isn't he angry?

I dropped my forehead to his wide chest. "I'm sorry."

He lifted his embrace to the middle of my back, pulling me closer to him. Keeping my arms against my chest, I settled into his warm and fresh-scented bubble. It was at that moment when I realized the erection I'd felt earlier was no longer an issue.

He must have masturbated in the shower—again.

I was a failure as a wife.

I lifted my gaze. "I'm sorry," I repeated.

"I'm not good at this."

My lips twitched. "Define *this* because earlier you were very good."

"I think you can take not-coming-with-oral off your list."

"I didn't hate it."

Aléjandro's laughter filled the air and floated out to sea. "That was obvious."

"I didn't mean to..." To what? "...freeze. I wish I could be different for you."

"Be you, Mia. What I'm not good at is this—talking isn't my forte. Actions are where I excel. I'll probably say it wrong."

"Say what?"

"Be you," he repeated. "Be the you who slapped me in the hallway and the you who told me you didn't want this marriage. That's who I married. And I fucking signed up for you. If I have to wade through some shitty, scum-laden waters to get to that self-assured firecracker, then I'll put on my boots and do that because I know you'll be worth it."

Swallowing became more difficult. I sniffled. He was better at talking than he gave himself credit for. Yet, I still had questions. "Why aren't you...? I expected you to be upset."

His eyes narrowed. "Should I be? Did you purposely set out to anger me?"

"No." My neck straightened. "I didn't...I was...it was...I've never come twice in one night before. We were kissing and I liked that." I exhaled. "But then your erection...when I felt it...I froze. Then I couldn't take my reaction back, and I thought you were mad."

"I told you it wouldn't bite."

Sighing, I let my head drop to his chest. "I feel like I need to keep apologizing."

"That fucking asshole should apologize for what he did to you. I won't, but I'll hold you, touch you" — he ran his hands up and down my back— "and stay with you until you forget everything about him."

"I panicked. I was so afraid."

"Of me?"

I nodded against his warm skin.

Aléjandro shook his head. "I don't hurt women, Mia." I looked up, seeing his growing smile. "*Mi mamá* would never forgive me."

"I like her."

"That's good. She likes you." He inhaled. "When you froze, I knew I'd fucked up."

"No. It wasn't you."

"I'm not him."

"You're not him," I repeated.

He reached for my hand. "Let's get some sleep."

I let Aléjandro lead me inside the suite. Once we were within, he closed the glass doors to the balcony and hit a switch that turned the panes opaque.

"What was that?" I asked.

"Magic. It will keep the sun out in the morning."

Aléjandro came closer and tugged on the sash of my robe. "By the way," he said with a less seriousness to his timbre. "If anyone has ever complained about eating your pussy, they don't deserve to be in your thoughts. It's perfection."

My cheeks rose. "Are you a connoisseur?"

"Maybe in the past. Now, I'm a satisfied customer. There's never been one that tasted as sweet and fu-ck" —the word was elongated— "the sounds you were making." He grinned. "I better stop, or I'll need to take another shower."

Once we were both in bed and under the blankets, Aléjandro wrapped his arm around me and tugged me to his solid shoulder. His chest reverberated with his words. "I'm going to get mad. Someday." He lifted my chin, bringing our gazes together. "When it happens —because it will—I want you to remember the sentence you keep repeating."

"You're not him."

Aléjandro nodded. "Fucking cowards bully those without the strength or ability to fight back. I'm not a coward. I face fights without hesitation."

I reached for his bandage. "Maybe a little less chasing Russians?"

"I won't be the perfect husband, Mia. I know that. I know me and I'll fuck up, but never fear me."

Inhaling and exhaling, I let his words sink in. "Your mom said tonight that all marriages are unique. I know I said I didn't want this marriage."

"You've changed your mind?"

I shrugged. "Jury is still out, but I'm at least seeing that what we have going on isn't the same as what I had before."

"It's a good start," he said.

Laying my arm over his trim torso, I settled back on the hard pillow of his shoulder, closed my eyes, and listened to the sounds of his breaths and the rhythm of his heart beating. When I woke from a dreamless sleep, I was alone. With the window magic, I couldn't get a grasp on the time of day. It was the clock that let me know that I'd slept until after eleven.

That same clock said noon before I was showered and dressed and ready to meet the others on the yacht. The sunshine warmed my skin as I made my way outside and back up a level. When I entered the living room and dining area, a woman in white appeared.

"*Señora* Roríguez, may I get you anything to eat or drink?"

"I know it's past noon, but coffee would be wonderful. With cream."

"*Sí.*"

I scanned the large open room and farther out to the helipad and the ocean beyond. "Do you know where my husband is?"

"No, *señora. Señora* Roríguez is at the pool. Maybe she knows."

"Could you please bring the coffee to the pool?"

"*Sí*," she responded with a nod and a smile.

Pool.

I tried to recall. I'd seen it from the helicopter last night. Going out toward the helipad, I found a staircase leading to the deck above. That brought me to the outdoor seating where Josefina and I sat last night. Climbing one more set of stairs, I found myself on the pool deck. Josefina was wearing a bathing suit and lying on a lounge chair in the water, looking more like Aléjandro's sister than mother.

"Good afternoon," I greeted.

Beneath a large floppy hat, she lifted her sunglasses, and smiled. "I'm glad you were able to rest."

Aléjandro's words about not letting me sleep until I was too wrung out to dream came back to me. "I slept very well. Do you know where I could find my husband?"

"He and Rei left early this morning."

"He left the yacht?"

SEVENTEEN

J osefina must have seen the concern in my expression. She twisted until she was sitting with her bare feet in the pool water and looking in my direction. "They left before I was out of the cabin. Jorge told me that something happened last night, and they were both needed on the mainland."

My empty stomach twisted.

She feigned a smile. "Did you bring a bathing suit? If not, I'm sure I have one that could fit you."

"I did." I looked around. The ocean went on in every direction for as far as I could see. "Is Patrón concerned?" I hoped using the term I'd heard Catalina use was acceptable. "Is he with them?"

"He's not alarmed." She stood and walked to me until she was out of the pool and on dry travertine. "What my sons do is not safe, but they're very good. Jano will come back to you."

"He didn't tell me he was leaving."

"Well," she said matter-of-factly, "that is something he needs to be told, by you."

I swallowed. "I'm just feeling sorry for myself." I scanned beyond the deck into the blue waters. "And that's probably the most ridiculous thing in the world. I mean, look where we are."

"*México*," she said with a smile. "It's always beautiful."

The woman from earlier arrived with a tray. A silver coffee carafe, a silver pitcher of cream, and a cup were placed on a nearby table, shaded by an umbrella. "*Gracias*," I said.

"If you need anything else..."

Josefina spoke. "I'm about to have my midday meal. You should eat, Mia. Would you like lunch or breakfast?"

I didn't want to be any trouble. "I'll have whatever you're having."

She spoke to the woman. While her words were coming fast, I thought I picked up on *ceviche*. Josefina stopped and turned to me. "Any allergies? Shellfish?"

"No." I shook my head and went to the table where my freshly poured cup of coffee sat.

Aléjandro's mother reiterated what she'd said to the woman. The lady in white nodded affirmatively and walked away, leaving us alone.

"Do you have sunscreen?" Josefina asked. "I hate to

mention it, but with your fair complexion, I don't want you to burn."

That made me smile. "I didn't think to bring any."

"I'll have the staff take some to your suite. After your coffee, you can go change into a bathing suit and be sure to apply sunscreen. I don't want Jano upset because his new wife is too burned to be touched. Oh, and on the first level I have a small office, much smaller than Jorge's. The bookshelves are filled with books. If you'd like to borrow one, help yourself." Before I could question, she added, "There are some in English."

"That's good. I'm better at speaking Spanish than reading it, and I can't speak it."

"I'd be glad to help you."

"*Gracias.*"

"*Buen comienzo.*"

By the time I finished my coffee, found Josefina's office, selected a book, changed into a bathing suit, applied my sunscreen, and made my way back to the pool deck, our food was waiting along with a pitcher of hibiscus *agua fresca*.

Josefina pulled a second hat from a bag near her feet. "I went and got this for you. The sun can be harsh. We must protect your beautiful skin."

"Thank you." I took the hat and placed it on my head. "You look too young to be a mother of grown men, but you do the mothering thing well. I guess I miss mine. After Rocco, my first husband, died, my brother didn't want me to live on my own. He sent me to live with my mother. Since my father passed at the same time, we were in mourning together."

"Oh, *lo lamento*." She shook her head. "That must have been hard."

"It wasn't. When you're young, you think you know so much more than your parents. I didn't want to live with her, but after a while, it was...comfortable. I think as adults we were able to be friends."

Josefina smiled. "Her home is beautiful. We were there for Catalina's wedding."

I nodded.

"You've been through so much."

"It's been a whirlwind." I took in the stunning views. "And that whirlwind is still swirling."

For a while, we ate in silence. Perhaps my filter was broken, but when a question popped into my head, I asked it. "Did you have a choice to marry *el Patrón*?"

"Everyone should have a choice of whom they marry."

I didn't respond.

"*Mi padre* believed in Jorge. He was honored when Jorge asked for me."

"Were you honored?"

"*Sí*, he was the most eligible bachelor. And he wanted me." Her smile faded. "You weren't honored?"

This conversation had the potential to end badly. I chose my words carefully. "Dario believes in Aléjandro. Catalina too. She spoke about Aléjandro's position—

second to *el Patrón*—as a place of honor within the cartel. And now, I can't believe I'm here on this yacht. I wasn't *not* honored." I tried to make sense of my twisted batch of emotions. "I just didn't think I'd have to remarry this soon. I've been married since I was eighteen. I guess I was hoping to live first."

"What does that mean...to live? Can you not live and be a wife?"

"I don't know," I replied honestly. "Not with Rocco."

"Mia, that man is dead. I'm not insensitive." She sat taller. "Tell me, was he a good husband?"

I picked at the food on my plate.

"I'll take that as a no," Josefina said. "If after ten years, he didn't earn a place in your heart, then after his death he doesn't deserve a place in your thoughts."

There weren't words to say—at least none that I could think of uttering. The truth was I'd thought more about Rocco in the past week than the first five months after his death. I was running every thought through my old Rocco meter.

Would he approve?

Would he be angry?

Would he react?

Was it better not to tell him?

Would he accuse me of deceiving him if he found out?

The questions went on and on.

"It has only been a short time," she said, "and

please, I'm not trying to..." —she pressed her lips together— "*fish*. I'm not trying to fish for intimate details. Just tell me, if your only two choices are good or bad, how is my Jano doing?"

Warmth filled my cheeks as I peered across the table. "Good."

She sat back with a satisfied expression. "I always believed he would be. To be honest, he needed to grow up. How old was this rock when you were eighteen?"

Rock. Rocco.

I smiled.

"Only a little older than I was, twenty."

"I don't think Jano was ready to marry that young. I was only seventeen when Jorge and I wed. I had no idea how to be a wife. Now you and Jano are older and wiser. That's why I know the two of you will be happy." She scoffed. "Throw that rock overboard. Let him sink to the bottom of the ocean."

'You're not him.'

Josefina continued, "I can't imagine your situation, but think of it in reverse. Would you like Jano to compare you to other women he's known before?"

Beneath my sunglasses, my eyes prickled.

Other women.

Younger.

Thinner.

Virgins.

I knew my answer. "No."

"Doesn't he deserve the same?"

"Has he said anything to you...about me?"

She shook her head. "I watch and listen. I'm older and wiser than I look."

"You are. *Gracias*. I'll try to do better."

"No. I never said you weren't doing your best. And that is all Jano can ask."

"You love Jorge?" I asked, using his name for the first time with her.

"*Sí*, with all my heart. It took time. Thankfully, that is what we all have."

During the next three to four hours, we alternated between talking and reading. Somewhere during that time, I found a new peace with my marriage. I even felt a bit sad for Catalina. None of the women in the famiglia did what Josefina was doing, not even my mother. I should have reached out to her and worked to make her feel wanted. It was a mistake on my part that I would try to rectify in the future.

While it occurred to me to ask what, if anything, Josefina knew about Liliana and Gerardo Ruiz, I was still finding my own way. As much as I wanted to help the young girl, I knew I needed to be on solid ground before I could be of any assistance to her.

The time was around four-thirty when Jorge made an appearance on the pool deck. I had a sudden flashback of the first time I saw him at my mother's pool. I quickly reached for my cover-up.

Jorge went straight to his wife, giving her a kiss. They lingered longer than I expected.

I stared in awe, wondering if I'd ever in my entire life seen that kind of affection between my parents. When he turned in my direction, he smiled. "Mia, I'm glad you're comfortable. Unlike your father, I don't see the need for you to cover yourself. Unless it makes you more comfortable, then by all means, do it."

"*Gracias*," I said, deciding my Spanish was improving by one word a day. At that rate, I'd be fluent by the time Aléjandro and I had grandchildren. "Have you heard from Aléjandro or Rei?"

He nodded. "They have been busy, and" —he gestured— "they will be back before dark."

I let out a breath. "Thank you. Are...? Will...?" I shook my head. "Do you know when it will be safe for us to return to our home?"

"Silas and Viviana arrived today. Jano is working to make it safe for his *novia*."

"Bride," Josefina whispered.

I nodded, content that Aléjandro was coming back to me and that he and this Silas would make sure our home was safe.

After Jorge walked away, Josefina began gathering her things. "I love the sun, but it makes me sleepy. You're welcome to stay here or roam wherever you'd like on Bella. I'm going to rest and then get ready for dinner. I'd say eight thirty, based on Jorge's timetable."

"Thank you again for making me feel welcome."

"I've never had a daughter. If I become overbearing, please let me know."

"Not overbearing."

My concentration unsuccessfully went back to the book in my hands. It was difficult to think about the story when my own life was more twisted than the characters'. As I read a kissing scene, I found myself thinking about Aléjandro. The unexpected fluttering of butterflies flittering within my stomach caught me off guard. Closing my eyes, I rested my head as I recalled last night before I ruined everything.

It wasn't wrong that I found my husband attractive. Then why did it make me feel guilty? My mind slipped back to the day at my mother's pool, the first time we met. I recalled the heat of his eyes on me. Maybe Aléjandro made me uncomfortable because I'd never seen that degree of hunger laser focused on me. It was the same way he looked at me after our ceremony. For a moment, I believed he wanted to sneak away and consummate our marriage.

As I lay under the sun and felt the dampness between my legs, I remembered the ferocity of his kisses, the way the muscles in his shoulders flexed as he lay over me, and even the weight of his body. No one was more surprised than I was that the mere thought of him caused my nipples to bead.

If I gave it more thought, I might come to the realization that what frightened me last night wasn't what Aléjandro was doing or could do, but instead, it was my reaction to our intimacy. I liked it. More than that, I wanted more of it. There was no denying that after he brought me to orgasm twice, I was a hot tangle of satiated goo. My mind was too overwhelmed to compute that I wanted what I'd grown to hate.

I still marveled at his reaction.

No anger.

No yelling.

No forcing himself or bruising my skin.

After our first few encounters, the last word I would have used to describe Aléjandro Roríguez was gentleman. However, after seventy-two hours of marriage, it was the perfect description.

Whenever Rocco would try to weasel his way into my thoughts of Aléjandro, I made a point to ignore him. Josefina was right. If in ten years of marriage, Rocco hadn't earned a place in my heart, then he didn't deserve a place in my head.

Aléjandro wasn't him.

I'd made the decision. I was Aléjandro's wife, and I was ready to move forward with our union. He deserved a reward for his patience. And I deserved to have pleasurable, consensual sex.

It was a liberating decision, making me happier than I could recall being—especially since Dario gave me the news of my nuptials. If I had a phone, I would give Giorgia a call to share my surprise.

Had she tried to reach me?

Had anyone from my family tried to reach me?

Did they know I was in international waters floating on an opulent Mexican island?

217

Gathering my things, I headed back to our suite. I stood staring at the bed with the knowledge that tonight would be different. In the bathroom, I stripped out of the bathing suit. My pinkened reflection made me glad I'd listened to Josefina about sunscreen. In the mirror I saw the paleness where the suit had been. Maybe I could sunbathe naked on our balcony to avoid tan lines.

As I turned on the shower, I half laughed. I'd gone from fearing a sexual encounter to wanting one and also considering exhibitionism.

Who am I?

My reflection also showed the sun's effects on my hair, light caramel highlights streaked the brown. Stepping under the shower's spray, I lifted my face to the warm water, feeling the prickle on my sunned flesh.

I took more care with my appearance than I did on our wedding day. Of course, I didn't have the stylists on Bella that I had on my wedding day. By the time I was satisfied, I was cleaned, shaved, and waxed. My long hair was styled with the sides pulled up and the length curled. Tonight's dress was the color of sage, making the hazel of my eyes greener and contrasting nicely with my new tan. With the cut of the bodice, wearing a bra wasn't an option.

Nervously, I paced the length of the suite, afraid I would talk myself out of tonight's plans. There was always the pros-and-cons approach. As I compiled the pros, the only con I could think of was my own fear.

"Don't overthink it," I said audibly.

Great, now I am a sex-craving exhibitionist who talks to herself.

I spun toward the sound of the opening door.

Blood.

I gasped at the sight and aroma of my husband. Crimson speckled his face, streaked across his light gray t-shirt and over his dark jeans. Before I could ask if Aléjandro was hurt, his expression stopped me in my tracks. It was as if he were made of stone, completely devoid of emotion. His penetrating stare skirted over me as he stalked to the decanter and poured himself a hearty drink.

"What happened?" I asked, my voice sounding weaker than I intended.

Closing his eyes, Aléjandro's nostrils flared. His Adam's apple bobbed as he emptied the tumbler and slammed it down on the table. His biceps bulged and the muscles in the side of his face pulled tight.

Bravely, I took a step toward him. "Are you hurt?"

He shook his head once before pouring more tequila. Taking the glass with him, he turned and disappeared into the bathroom. The door closed with a loud thud.

Emotion clogged my throat as I turned away, shaken by his cold response. Out on the balcony, the sun was nearing the horizon, casting orange and red hues over the glistening water. The clock on the bookcase told me it was only a little after seven. We had an hour and a half until dinner. The sound of a shower came from behind the closed door.

Looking down at my dress, I lamented the time I'd spent preparing for his arrival. He'd barely noticed my presence. While I considered imbibing on the tequila, I had another idea.

He isn't him.

My husband needed a wife, a wife who understood the dangers and pressures of his livelihood, and one who offered support rather than wallowing in self-pity.

CHAPTER
EIGHTEEN

Aléjandro
Fifteen hours earlier

T he clicking of the lock woke me from whatever sleep I'd managed to drift into. It was nearly impossible not to spend the entire night with a damn boner with Mia sleeping at my side. Her soft skin smelled of scented lotion and radiated warmth. I could get lost in the way her lips parted as she slept.

Click.

Instantly, I was on high alert.

Who the fuck would try to enter my suite?

Quietly, I scooted away from Mia, careful not to wake her. Moving without sound was an asset in our world, the element of surprise. Wearing only my pajama pants, I padded barefoot to the bookcase where I'd laid my weapons last night before feasting on my wife. One last glance at the beauty sleeping in my bed before I reached for one of my knives and made my way to the door.

As the doorknob turned, I pulled the door open and lifted my knife, the point of my blade landing squarely on the intruder's throat. His eyes bulged and his lips parted as I shoved him into the hallway and against the far wall, my arm against his chest as a droplet of blood oozed from where the tip of the blade penetrated his flesh.

"*Qué chingados haces*," I asked, my voice low.

The man babbled an apology as his stare stayed fixed on me.

I angled the knife under his chin, where the soft flesh was easily slit. The windpipe put up more resistance than the carotid, but once sliced, the victim quickly died from the combination of blood loss and suffocation.

I recognized this man as one of *mi padre's* guards. That didn't mean that he wasn't a traitor, looking to kill Mia and me in our sleep.

His hands went up in surrender. "Your father sent me," he said in Spanish.

"No one walks in on my wife." I pressed the blade for emphasis and ripped open his suit coat, taking the revolver from his holster. Once he was unarmed, I took a step back.

"*Señor* Roríguez, there's been an incident. Your *padre* wants you and *Señor* Reinaldo to go to the mainland right away. He sent me to wake you."

"We're going to *mi padre*," I said, flicking the knife in the direction of the hallway. The guard walked a few paces in front of me as we made our way down to the first deck, to the door of *mi padre's* office.

Rei's voice came into range as we approached the open doors.

The guard stepped to the side before entering and turned to me. "*Mi pistola?*"

I shook my head and entered. "Did you send this asshole into my fucking suite?"

Instead of answering, *mi padre* and Rei turned in my direction. "Andrés's home was attacked tonight," *Padre* said.

The house where we'd just had our wedding and where Rei and I had been staying.

"Attacked?"

"Four Russians. They killed one of their guards, Luis Bosco."

"The Ruizes?"

"Alive."

"Russians?" I asked.

"Three dead. Emiliano wounded the fourth. Now, he has him in the basement at Wanderland."

I inhaled and looked at my brother. "Sounds like we have some questioning to do."

Interrogation was our specialty. For the record, we didn't follow the wartime rules of the Geneva convention. There was no humanity in our tactics.

"This invasion was meant to send two messages," *Padre* said, "one to us and one to the *famiglia*." Andrés's eldest daughter was now married to the Kansas City capo. "Get all the information you can from him. The bratva is getting bolder, and it's going to stop. I want the other three bratva soldiers delivered to their doorstep in pieces. Give them a message that the Roríguez cartel is done with this fucking game."

"Their doorstep," Rei repeated. "Do we have a location?"

Padre grinned. "No, but I trust the two of you will have one before the fourth is dead."

Rei and I nodded.

"I need more clothes," I said, looking at Rei dressed and ready to go. "When did you call for Rei?"

"Earlier. I wanted details before interrupting you and your new *novia*."

"Yeah, that wife. In the future, send a message. No one walks in our suite when Mia is asleep. You almost lost a guard tonight."

Mi padre's forehead furrowed, and his eyes narrowed.

Patrón didn't take orders from anyone, including me. I knew that. One day, it would be me not taking orders. In the meantime, I had a few ground rules to make clear. Entering my suite with my wife present was a hard no. Before *mi padre* could respond, I turned, headed out of the office, and handed the guard back his gun.

Mia was still sleeping when I returned to the suite. I wasn't certain how she slept through the intruder, but I was glad she did. Before our night went south, I'd wrung multiple orgasms out from her. My lips curled as I thought about what I'd said, telling her she'd sleep a dreamless slumber. Hopefully, she was because Rei and I were about to enter a nightmare.

In less than five minutes, I was down on the lower deck with Rei.

"Too bad this shit is taking you away from all the action in your suite," Rei said.

I was too tired to pretend, besides this was my brother, the one person who always got my truth. "Most of the action has been with my own hand."

Rei's eyes opened wide. "Hey, fuck. I'm sorry."

"Me too." I shook my head. "Her asshole first husband did a number on her." A smile curved my lips. "She gives off a confident air that's sexy as hell." I sighed. "I'm biding my time. If I forced her, I'd be no better than him."

Rei patted my shoulder as Joaquín, one of *Padre's* guards and boat captain pulled a forty-eight-foot cigarette boat up to the floating platform. Rei and I stepped from the deck to the platform and down into the boat. This mode of transportation would allow us to get back to the mainland under the radar.

"Diego and Felipe will meet us at the docks with supplies," Rei said as Joaquín pulled away from Bella and accelerated through the darkness. The five outboard engines roared to life as we skimmed over the waves with the wind in our faces. The sun wouldn't rise for another two hours. There'd be no sightings of us coming on land. When the sun rose, Joaquín and the cigarette boat would be back out to sea.

Wanderland was closed to the public by the time we arrived. With Diego and Felipe as our backup, Rei and I entered through the back of the club.

Nicolas met us with a solemn expression. He scanned our backup. "You brought company?"

"Diego and Felipe go most everywhere with us."

"Out on Bella?"

"*Most* everywhere," I replied as I looked around. "It's quiet in here." Down a long hallway on our right was where the whores slept and lived. It was like a fucking sorority house with dorm-style sleeping and common areas such as a kitchen and television room. I didn't like the setup for the way it dehumanized the sex workers. That subject was one of the issues I'd recently brought up to Nicolas.

"Whores are sleeping, except the two in my office. Cleaning crew won't be here until eight." He inhaled.

"It's quiet down in the basement. The moskal isn't talking."

My gaze met Rei's.

"Five hours is the longest it's taken us to get information," Rei offered.

Nicolas shook his head. "Not this one. He'll die before talking."

"Oh, he'll do that too," I replied, "but not in that order. Where are the other three bodies?"

"Em has them at the hideout. I can't have dead bodies on the premises. It's bad for business."

"You'll have one, but not for long. *Mi padre* wants these men delivered in pieces to the bratva's doorstep."

Nicolas's jaw clenched. "*Carajo.* Patrón is making this war worse. He's just asking for more attacks."

I took a step toward Nicolas, meeting him chest to chest. "Don't question Patrón's decisions. He's sending a message. Fuck with us and get fucked." I looked at Rei. "Come on, let's go talk to our new friend."

"What's that?" Nicolas asked, tilting his chin toward the duffel bag in Felipe's grasp.

"Tools," I replied.

"We already have—"

I lifted my hand. "You're welcome to watch."

When we entered the small room at the far end of the basement, our guest was nude, tied to a metal chair, with swelling and bruising already forming on his face and body. His left eye was swollen, his blond hair was matted with blood, and his left leg was bent at an angle that suggested it was fractured.

As I went to work with the regular incentives like cutting off fingers and toes, Rei did what he does. Rei's technique was more psychological. All he needed was the help of a computer and hacking skills, getting him into databases that the US government assumed were secure.

My techniques were doing very little to make our friend find his voice. When he did, he only cursed in Russian. I might not understand the language, but I could easily decipher the tone.

"*Inglés,*" I said, doubtful he could speak Spanish.

"What the hell is Rei doing?" Nicolas asked.

I glanced at my brother as his fingers flew over the keyboard. "You'll see."

My hand ached as I delivered another kidney punch. "Talk, motherfucker."

About two hours into our interrogation, Rei spoke up. "I have it."

I staggered back away from the man about to sing. There was no doubt. This was what got them all singing like songbirds. They could take the physical pain. Like most of us, they'd endured it most of their lives. It was that every man who hadn't lost all his humanity had a soft spot whether he admitted it or not.

My thoughts went to Mia.

She was now mine.

That was why she needed to be protected.

Rei stood and carried his laptop toward our naked prisoner. "Danill Petrov, thirty-eight years old and illegally in the States. Labeled as a member of the Kozlov bratva, a recognized terrorist organization by US Department of Homeland Security."

Danill's blue eyes opened wide in horror.

My lips curled into a grin. "Danill, nice to meet you."

"Not me." He repeated the sentence multiple times.

"How?" Nicolas asked.

"Face recognition. It's why I took his picture when we arrived." My brother looked down at his information. "Wife, Kira Ivanov, last known address Simi Valley."

"Why did you come all the way down to San Diego," I asked, "and fuck with us? You should have stayed farther north."

A few more taps of the keys and Rei brought up a picture of an apartment building. He showed it to Danill. "If you want her to live, you'll talk."

"I don't trust you. You will kill her either way."

His English had remarkably improved.

"You don't have to believe us," I said. "She's dead if you don't talk. That's a promise. If you talk, we might let her work here at the club."

Danill pulled against the bindings. "I'll fucking kill every one of you."

A laugh bubbled from my throat. "Do you think we should be kinder to women? That's rich coming from the man who would have killed two innocent women if you hadn't been stopped." Andrés's wife, Valentina, and his daughter Camila were both home during the invasion. I picked up my knife, walked to Danill, and aimed the tip under his chin as I'd done earlier to the guard. "Did you know that? Did you know you were ordered to kill an old and a young woman?"

With his chin held high, Danill shook his head.

"Liar," I said, slicing across his neck, not deep enough to cause real damage.

Danill growled, letting out a breath and trying to assess his minutes of survival. "I follow orders. They said to scare, not kill."

"Whose orders?"

"Pakhan's."

Now we were getting somewhere.

NINETEEN

N ow to learn from this piece of shit where this boss was hiding. "Kozlov?"

He nodded. "I can't say more." Snot and blood dripped from his nose. "Kira. They will kill her if they find out I gave up information."

"Maybe you should have considered that," I said, "before getting involved with Kozlov." The truth was that Danill probably didn't have any choice in his recruitment into the bratva. His fuck-up was attacking the Ruizes. Stay in the bratva's territory.

The grown man alternated between curses and tears. The sadness wasn't about physical pain. I could have chopped off his leg, and he wouldn't tell the bratva's secrets. It was the threats we made against his wife.

Vile.

Hideous.

Disgusting threats.

Four and a half hours after beginning our interrogation, we had Ivan Kozlov's address in Hidden Hills. The bratva was doing well for him to have a home in such an affluent neighborhood. It was a drivable trip, but with weekday traffic, it would take us about three hours.

So much for getting back to my wife anytime soon.

"It's going to be a long fucking day," I said as we left Danill still breathing under Wanderland. If his information didn't pan out, we'd need him conscious to extract more. Of course, that would involve a stop on our way back to get Kira Ivanov.

Seeing her picture, I had no doubt Nicolas would want her for the club. She'd bring in a line of cartel men waiting to fuck a Russian whore. It might be a better outcome than the bratva learning her husband narked.

The Russian cunt wasn't my concern. Following *mi padre's* orders was.

Laying my head against the seat, I closed my eyes as Diego drove us to the hideout near the boatyard. Less than twenty-four hours ago I was upstairs being treated by the cartel doc. Today, with my arm throbbing, we were picking up a van packed with plastic totes. Thankfully, Em, Nick, and their soldiers had already followed *mi padre's* directions. The men's bodies were chopped into pieces and placed inside the totes, ready to be distributed around Ivan

Kozlov's forty-million-dollar mansion in the mountains.

"You know his place is guarded," Rei said as the four of us drove north toward Hidden Hills. "We could be walking into a trap."

The permeating odor throughout the van was one of rotten eggs combined with rotting meat. Shouldn't the plastic totes keep the stench inside?

Diego cranked the air conditioning. "Two hours of this and I may throw up."

I cracked the window at my side. The chopped Russians were already beginning to stink. "We need a refrigeration unit at the hideout. Something big enough to keep bodies on ice, because fuck this shit. They reek."

"Watch your driving," Rei said to Diego. "If we get pulled over, we'll need to add the cop to the totes. There's no way he won't smell this."

Once the windows were open and the air conditioning running full blast, the four of us went to work on what Rei had been able to learn about the six-bedroom mansion, the grounds, and the roads leading in and out of there. Waiting until after dark would be safer and easier. Then again, sending a message in the light of day was brazen and would show the cartel's strength.

Rei studied aerial views of the mansion. "The house is officially listed as belonging to a trust. Kozlov's name is nowhere on the records."

"My name isn't on the house I just bought either."

The property that these same bits of bratva may have broken into last night.

Rei nodded, his thoughts focused on the task at hand. "Looks like the property is just over two acres. Our best bet is to go through their neighbor's property. There is a steep grade for the illusion of their infinity pool. The front and back of the house is all fucking windows, but if we stay below the downgrade, we probably won't be seen."

"Probably?"

"Most likely," Rei replied.

I wasn't thrilled with his qualifiers. We needed a cover. "Who could be on the grounds without being questioned?"

"*Jardineros,*" Felipe said.

"Genius," I said. "We'll dress as gardeners. No one will think twice about our presence."

The gardening crew who we borrowed a truck from would most likely wake within an hour or two. If things went as planned, they'd even have their truck back by the time they woke. The four of us donned the crew's long-sleeved shirts with the same name as on the side of the truck, large sun hats, sunglasses, bandanas to cover our lower faces, and latex gloves. My arm protested, my bandage turning red as we moved the heavy totes from the van to the trailer, stacking them inconspicuously near the lawn mowers and other lawn equipment.

Diego drove the van to a grocery store parking lot. After picking him up, Felipe drove the lawn service truck while Rei and I crammed into the back seat.

I wondered if the people living downhill from Ivan Kozlov's property knew they were neighbors with a bratva boss. It wasn't like we were going to chat with them to find out. As we pulled the truck and trailer up near the neighbor's house, no one questioned our presence.

Rei and I ran reconnaissance up to Kozlov's property line. We didn't see any guards, but there were probably cameras. We'd have to work fast. The first feat was carrying the damn totes over half an acre uphill. I claimed the wheelbarrow for myself.

Wearing surgical gloves, we emptied the totes along the western border of Kozlov's land. Jobs like this ate away at one's humanity. There should be remorse for the lives lost, but I didn't feel it. Mostly, I was hot, sweaty, and disgusted. In short, I wanted to be done. The rotting stench of flesh and the copper tinge of blood was a magnet, drawing insects, birds, and other predators. It would be like putting together a gruesome puzzle, but there were enough fingers and teeth to confirm identification if the bratva wanted to go the extra mile.

The four of us made it back down the hill before setting off any alarms.

We returned the landscaping truck, trailer, and uniforms to the crew before they woke. I imagined them waking from their *siesta* and wondering what the fuck happened to their clothes and having no realization of their role in our long-ass day. They should be thankful. It could have gone worse for them.

It was late afternoon before we arrived back at the hideout to deliver the van and now-empty totes. My skin itched, feeling tight as if it had shrunk throughout the day. An inescapable darkness lurked below my consciousness, one that showed its ugly head with so much death.

Em and Nick took over the cleanup. Our next stop was Wanderland.

"Danill told the truth," I said to Nicolas.

"What do I do with him?" he asked.

"He's seen too much. Kill him." I thought about his wife. "Dispose of the body with acid. The bratva doesn't need to know he isn't part of the puzzle we left."

Nicolas's nostrils flared as he nodded. "You look worn out."

"Not worn out, fucking itching with energy and not the good kind."

He slapped me on the shoulder. "How about you spend some time with one of our whores, you know, blow off some steam?"

While I didn't give him a verbal response, I was confident my expression let him know I wasn't interested. Truth was that I wanted to blow off steam, but it wouldn't be with one of the whores from Wanderland. If I were honest with myself, it would be with my own hand in the shower. I fucking needed to be disinfected before touching my wife. As we stepped back into the sunshine, my phone rang.

"Fuck," I mumbled.

Rei turned in my direction.

"Silas and Viviana. I forgot they were arriving today."

"To Jano's house," Rei said, throwing the keys to Felipe.

By the time Rei and I stepped foot back on Bella, the sun was nearing the horizon. As much as I'd like to shower and spend time with my wife, we knew the routine and what was expected of us. Together, Rei and I went to our *padre's* office to give him a full report.

After listening, *mi padre* leaned back in his chair and templed his fingers. "Why not leave the nark as another calling card?"

I shook my head. "Business is good. Too many dead bodies and the authorities get suspicious. They start snooping around. We don't need that headache."

Padre nodded.

If I told him about the wife, he'd tell me I was too soft. He'd probably agree with Nicolas that she could have made us green by working the back rooms at Wanderland.

Padre continued, "We should hear soon if our

message was received." He scanned both of us. "Get rid of those clothes and clean up before *vuestra madre* sees you."

Rei and I walked silently toward our suites. With each step, I tried to blot out the horror of our day and what we'd done. Only a monster could threaten a man's wife, transport and distribute human remains, and face his own wife with a smile. I was close to a monster, but the dread coiling through me at the thought of Mia's innocent smile was evidence that I hadn't fully made that transition.

Rei stopped me in the hallway. "Maybe we should have taken Nicolas up on his offer for whores."

"What the hell?"

"I've been thinking about what you said earlier. I know how days like today fuck with our minds. Mia shouldn't be a victim too."

My fingers flexed, ready to ball into a fist. "I wouldn't hurt her."

"I know that. I'm just saying—"

"What?" I growled. "What exactly are you saying?"

Rei lifted his palms in my direction. "Get yourself into a better headspace."

"Go fuck yourself."

Headspace.

Straightening my neck, I took a deep breath and opened the door to our suite.

Mia turned my direction, standing near the open doors to the balcony. The setting sun glowed around her like the aura of an angel. I couldn't peel my eyes away. She was a fucking goddess in a long green dress. Her soft skin glowed pink and tan and streaks of gold highlighted her hair.

She was exactly what I needed and wanted, the light to balance out my darkness. My muscles tensed with the hunger to not only go to her but to consume her. The darkness in my soul longed to ravage her mercilessly. The craving was so intense, it was almost more than I could restrain.

Her wide eyes met mine. "What happened?"

Closing my eyes, I clenched my teeth and walked to the decanter of tequila. Pouring myself a generous portion, I brought the tumbler to my lips and emptied every drop. The sweet burn attempted to douse the flames of destruction sparking to life beneath my skin. The slam caused by lowering the glass too hard to the table echoed throughout the suite.

She came closer. "Are you hurt?"

I shook my head once before pouring more tequila. Holding tight to the tumbler, I contemplated trying to explain my state of mind, but the memories were too raw and fresh. Hell, the smell of death hung around me like a thick fog. If I opened the faucet, I was afraid I couldn't shut it off. I'd spent the last few days and nights trying to ease Mia's fear of me and about this marriage. All my effort would be for naught if I didn't get myself under control.

Headspace.

Instead of replying, I turned, disappeared into the bathroom, slammed the door, and turned on the shower as hot as it would go.

TWENTY

Mia

A minute passed and then another. An unusual flicker of need came to life within me. Yes, it was the desire to follow through on my plans, but it was more than that. There was a yearning to be what Aléjandro needed.

Though I didn't want to give my first husband time in my thoughts, I knew Rocco wasn't faithful during our marriage. He often used the whores at Emerald Club to take the edge off. I appreciated the reprieve.

Aléjandro wasn't Rocco. I'd come to terms with that. I also wanted to be more to him, to be who he sought when he had unfulfilled needs.

Steeling my shoulders, I opened the bathroom

door. As steam billowed from the shower stall, Aléjandro stood under the hot spray with his back to me. Nibbling on my lip, I watched the muscles in his wide shoulders move as his right arm pumped ferociously. There was no shock or surprise at what he was doing. I'd known what I would walk in on, and as it was like the first time I'd witnessed his self-pleasure, the act in itself was hauntingly beautiful.

My gaze skirted down his back littered with silver scars, landing on the sexy dimples at the base of his spine. I caressed his firm ass with my eyes while longing to touch him with my hands. Even his thighs were defined, muscular and strong.

Slipping my dress over my shoulders, I let it fall to the ground. My nipples beaded as I pushed down my panties and stepped out of my sandals. Aléjandro didn't turn or acknowledge my presence until I slid open the glass door.

He spun all at once, his massive cock in his moving hand. His facial features contorted as if he was causing himself pain not pleasure. I stepped into the glass stall and pulled the door closed. The hot water accosted my tender sun-scorched skin and flattened my hair that I'd so painstakingly styled.

The blood from earlier was gone.

Bravely, I reached for his erection. "May I change the rules again?"

Aléjandro's Adam's apple bobbed as he slowly shook his head. "No. Not right now."

There was an edge to his voice I'd never heard before, one that both frightened and excited me. Whatever happened today had been draining and taken him down a dark path. I was familiar with the evil in our worlds. As I worked to keep my courage, I spoke, "I don't need to know what happened today."

Aléjandro turned away from me.

I reached for his shoulder, encouraging him to turn back in my direction. "The only thing that's important to me is that you came back, that you're here." He turned, his dark stare devouring me. "I made a decision today."

"Fuck, Mia. Not now."

His volume caused me to flinch.

He went on, "I don't want to scare you, and you're right; I don't want you to know what happened today. But know it was sick and perverse. That's me or who I can be. That's the man you married. I don't want to be that man for you."

Lifting my hands to his shoulders, I ran my palms over his strong arms, seeing the water and blood-soaked bandage. "I want to have intercourse. I will never mention him again, but I know you're not him. Your restraint has been..." I fought tears. "I want to be your wife in every way."

He shook his head. "Later."

My cheeks rose as I smiled. "No, Jano." I'd never before used the name his family called him. "Now. Right now. In this shower or out on the bed. I don't care where… I promise I can take whatever you give because I want to be close to you. I don't care what we do, this is me giving you permission." When he didn't answer, I added, "I can beg."

He'd said I would beg. Now, I didn't care.

His palm cupped my cheek as he inhaled. "Fuck, Mia. I don't want to hurt you."

"Any more than I want."

"What?" he asked, tilting his head.

"That's what you said, you wouldn't hurt me more than I want. I'm done hurting you. I blamed you for wanting me, for taking me away from my family. I've given you every reason to lash out at me, but you've shown restraint at every turn." I reached for the faucet and turned off the water. "Come, I know you won't hurt me. Use me."

Aléjandro~

Fuck, Mia didn't understand what she asked for. There's no way she'd willingly put herself in my crosshairs, not today, not after the day I'd had. She turned and stared up at me with wide hazel eyes swirling with flecks of desire. Water dripped from her long hair down her perfect body as she led me out of the bathroom.

She will hate me for this.

"Come." Her one word was filled with hope.

Hope that I would crush the darkness inside me.

I stopped walking and reached for her chin, pulling it up as my lips savagely took hers. She tasted like fresh mint. Mia gasped as my tongue prized open her mouth, ruthlessly taking what she'd offered.

Each lick and moan were fuel for the fire I'd tried to keep contained. My need to be inside her was all-encompassing. Once we were done, she may call her brother and demand to go back to Kansas City.

I couldn't think about that now.

When I pulled away, her lips were gloriously swollen and pink.

"Last chance, Mia." She didn't speak or move, just stared up at me with a tornado of emotions in her eyes. "Here's the thing, if you don't stop me now, I'm in charge. It's the way I work."

Swallowing, she pressed her lips together and nodded.

"This won't be gentle."

"I never said I needed gentle." She squared her perfect, slender shoulders. "I need consensual, and that's what this is."

Fuck.

Wrapping my arm around her waist, I pulled her against me, smashing my hard cock between us. Mia didn't freeze or frighten as she had. Her tongue battled with mine as her small hands reached up to my hair, weaving her fingers through my locks.

She smelled like sunshine and life, the exact opposite scent that we'd been immersed in earlier today. My mouth trailed over her skin, nipping and licking as she filled the suite with erotic sounds. Step by step, I walked her backwards until her shoulders collided with the wall. Reaching down, I palmed her firm ass and lifted her, her legs wrapping around me, giving me the perfect access to her pussy. My fingers dipped between her folds as Mia hung tightly to my neck and arched her back.

Her wetness coated my fingers as I relentlessly finger-fucked her. As she bounced in my grasp, I leaned forward, seizing one of her pert nipples between my lips and sucked. She quivered in my arms until I sat her on the edge of the table.

"I want a good look at your cunt."

Mia looked up at me through veiled lashes.

"Spread those legs."

My heart beat in double time as she obeyed.

I lifted one of her heels to the table and then the other, opening her wet, swollen pussy to me. "You're fucking beautiful." A rose hue climbed from her neck to her cheeks. "Touch yourself."

"I want you to touch me."

I shook my head and deepened my tone. "I'm in charge. If you want to come, you'll do as I say."

Mia's bottom lip disappeared between her teeth as she brought her fingers to her swollen clit and began to rub. I grasped my length, running my fist up and down as she continued her slow and torturous caress of her bundle of nerves. My already-hard cock turned to steel.

"I'm going to fuck you."

Mia nodded.

As I came closer, she lifted her arms to my neck. My cock twitched with need as I lined up my weeping head and pressed within. Her silky cunt sheathed me, contracting like a damn vise. Mia wiggled, her fingernails biting into my shoulders as she adjusted to my size.

I peppered kisses along her neck and shoulder. "Are you still with me?"

She turned, her lips attacking mine with a sloppy, tongued kiss. "Fuck me."

Holy Lord Almighty.

After a day in hell, this was heaven. The pearly gates and singing angels were only the backdrop. The real paradise was being balls deep in Mia's perfect pussy.

"I'm in charge," I said, thrusting in and out of her.

Mia continued to cling to my neck, her heels digging into my lower back as she took all I had to offer. In and out, it was fast and hard. Perspiration coated my forehead. Holding her away from me, I stared down, taking in the sight of my hard, angry dick glistening with her juices.

When I looked up, I saw that Mia was watching the same show, her soft hazel eyes enthralled with the way her body took me in. She lifted her gaze to my eyes as a smile curled her lips. "You...I feel so full."

"You're fucking tight." Her damn husband probably had a pencil dick because she was not stretched out.

I lowered her feet to the floor.

"What are you doing?" she asked as I pulled out.

My cock instantly missed the warmth of her slick haven as I spun her around. Pressing on the small of her back, I lowered her torso to the flat of the table and pulling her ass toward me, encouraged her feet to spread, with my foot.

Her round ass was stunning up in the air, giving me a view of both holes. Rearing back, I landed a palm on her ass cheek. Her neck swiveled as her stare met mine. I rubbed my hand over the bright red palm print before landing another blow to her other ass cheek. "No questions. Just obeying."

Her lips curled. "Yes, sir."

Oh fuck. My wife had been holding out on me. Without any prelude, I speared her, ramming my solid cock into her pussy. Mia called out as she reached for the edge of the table to hold herself in place.

Over and over, I pulled almost out only to bury myself to the hilt. Reaching around, I found her clit and rolled it between my fingers. Mia's body quivered around me as she tensed under my touch. It was the same as last night with my tongue. She pushed up on her tiptoes as her orgasm rushed through her. The way her core strangled me was both pleasure and pain.

Pulling out, I lifted her, cradling her against my chest. Her eye makeup was smeared, her lips swollen, and her cheeks flushed. Mia was absolutely, breath-takingly stunning.

"Are we done?" she asked.

"Just getting started."

I laid her on the bed and climbed over her, kissing her toes, ankles, calves, knees, and inner thighs. She called out my name as I lapped her essence. My kisses continued over the dip of her stomach and up the swells of her breasts. As my tongue danced with hers, I pressed her thighs back, pulling her legs over my shoulders and thrust deep inside her.

We were a loud chorus of sloppy bodies slapping against one another. My grunts and her moans were a symphony of sounds uttered since the beginning of time. Mia came again, gripping my shoulders, her lips forming a silent "o," before biting my shoulder, muffling her screams of ecstasy.

Sensing her bliss, I didn't slow or allow her time to bask in the afterglow. I couldn't. This was a marathon, and I wasn't stopping before the finish line.

When the sensation hit—drawing my balls tight— it was if someone lit a fuse, scorching my body from my head to my toes, ripping me apart from the inside out. Holding tight to her hips, I surrendered to the pleasure as I filled her with everything I had.

My circulation roared in my ears as I panted for air. Beneath me, Mia too was languishing in the satiation. Her eyes fluttered closed.

I lowered my forehead to hers, concern fighting its way out of my dark state. "Do you hate me now?"

Her sleepy eyes opened wide. "Only for making me ruin my hair. I had it all ready for dinner."

Fucking light—blinding light.

My cheeks rose as I peppered hers with kisses. "Yeah, your eye makeup is a bit..." I touched under her one eye and the other.

"What time is it?"

I turned to the clock. "8:20."

Mia's hands came to my shoulders, and she pushed. "Oh God. We're supposed to be at dinner in ten minutes."

Laughing, I rolled to my side, freeing her.

"You think this is funny?"

I seized her hand. "I do."

Mia tilted her head.

"This night turned out a hell of a lot better than the day."

She leaned close and kissed my cheek. "I'm sorry I was so awful to you."

Today was awful. Lying beside my gorgeous wife and jacking off in the shower wasn't awful. If anything, it made what just occurred all the better.

Placing my elbow on the pillows, I lifted my head

and watched her round ass as she walked naked to the bathroom.

Mia.

Mine.

Laying my head back on the pillow, I stared up at the ceiling with one thought going through my head. I'd walk through fire for that woman.

TWENTY-ONE

Mia

Tomorrow Aléjandro and I would be married for an entire week. It seemed like it should be months. It's felt like that long since I'd spoken to my family. There was an issue with me having a phone on Bella. The way Aléjandro explained it, I agreed that I wouldn't risk his parents' safety with a means to pinpoint my location.

Since I spent most of my time over the past week with my mother-in-law, this getaway couldn't be considered a honeymoon. That said, my golden tan and sun-streaked hair showed visible signs of a week in paradise.

Most mornings when I woke, Aléjandro was

already gone. He didn't tell me much about the work he did. The lack of knowledge gave his absences a sense of mystery as well as danger. Thankfully, other than that first day he was gone, he hadn't returned in such a dark state. Not that I minded the less gentle version in the intimacy department. In some ways, his ravenous hunger was my perfect initiation back into the world of sex.

Even that evening, the restraint he'd shown with my initial boundaries was still present in a different way. It was hard to explain, but those first nights set a stage that gave me a sense of peace I couldn't articulate. And then the evening we were almost late to dinner, well, it reassured me that we can share in voracious hunger for one another without violence. To say he'd reawakened my libido, my desires, and my wanton needs would be inaccurate.

There wasn't a reawakening.

Never before had I felt as free with my body or a man's as I did with Aléjandro.

He took control while also encouraging my desires, showing him and telling him what I liked. It almost felt wrong to discuss such things so freely, like two consenting adults, but that was what we were.

Aléjandro didn't marry a frightened virgin. He married a bruised soul, who never learned that sex could result in mutual satisfaction. Sure, I'd heard the stories. Giorgia didn't hate sex. From the way Dario and Catalina cling onto one another, I'd guess they were both satisfied. Dante fucked whoever he could. Our parents weren't shining examples of monogamy or consent.

Growing up, my brothers and I heard Mom's pleas for restraint fall on our father's deaf ears. That could possibly be one reason I suffered through Rocco without complaint. It would take years of therapy to unwind the knotted mess of my psyche.

And still, in a short span of time, by not pressuring me, Aléjandro gave me something simple that I'd never had before.

He gave me choice in a world where the concept was new.

To some people it may seem like a small thing, but those would be the people who have always had it. To me, choice was monumental and significant. I hadn't chosen Aléjandro as my husband, but I also wasn't powerless.

Now that I had that freedom of choice, I found myself choosing intimacy whenever it was an option. I didn't plan on us fucking on the dining room table, but it would be nice to not be living under his parents' watchful eyes.

My cheeks rose as I recalled Josefina the day after our nearly missed dinner. I met her on the pool deck for breakfast. And in no time at all, she casually asked me if *it* splashed.

I looked up, unsure what she meant.

"Look at your smile," she said. "Something has changed about you."

"I'm not sure."

Josefina pressed her lips together. "You didn't answer me. Did it splash, or was it so insignificant it didn't make a ripple?"

Slowly, I understood what she was saying, and my cheeks warmed. She was asking if the rock *splashed when I threw it overboard. I looked into her lovely dark eyes. "You do watch and listen."*

She nodded.

"I would say there was a splash. To claim no significance would be to say not only did I waste ten years of my life, but also, I allowed those memories to threaten my future."

"Any element in life that forms us into the person we are is significant. Depending on how that element molds us, it can either be bright" —she wiggled her large diamond ring — *"or burdensomely heavy. Those are the ones we must throw overboard." She lifted her coffee mug to her lips and smiled. "You will be good for Jano, Mia. Keep him on his toes."*

I recalled being on my toes as he shattered my world in the most pleasurable of ways.

My thoughts came to present as my husband entered our suite.

"What are you smiling about?" Aléjandro asked.

Scanning from his wavy hair to his prominent brow, dark brown eyes, and freshly shaved cheeks, I stepped closer, the scent of his sandalwood cologne filling my senses. "Am I smiling?"

"You most definitely are. It's a gorgeous smile. I especially like it after your cunt convulses around my cock and your fingernails try to shred my shoulders."

This banter was foreign to me. That kind of talk should make me uncomfortable. However, evidenced by the twisting in my core and tightening of my nipples, the only part that was uncomfortable was the way my husband could dampen my panties with only words and a sexy smile.

My smile.

I hadn't told Aléjandro the specifics of my talks with Josefina, so I went with another truth. "I think this time away has been good."

He wrapped his arm around my waist and tugged my hips toward his. I craned my neck to keep sight of his dark mahogany orbs. "If it's only been *good*, I need to up my game."

More warmth filled my cheeks as I tilted my forehead to his shirt.

He lifted my chin with his thumb and forefinger. "Just say the word, Mia. We'll up it to three, four, five times a day. We're going to need to work out a morning and night schedule." He shrugged. "Maybe during the night, too, but I think it's doable."

Ignoring his comments—because I was beginning to realize his jest was often only a cover for his truth—

I changed the subject. "I'm smiling because we're going home."

"Our home." He nodded. "I'm glad you're ready to go back."

"I've been thinking about furniture. Your mom got me some decorating magazines. They have great ideas."

He released my chin with a kiss to my nose. "I'm glad you're excited about it."

"I am." My smile dimmed. "We'll be safe there, right?"

"Yes. I promise."

"I trust you. Has anything else happened with the bratva?"

"Else?" His forehead furrowed.

"Since the break-in at our place."

Aléjandro took a step back. "I told you about the attack on the Ruiz home."

I shook my head, concern twisting in my stomach. "No. Which one?"

"Andrés's."

My fingertips came to my lips. "Catalina's family. What happened? Is everyone all right?"

"One of their guards was killed. Em said he'd been with the family for a long time."

"Were the intruders caught?"

My husband nodded.

"They won't be bothering any of us again." It wasn't exactly a question. I knew how Dario's men would deal with people who terrorized anyone in the famiglia.

"No. We don't need to worry about them."

I had an idea. "Are they the same ones who broke into our house? If they were, the threat level can go down."

Aléjandro feigned a smile. The muscles pulled taut in his temples. "Silas has been working tirelessly. Rei too. We will be better protected than the crown jewels."

"Rei?"

"He's a genius when it comes to technology. I don't know how he's learned all that he has, but damn, I'm glad he's on our side."

My lips curled. "*Our* side."

He took a few steps closer and sandwiched my cheeks with the palms of his hand. "Yes, *Señora* Roríguez, our side."

"What did Dario say?"

"About what?" he asked.

"The break-in at Catalina's family's home. I'm sure he was upset."

Aléjandro furrowed his brow. "I got the impression that because the break-in upset Cat, your brother was extra concerned. Valentina and Camila are currently in Kansas City staying with Dario and Cat. Andrés agreed that it would be best until they improved security."

It was interesting which two homes were hit. "By targeting us and them, it seems the bratva is trying to harm both the famiglia and the cartel—trying to harm the alliance."

"The alliance is solid, but we've drawn the same conclusions. There's a man who believes he should take over the Roríguez cartel."

My eyebrows knitted together. "You'll take it over."

"One day it will be mine. Elizondro Herrera wants to take it over and add our men, our products, our business...all of it to his empire. He built his kingdom after *mi padre*, and he's thirsty for more."

"You mentioned him before." I remembered. "He was the one who was working with my father and... rock."

Aléjandro's eyebrow arched.

"You know, like an annoying pebble in your shoe." My eyes widened. "It's not really a name, so I can use it to refer to someone whose name you don't want to hear."

My husband grinned and shook his head.

"Josefina came up with it. Anyway, Dario took out the rats in the famiglia after the attempted coup. Can't *el Patrón* take care of Herrera?"

"Not without furthering a war." He shrugged. "Herrera isn't under *Padre's* control." Aléjandro's nostrils flared. "Honestly, the war is already happening. Especially if Herrera has enlisted the bratva."

"I'd forgotten you said that."

"It's more than I want you to worry about."

"Please don't do that," I said. "I'm not breakable."

"Fuck no. You're very bendy."

I slapped his chest. "I want to be your wife in more than sex. Confide in me. Talk to me. Nearly thirty years in the famiglia, I promise I can handle whatever you throw my way." I laid my hand in the center of his wide chest, feeling the soft cotton beneath my fingertips. "Maybe I can even give you the perspective of the famiglia."

Aléjandro took my hand from his chest and lifted it to his strong lips, kissing my knuckles. "I will. And if I don't, ask. I don't mind. *Mi madre* doesn't want to know what goes on. I don't want to scare you away."

"I'm afraid we're stuck with one another. Dario won't take me back, well, unless..."

"I die."

"Yeah, don't do that."

Josefina met us on the lower deck, looking as elegant as ever. When she lifted her arms, I willingly went forward hugging her back. Tears came to my eyes, and my throat felt tight. I didn't know how to tell her how important her acceptance had been or how she helped me without ever telling me what to do. I pulled back and forced a smile. "Thank you."

She lifted her hand to my cheek. "Take care of my Jano."

I nodded.

Next, she hugged Aléjandro. "You chose well. Show her every day why accepting your proposal was a good thing."

He curled his lips. "Actually, she didn't."

Josefina looked in my direction and smiled. Her attention went to my husband. "Then spend every day showing her why she should have."

He nodded. "Maybe in a few months, you and *Padre* can come visit and see the house."

"*Sí*," she said excitedly, "I can't wait to see how you decorate it, Mia. Make it more than a house. Make it a home."

"I'll do my best."

"It's all that can be asked."

We all turned as a long shiny silver boat pulled up beside a floating ramp. Two men from Bella's staff hurried to moor the boat with the mooring lines. Aléjandro took my hand and helped me down to the platform and into the speed boat.

Once we were seated and our suitcases were aboard, the men in white untied the mooring lines. The waves took us away from Bella before the driver pressed the throttle and the engines roared to life.

Aléjandro reached for my hand as the speed boat soared over the ocean. Even through my sunglasses, the sunshine on the water was nearly blinding, thousands of points of light glittering over the blue waters. The boat pounded up and down until land came into view. The city of San Diego grew larger and taller as we approached the marina.

The two guards, Diego and Felipe, who had searched our house were waiting with a large SUV. I sat beside my husband as we were driven north along the coast and through the city. Before reaching our destination, Diego turned from the front seat and handed me a small bag.

"*Señora.*" His gaze went to Aléjandro and back to me. "I was told to have this ready for you when you arrived back on the mainland."

I peered between Diego and my husband as I took the bag and peeked inside. My cheeks rose as I saw the contents. "A new phone."

"I told you," Aléjandro said. "Our people have done some work on it. They made it impossible for anyone outside our organization to track your location. They've also transferred all your numbers and other information from your old phone."

This was my lifeline. I hugged the bag to my chest. "Thank you." I looked forward to Diego. "And thank you."

"*De nada.*"

A few minutes later, Felipe pulled the SUV up to our house. He paused, and the gate opened.

"Is there a transmitter in the vehicle?"

Aléjandro nodded. "If a vehicle doesn't have one, the gate can only be opened from within. Silas receives the alert. I didn't want a keypad. Four-number random patterns aren't that difficult to hack."

"I can't wait to meet Silas and Viviana."

TWENTY-TWO

As soon as Diego opened the door between the garage and house, my stomach growled at the delicious aroma permeating the kitchen coming from a stock pot on the stovetop. The woman at the counter looked up and smiled. If I were to guess, she was older than Josefina. Her dark hair had gray highlights and was pulled back in a stark bun. Her trim figure was covered by a black dress and apron. Her eyes shone as she looked at Aléjandro.

"*Bienvenida a casa,*" she said.

"Thank you," I replied. "Something smells divine."

Aléjandro greeted her with a hug and returned his arm to my waist. "Viviana, this is *mi esposa*, Mia Roríguez. Mia, Viviana, the master of everything. I swear there's nothing this woman can't do." He looked out over the living room.

My gaze went with his. We both chuckled, seeing the temporary furniture that had been set up since we were last here. Nothing said a multimillion-dollar home like lawn furniture in the living room. Before we could comment, an older gentleman in a black suit with a white shirt and an open collar entered from the direction of Aléjandro's office. He wasn't as tall as Aléjandro, but he had a distinguished air about him, much like Jorge with a bit more silver than black in his hair.

"*Señora* Roríguez." He bowed. "A pleasure to meet you."

Aléjandro had warned me about a language barrier. Maybe I'd gotten used to Josefina's and Jorge's thick accents. I had no trouble understanding either Silas or Viviana. I stepped forward offering my hand. "You must be Silas. I've heard all about your expertise."

He took my hand, and we shook.

"Please, call me Mia."

"Mia. A beautiful name."

I turned to Viviana. "Whatever you're cooking smells wonderful."

"Pozole," she said, going to the pot and lifting the lid. "It needs to simmer for a few more hours."

"Hours?" Aléjandro questioned.

She opened the refrigerator. "I haven't forgotten your appetite, Jano. I'm prepared if you're hungry."

While I didn't recall looking in the refrigerator the

last time we were here, my eyes opened wide at the fully stocked appliance. "Goodness. You've been shopping."

"*Sí*," she said with a smile. "I've cooked pork and beef. I can make you sandwiches?"

"Pork," Aléjandro said before walking with Silas toward the front office.

"I'll have roast beef. I can make them," I volunteered, walking around the counter and wondering where anything was located in my own kitchen.

Viviana shook her head. "It's my pleasure. We're happy to be closer to our grandchildren—*nietos*."

"Josefina told me that your daughter is in the States."

"*Sí*, and we'll be able to see them more often." Viviana reached her hand closer to me on the countertop and met my gaze. "When Aléjandro called Silas, I was surprised to hear he was to marry."

"It was surprising to us all."

"Silas and I, we watched him grow and always knew he would be a good man." She smiled. "It took him a little longer. Some boys need to find their way to becoming a man even when it's mapped out for them. When he looks at you, I see that he's become what Josefina always knew he could be."

"A good man," I said, a lump forming in my throat.

"*Sí*. And he has Silas working to make your home safe, which means he cares. I believe Silas wants to show you all he's done."

265

"Thank you for accepting Aléjandro's invitation. I know it was a big move. I don't know what you've heard about me." I thought honesty was the best. "I was married before. I'm a widow...or was. I'm not sure how that works now that I'm married again. In my first marriage, we didn't have the means for live-in help or any help, but my husband liked to keep up appearances. I'm capable of cooking and cleaning."

Her smile softened. "We can work together to make you and Aléjandro happy."

I nodded. "Just know that if you and Silas need time off to visit *su nietos*, we'll manage."

"*Gracias*." She inhaled and straightened her shoulders. "Now, I'll make sandwiches. From what I've seen and heard, you have furniture to buy."

"I do, and I think Aléjandro's office needs to be at the top of my list."

Viviana laughed. "Silas has been working on a folding table and sitting on a milk crate."

Office furniture was definitely on my agenda.

Turning to the stairs, I remembered the break-in. "I'm sorry our bedroom was such a mess."

"That reminds me. Let me show you something we found."

"You found?"

She nodded. "It's upstairs."

I followed Viviana up the staircase and into the bedroom I'd decided to make an exercise room. The large picture window that looked out over the ocean would be the perfect place for a treadmill with a view.

"I put it in here," she said, opening a drawer within the closet and removing my jewelry box.

My eyes widened as I gasped and reached out. "I thought they took this."

"It is yours?"

"Yes." I opened the lid and peered down into the depth. "Where did you find it?"

"Silas found it outside beyond the pool. It was discarded in the brush that grows on the steep hill to the shore."

"That means Rei was right about the way the people who broke in came and went."

"I hope everything is there. The jewelry was scattered. I tried to find everything."

"Let's find out." Viviana followed me as I took the jewelry box into Aléjandro's and my bedroom. I emptied the contents on top of the comforter. The pieces settled on the soft surface. I lifted a knot of tangled gold necklaces and set them aside. Running the string of pearls I received for my high school graduation through my fingertips made me smile. Various sets of earrings in all styles were present. I arranged them in pairs.

"Is there anything that stands out as missing?" she asked.

The ache in my chest was back. "There was a ruby ring that belonged to my grandmother."

"I didn't see any rings." She tilted her head. "Should there not be your first wedding band?"

"No. I sold them."

Viviana's lips curled. "I don't judge." Her gaze went to my left hand. "Aléjandro's rings are lovely."

I looked down and wiggled the fourth finger on my left hand, appreciating the rings more than I did the first time I saw them.

"I can show you where Silas found the box," she said, "and we can search together for any other jewelry that I may have missed."

I lifted the box to my chest. "I'm so happy. I never thought I'd see this again." Swallowing, I looked around the tidy bedroom. "Thank you for cleaning up the mess."

"Thank you for welcoming us into your beautiful home. We should go back downstairs. I can make lunch while Silas shows you the safety measures he's put into place."

It didn't seem as if there was anything Silas hadn't thought of. The house and outside property were secured with top-notch security equipment. With the sun still high in the sky, I was able to see beyond the yard, down the steep slope, and all the way down to the beach below. "That would be hard to climb," I said with Aléjandro at my side.

"Difficult," Silas said, "but not impossible. No one will climb up the cliff or disappear down it without tripping one of my alarms. There are motion detectors and cameras. If an alarm sounds" —he pointed at the watch he'd just given me— "your watch will notify you. It's waterproof, so please wear it at the pool."

"You won't be alone," Aléjandro added. "Someone will always be here."

He must have read my mind because my husband grinned and shook his head. "They aren't jail keepers. They're for your safety. If for any reason Silas isn't here, Felipe, Diego, Rei, or I will be. If the alarm sounds, go inside to my office."

"Your office?"

"Come," Aléjandro said, "we'll show you."

The three of us walked past the pool, up the steps, and through the open doorways into the living room. Viviana didn't look up from the kitchen where she was preparing our sandwiches. In Aléjandro's office he led me to the closet door. The interior of the closet was lined with shelves. He reached for the back shelves and pressed a button. The bookcase swung back.

My eyes opened wide. "Is this why you bought this house? Because it had a secret room?"

"It didn't have one until a few days ago," Silas answered. "The construction was done by trusted members of the Roríguez cartel. Officially, this room doesn't exist." He stepped past me and turned on a light. The room was rectangle, longer than it was wide. "Currently, it's without furniture. I was happy to get it constructed on such a short timeline."

"Most of the house is without furniture. I'll add

furnishing this room to my list" I tried to figure out where the room came from—how it fit into the grand scheme of the house. "Did you build this in the garage?"

Aléjandro smiled. "You didn't even notice the loss of space in there."

"I didn't. I'd only been in there once before, but it doesn't stick out."

"From the garage, it looks like storage," Silas said. "The contractor was talented."

"Let me know what kind of furniture you want to have inside," I said. "I better get busy."

"That room is only for emergencies," Aléjandro said. "Hopefully it will never be used, but if the alarms are tripped, I want you to go in there and let the guards take care of whatever is happening outside."

I leaned against my husband's side. "I've always wanted a secret room."

He wrapped his arm around my waist. "Look at me, fulfilling wishes I didn't even know you had."

Later that night as I readied for bed, I marveled at the change a week could make. Between lunch and dinner, I used my new phone to call my mother and Giorgia. They were both happy to hear from me. I told them about spending a week on Bella. I didn't mention the break-in. Instead, I made it sound like we'd escaped real life for a honeymoon at sea. Of course, Mom knew about the break-in at the Ruiz home. She mentioned that Catalina's mother and sister were in

Kansas City and even sounded a little jealous, which didn't surprise me.

I shared more personal information with Giorgia.

She screamed when I told her. And even from thousands of miles away, my cheeks filled with warmth as I admitted that maybe sex wasn't as horrid as I'd previously thought.

Wearing a short nightgown, with my face washed, teeth brushed, and hair combed, I walked into the bedroom suite and spotted Aléjandro out on the balcony with a tumbler of tequila in his hand. The whoosh of waves came from the shore. I stood in the open doorway, leaned against the jamb, and bit my lip, appreciating the specimen that was my husband. He was leaning forward on the railing, looking out toward the dark ocean, and unaware that I was dissecting him inch by inch.

His shirt from earlier was gone, giving me an unobstructed view of his shoulders, the concavity of his spine, and the sexy dimples near its base. My insides turned to liquid as I scanned his bronze skin. His torso slimmed to a V, and his pajama pants rode low on his hips, giving me a hint of his tight, muscular ass.

How hadn't I seen how sexy he was the first time I saw him?

Maybe I did.

I did.

I refused to admit it.

Aléjandro turned, resting his ass on the railing and crossing his arms over his chest. His eyes appeared black, as if the pupils had taken over the brown, melting it away. His lips curled above his chiseled jawline, and his dark hair was smoothed back in waves, the lights from below reflecting in its raven black shine.

"You're overdressed, *señora*." There was a rasp in his voice that set my blood racing.

"I'm dressed for sleep."

Aléjandro drained the last of the tequila and set the tumbler on the tile floor, all while his stare didn't leave mine. It was as if he didn't even blink. The black holes of his orbs were magnets, beckoning me toward him.

"I was just thinking," he said, coming closer and lifting his arm to the doorjamb above the top of my head, "about the first time I saw this house."

I lifted my chin to see him better, the sharp cut of his jaw and the bobbing of his Adam's apple. "I love it. You said you wanted me to like it. I do."

A gasp escaped my throat as he seized my wrists, lifted them over my head, pinning me in place. "This suite." He tilted his chin to the bedroom. "I imagined you here." He tugged my wrists higher, making me push up onto my tiptoes. "I envisioned the things I could do to you here."

Beneath the fabric of my nightgown, my nipples hardened.

Aléjandro leaned forward and nipped my neck, sending shockwaves throughout my nervous system. "Would you like to hear all the things I thought of?"

"No." I shook my head, my toes stressed, wrists aching, and imagination in overdrive. "Show me."

His lips crashed down on mine, taking my breath as his tongue plunged within. I wiggled and fought against his hold of my wrists to no avail as his kiss devoured my need for freedom. With the hardness of his chest pressed against me, I sensed his kisses everywhere. Fire raged through my circulation, leaving smoldering ruins in its wake. By the time he released me, my muscles had softened, and I staggered to remain standing.

Aléjandro stepped inside the bedroom, offering me his hand. Once we were both within the room, he closed the glass doors and blinds. As he turned, his voice deepened, and his accent thickened. "Suck me, Mia. Like you did in the shower."

The shower.

My first revision of my declaration.

My modification.

My decision.

Without hesitation, I fell to my knees, willing to let Aléjandro take command of our evening, giving him the control while knowing that I had the option to tell him no. As his erection grew beneath his pants, my mouth watered, and the word 'no' was suddenly absent from my vocabulary.

Looking up through veiled lashes, I straightened my neck, sitting back on my heels. Wanton need stirred within me as he lowered the waistband of his pajama pants. Oh God Almighty, he was commando. No wonder his pants hadn't hidden his erection.

I fidgeted, needing to feel friction between my legs, but my efforts were in vain. My hunger grew as he reached for my chin with one hand while grasping his length with his other.

"In the shower," he said, "I was at a disadvantage."

He was talking about his arm.

"Now, I'm not..."

I was listening to his words while mesmerized by his actions. I nibbled my lip as his hand moved, up and down. His penis was glorious, beautiful, and angry at the same time. The length and width multiplied, veins coming to life and come weeping from the tip.

His voice deepened. "Take all of me like a good girl, and that ache between your thighs will be thoroughly fucked until you're not sure you can come again."

My lips curled. "I never said there was an ache."

"You don't have to. I see your hard nipples, and I can smell your arousal. Your panties are soaked, and you haven't even gotten a taste of my come." He lifted a brow. "Tell me I'm wrong."

My head shook from side to side. "Not wrong."

"Keep your lips closed."

I obeyed as he wiped his salty come over my lips like lipstick.

"Fuck, Mia. I could come all over your beautiful face."

My core twisted at the idea of Aléjandro marking me, fully denoting me as his, and making his possession overtake memories of anyone who came before.

"Open your mouth before I do."

I instantly opened my lips as Aléjandro pushed his way to the back of my throat. Resisting the urge to gag, I worked my tongue, swirling it around his shaft. Bobbing my head, I sucked in a breath only to tighten my lips and slide up and down his glorious cock.

His fingers wove through my hair, tugging on the roots as he pistoned his hips, thrusting in and out of my mouth and filling the air with curses in two languages. Behind my closed eyes, I imagined his cock satisfying the growing and unbearable need between my thighs.

It was as his body tensed that I sucked, pulling away with a slobbery pop. Closing my lips, I lifted my face and closed my eyes.

"Fuck," he growled seconds before his warm come painted my face, neck, and chest.

When my eyes opened, Aléjandro was kneeling before me, his hands on my shoulders. Blinking, I saw the uncertainty in his gaze. Before he could speak, I smiled and leaned forward, capturing his lips and sharing his salty taste.

We fell back, me on top of him, kissing, lapping, and licking. Aléjandro reached for the hem of my nightgown and pulled it over my head, wiping away some of his marking. Then he palmed my cheeks and focused his intense stare on me. "You're mine. Mine. I'm who you think about before you fall asleep and as soon as those gorgeous eyes open. Mine."

I nodded. "Yours."

TWENTY-THREE

Aléjandro

Rei and I sat in my newly furnished office.

It didn't take Mia long—a little over a week. With Silas at her side, she visited furniture stores far and wide. She asked Silas to work with the contractor who constructed the secret room to fill one wall of the office with bookcases. The day after those were complete, the furniture arrived. She was almost giddy with excitement, promising me it was fit for the future leader of the Roríguez cartel.

Now my wife was concentrating on other rooms. If I remembered correctly, by the end of this week, we'd have a real dining room table, and the lawn furniture in the living room would be replaced by sofas and plush chairs. The other night when I came to bed, she was lying with open magazines scattered about, deciding on artwork and other decorations.

"You don't need to furnish every room immediately," I said, crawling under the blankets beside her.

She lowered the magazine in her grasp and looked at me in a way that made the world stop spinning. There were tears in her eyes. My breath caught in my chest. "Is something wrong?"

Mia shook her head. "You could have hired a decorator. I'm glad you didn't."

"So glad you're crying?"

She wiped a tear with the back of her hand and forced a smile. "Happy tears, Aléjandro. Not sad. By leaving the decorating to me, you're letting me...well, this house is our home and your trust in me makes it feel like it is part me."

"Did you decorate your first house?" I wasn't sure why I asked. I wasn't a fan of hearing about her first marriage.

Mia shrugged, her smile dimming. "We were young. Rocco's parents gave us money for our wedding. He wanted things to appear as if we were better off than we were. Instead of budgeting the money, he insisted we make the first floor look like a showroom." She shook her head. "In retrospect, I realize it was a cheap imitation. For the first two years, we slept on a mattress on the floor, and our clothes were in those plastic dressers." She inhaled and looked down at her lap. "No one was allowed to go upstairs."

I reached for her hand and gave it a squeeze. "I don't give two shits about other people's opinions. The only person whose opinion matters is you."

"I want you to like it too."

"The office is even better than I imagined. I've never had my own office," I admitted. "At my parents' house, Rei and I would talk in *mi padre's* office. Our work was done throughout the house." I laughed. "It's a big fucking house, so we were never without space."

She lifted one of the magazines and showed me different sets of outdoor furniture. "I was thinking about this for the back patio and pool area." She turned the page. "This is pretty, but I don't think it's worth the extra expense."

"Stop."

Her hazel orbs looked over at me.

"We're not on a budget. Get whatever you want."

"My mom has some amazing artwork. You know... real art. Not paintings you buy at a store but ones you purchase through dealers."

Mi padre and *madre* had artwork. I thought of it more as a status symbol than their love of the art or artists.

"Get art," I said.

"I wish I knew more about it."

"Cat's degree is in art something or the other. I'm sure she'd be open to talking to you about it."

Mia sighed and tugged on her lower lip. "I feel bad about Catalina."

"Why?" I asked, genuinely curious.

"I didn't realize until we married how lonely Catalina must have felt in Kansas City. I wish I'd done more to welcome her into the famiglia."

"Are you lonely?"

Her gaze met mine. "Sometimes. I was at first with the extra emotion of feeling sorry for myself." Before I could comment, she went on, "Josefina was a big help. It sounds ridiculous that I was feeling sorry for myself while sailing on a superyacht. It's a lot to leave your home, family, and friends."

"Valentina Ruiz and Camila recently returned from Kansas City. Maybe you could do something with them? I don't care where you go or what you do as long as you have Silas or another bodyguard with you."

She sat taller against the headboard. "I was thinking that maybe after the house is decorated, we could have a housewarming party or something."

My thoughts immediately went to the problems with the bratva and some unusual coincidences that had befallen a few of the cartel's recent transactions. For a party we'd need more than Silas's security; we'd need guards we could trust without question.

"If you don't want us to..."

I shook my head. "Give Silas and me time to manage security and we can have a party."

"What about Gerardo and Liliana Ruiz?"

"What about them?"

"Did you tell Gerardo after our wedding that we may visit?"

"I said something that morning, but honestly, with everything happening, I'd forgotten all about it."

Mia turned toward me, pushing the magazines out of the way. "If we could make the trip, I want to do it. I'm worried about Liliana."

I lifted my palm to cup her cheek. "I never took you for someone with such a big heart."

Her smile caused her cheeks to rise. "You didn't know me, nor I you. I admit I had my share of misconceptions about you."

"We're both guilty." As I lowered my touch of her soft skin, my thoughts went back to the wedding when Mia pointed out Gerardo and his new bride from among the guests. "I'm sure it's tough with how young she is. She'll adapt."

"It's more than that. She had bruises on her wrist."

"Like I said before, maybe Gerardo is into kink." I lifted my eyebrows. "The idea of you struggling under restraints is getting me hard as we speak."

Mia smiled in a way that gave me hope of that dream one day becoming a reality. It wasn't a secret that in the last few weeks, my wife had come out of her shell when it came to our sex life. While I didn't want to push her, the times I had...call it encouraged... she'd surprised me with her acceptance. Taking what we shared deeper into the fringes of BDSM would require her ultimate trust in me. I planned to earn that first.

"When your schedule allows, maybe we could make a surprise visit to Sacramento."

I nodded. "There are a few cartel endeavors up there I'd like to check on."

My wife's smile returned. "Don't warn Gerardo until the last minute."

"You're trying to set him up?" I asked.

"No. I'm doing no such thing. I'm utilizing the element of surprise to confirm or refute my concerns."

"I know you don't want to hear it, Mia, but Gerardo is Liliana's husband. She's his wife. What they do in private isn't under the jurisdiction of the cartel."

"The cartel sanctioned their wedding. Maybe the cartel should consider the consequences."

"Does your brother interfere with marriages in the famiglia?"

"Make the cartel better than the famiglia, Aléjandro."

Shaking my head, I leaned in closer and captured her soft, pouty lips.

Make the cartel better than the famiglia.

The health of individual relationships seemed minimal in the grand scheme of the bratva, the alliance, and the dangers that lurked outside our safety zone.

When I pulled away and our noses were nearly touching, I looked into her soft hazel eyes and asked, "Do you plan to challenge me forever?"

Her lips curled. "Until death do us part."

REI LEANED back in one of the leather chairs opposite my desk with his ankle resting on his opposite knee. "I have to hand it to Mia. Even you look important behind that desk."

"No more important than I was behind the folding table with the milk crate."

Rei laughed. "I know that, and you know that, but the soldiers will think otherwise when they meet with you."

"I'm not ready to have anyone in our home until we make sure our people are loyal." I changed the subject to another of my concerns. "How did our shipment get seized?"

Rei's expression darkened. "Fucking 500 kilos." He lowered his other boot to the floor and leaned forward. I saw the tension in the small lines near his eyes. "Doesn't make sense. Our man had it across the border without a hitch. Then he was pulled over for mistaken identity. What the fuck? There was an APB out on the same make and model beater."

"Someone knew the shipment was coming. They

even knew the damn car. It was a setup. That person wanted the shipment to be seized."

"A person or persons who want Roríguez to look bad or to prompt DEA's radar and have them start breathing down our necks." I let out a breath, clenched my jaw, and pushed back against the tall leather desk chair. "Where's our soldier?"

"Custody. He's not talking."

"Does he have papers or is he getting deported?"

"Has papers," Rei said. "*Padre's* lawyer is working to have him released, but we're fucked on product. Fucking agents are probably using or selling it themselves."

"Five hundred is too much to lose, but it's nothing compared to the shipment we have headed to Kansas City." I met my brother's stare. "Who knows about the shipment headed to KC?"

"Too many people."

"Then delay the shipment." I sat forward. "Delay it. Get word out among the soldiers that the glitch with the recent seizure is fucking with our network."

"That will make us look weak."

"Only temporarily. The shipment will proceed as planned, but I don't want anyone outside our top lieutenants to have that information. I've been thinking for a while that we may have a mole or a whole fucking nest, and we need to fucking exterminate."

Rei's cheeks rose. "And when the shipment arrives as planned, no one will say we're weak."

I thought about Mia's request. "How are things going up north with Gerardo Ruiz's crew?"

Rei shrugged his shoulders. "He reports to *Padre*."

"Andres and Nicolas report to me. What's Gerardo's problem with the chain of command?"

"*Padre* said to give him time. Gerardo's money-laundering network has exceeded expectations. With the loss of the horse tracks, Gerardo made headway with the casinos. We're not supposed to rock the boat."

"I don't like it," I said. "I think I'm going to take a day trip up north and get an eye on things. *Padre's* back in *México*. The stateside overseeing of the cartel is my responsibility, whether Gerardo likes it or not. I'll have Silas book one of *Padre's* planes, and I'm taking Mia." I scoffed. "No one has time for a fucking eight-and-a-half-hour drive." When Rei looked as if he were about to question me, I added, "Mia spoke with Gerardo's wife, Liliana, the morning after our wedding. Mia mentioned something about missing her family. Maybe talking to another recently married bride would be good for her." That wasn't one hundred percent forthcoming, but it was enough to pave the way for the trip I believed the Roríguez cartel needed and my wife wanted.

"I checked on Wanderland last night, unannounced," Rei said, changing from one fire to the next.

"And?"

He shook his head. "Nicolas is all talk and no

action. Nothing has changed with the whores. He had two new ones, and fuck, I didn't get the vibe they were enjoying their new employment."

"Did they say something?"

"Nicolas had them come to his office while I was there." Rei's nostrils flared. "Looked like frightened kittens. Wouldn't say a thing in front of Nicolas."

I gritted my teeth. "Did you get names?"

"Only first names."

"If they won't talk to you," I asked, "who do you think can get us the deets?"

"I was thinking Em."

My forehead furrowed. "You think Nicolas Ruiz's nephew will get us dirt?"

"If there's any to be found." Rei was still living in the Ruiz pool house. "Em's had it with some of Nicolas and Gerardo's shit. Em knows that if Wanderland is busted with underage, undocumented, or unwilling sex workers, it will be bad for the entire cartel. We clean millions through that club every year. If it were shut down, we'd be scrambling."

That made me think. "We might need to move the operation to Gerardo's territory."

Is that a plan?

Who will it benefit?

Rei sat straighter and the muscles in the sides of his face pulled tight. "Go see what's happening up there. I can keep things down here running smoothly."

"I'll go tomorrow and take Mia with me. We'll pay Gerardo and his wife a visit."

TWENTY-FOUR

Mia

My nerves were in tatters as the attendant on our twelve-passenger Gulfstream announced that we would be landing shortly. Sitting across the small table from Aléjandro, I peered out the window to my right, taking in the ground below. With the summer solstice quickly approaching, Northern California was greener with more trees than its southern counterpart. That said, there was still plenty of brown. For a moment, I thought about the vegetation around my mother's home. By now, it would be green in every direction for as far as you could see.

Twisting my wedding rings, I looked down at my

hand, but I wasn't seeing what was right in front of me. My mind's eye was remembering what it was like to hide bruises and walk on eggshells, never knowing exactly what to do or say. If my instincts were correct about their relationship, part of me worried that our visit might incite Gerardo's wrath on his young wife.

Maybe I was way off in my assessment. Perhaps it was my own ghosts I was projecting on Liliana. Maybe during this visit I'd learn that Liliana was simply shy but nonetheless, a happily married woman.

I turned to see Silas and Felipe sitting in seats behind us, closer to the cockpit. They were both busy reading something on their tablets.

Looking up, I saw Aléjandro's dark gaze on me.

"You're twisting your rings," he said. "Why are you nervous?"

"I'm not."

He reached across the table and turned his large hand palm up.

Begrudgingly, I laid my hand in his, both thankful for his concern while simultaneously, stunned by his ability to read me after such a short time. With Rocco, I'd learned to mask my thoughts and feelings. I could never do it with Giorgia. It seemed Aléjandro was falling into the no-mask category.

"What did you tell Gerardo?" I asked not for the first time since he announced our trip.

"Exactly what I told you. *Mi padre* is back in *México,* and he wanted me to see how things are proceeding in Gerardo's territory. I told Gerardo that his reports have been impressive." My husband grinned. "I even stroked his ego and told him that due to his success, we may want to implement some of his practices down south. As I said, he's having trouble recognizing my new role. It isn't easy for the old guard to bow to a younger man even if I am *el Patrón's* son."

I was pleased with Aléjandro's approach. If news of our visit was upsetting to Gerardo, he could take it out on Liliana.

"And you told him I'd be here?" I knew he had. I was simply trying to calm my nerves. I was more nervous about *Señora* Ruiz than about us.

"Yes, Mia. I told him that you would be with me as you'd never been to this area. I asked if we could join them for dinner after he showed me around his territory and the various casinos. I offered a restaurant, but he invited us to their home for dinner."

I nodded. Nothing he said was new. My husband was simply trying to pacify me, and I appreciated it.

The time on my watch was after ten in the morning. My job was to spend the day shopping and sightseeing around Sacramento. Silas would be at my side throughout my explorations. I didn't mind. In the few weeks since Silas and Viviana arrived, I'd grown fond of their company as well as their dedication to Aléjandro and by extension, to me. Silas and I spent many days shopping for furniture and décor. I was getting used to his presence. Today would only be different in that instead of shopping for home goods, I was supposed to shop for myself.

My closet was still filled with clothes I'd brought from Missouri. As the temperatures rise, I could use new dresses. I even thought I'd look for one for tonight's dinner. Something that wasn't too formal but still said I was the wife of the next in line in the Roríguez cartel.

"And we'll meet you and Felipe back at the plane before dinner?" I asked.

"That's the plan."

I nibbled on my lower lip. "Is it safe here?"

"*Sí,*" Aléjandro said comfortingly. "You have Silas. Felipe will be with me. We're visiting allies."

"Yeah, I didn't get a warm, cuddly feeling from Gerardo in our few interactions."

My husband laughed. "Tell me, did you get that feeling from me when we first met?"

"No," I answered with a grin. "I think it's better that I don't describe the feelings I got."

I reached for the arms of the chair as the airplane bounced on the tarmac. The change in motion caught me off guard. I hadn't realized we were that close to landing. The scenery sped by the window, finally slowing.

"Be careful," I warned.

Aléjandro shook his head. "I'm fine. You stay with Silas."

"Is he to go into the dressing rooms with me?"

"If he does, I'll have to kill him."

Two cars were waiting for us when we descended the stairs and stepped onto the tarmac. Aléjandro spoke to the drivers in Spanish, keeping their conversation from me. I turned to Silas and lowered my volume. "Why do we have drivers? You and Felipe can drive."

He didn't respond, but by the way Silas's lips were pressed together in a flat line, I had the feeling he agreed.

Aléjandro came back and reached for my hands. "Have a good day. I'll see you back at the plane before dinner. We're supposed to be at their house by six thirty."

As he leaned in to kiss me, I whispered the same question that I'd asked of Silas.

His response was equally as quiet. "Gerardo arranged the cars and drivers as an offering of good faith."

"Can we trust them?"

"Silas will be at your side."

I nodded and inhaled, failing to ignore the unease percolating deep in my stomach.

"*Hola, Señora Roríguez,*" the driver said, his countenance without emotion.

That was the first and last time he addressed me the entire day. I learned through Silas that his name was Ángel. He didn't fit his name.

We spent the next six hours in a game of translation. Silas would ask me where I wanted to go, and then he'd relay my answer to the driver. While there wasn't anything that was outwardly threatening about the man behind the wheel, there was also nothing friendly.

Ángel waited in the car as Silas and I went into various shops and boutiques. By midafternoon, the lack of acknowledgment was wearing on me. "Do you really think he doesn't speak English?"

Silas shook his head with a grin. "He speaks English. I guarantee it. What he's doing is his way of protesting your presence."

My feet forgot to walk as we stopped in the middle of a busy sidewalk. Turning to my bodyguard with my lips agape, I asked, "Why is he protesting me? What did I do to him?"

Silas's expression softened. "Nothing, Mia. Your offense isn't your actions but merely your presence. Many in the cartel have vocalized their displeasure regarding Patrón's alliance with the famiglia. You're a reminder of that coalition."

"So, they hate me because I'm famiglia?"

"Essentially," Silas confirmed. "I won't lie to you." His smile returned if only briefly. "I respect you too much for that. The others, they don't see what Viviana and I see, the way you and Jano are in private. They assume you're miserable and you're out to make Jano miserable. You may be out to harm the cartel."

"No," I said, shaking my head. "I don't want to harm it."

"I know that because I've taken the time to know you. Don't give the other people time in your thoughts. Eventually, the truth will be seen. In the meantime, it only takes one rumor to sour the attitude of the majority."

By four in the afternoon, I was shopped out, and my head ached from the unease of the unknown. In the time since Silas's and my conversation, I was acutely aware of each glance or comment made by the driver. The scrutiny was overwhelming.

"I'm ready to go back to the plane. I'd like to rest before I change for dinner."

Silas translated my request to the driver before calling ahead to the pilot.

When we arrived on the tarmac, the steps to the plane were open and the attendant was waiting at the top. While the Gulfstream was luxurious, it was basically one large cabin with a bathroom without a shower. After the day I'd had, the idea of soaking in a hot bath or under a steady spray was at the top of my wish list. Instead, I settled in one of the cream leather seats and reclined with a cool glass of water and a Tylenol.

I wasn't certain I slept, but the rest combined with the painkiller were helpful. Over forty minutes after settling in, I sat my chair up, gaining Silas's attention. A smile came to my lips. "Thank you for watching over me. And for being with me today." The thought of being alone with the driver sent chills over my flesh.

He nodded. "It's an honor. Jano called. He's on his way."

"I'd like to change, and the bathroom is..."

Silas lifted his hand. "I will be happy to wait outside."

"Thank you."

One of my finds today was a long fuchsia tunic dress with gold, pearl, and turquoise embellishments around the neckline. I'd purchased it before Silas's and my conversation, believing the minimalistic tailoring with the opulent trimmings made for the perfect statement. Elegant yet simple. I even found gold sandals, a turquoise beaded necklace, and turquoise earrings to complete the ensemble. Now, as I stood before the bathroom mirror, styling my hair, I was left wondering if I could be of any help to Liliana even if I learned my suspicions were true.

Did everyone in the cartel hate me?

Again, my thoughts went to my sister-in-law. We, the members of the famiglia, didn't hate her. If anything, she was insignificant. The truth hit me. Catalina was no more insignificant to Dario than I was to Aléjandro. The more time I spent in his world, the stronger was my realization of how selfish we'd been not to welcome her better.

The rumble of footsteps on the metal steps and the sound of deep voices let me know I was no longer alone. Thankfully, even in his native tongue, I recognized one particular baritone voice. With a smile, I stepped from the bathroom.

Aléjandro stood near the entry with his dark stare fixed on me. "*Guau!*" His smile grew. "You're exquisite, Mia. You look like a princess from India." He came closer, his eyes still scanning the length of the dress and back. He dipped his nose toward where my neck and collarbone met, sending shivers with the puff of his breath. "Definitely royalty."

"You approve?"

"Without a doubt. I also approve of what is beneath that dress." His eyebrows did a little dance. "That will need to wait until we're home."

Heat filled my cheeks as I looked over at Silas and Felipe pretending they were suddenly deaf. I turned back to Aléjandro. "Yes, that will need to wait." I knew what he was referring to; it was something he said that threw my misconceptions of men into a tailspin.

One night while we were being intimate, he made a comment about the lack of hair at my core, saying he wouldn't mind a landing strip or something to confirm he was fucking a woman and not a child. I was so taken aback I even questioned him. Aléjandro laughed, saying real men weren't afraid of hair.

Even the memory made me giggle.

"Did you buy me clothes for dinner?"

"No," I said, my eyes growing wide. "You didn't mention it. I would have..."

My husband's laugh rumbled through the plane. "I brought a change of clothes." He leaned in and kissed my cheek. "I was teasing."

Exhaling, I shook my head. "Because I'm not nervous enough about tonight."

"Tonight is only dinner, and we are honored guests."

Pressing my lips together, I nodded.

"I've spent the entire day with Gerardo." Small lines formed near the corners of his eyes. "I'd be happy to skip dinner and head home." He inhaled. "However, I promised you access to Liliana, and I'm a man of my word." He squeezed my hand. "I need to change, or I'll appear a beggar beside my wife's regal air."

Aléjandro changed from his blue jeans and black t-shirt into black slacks, a black button-up shirt, with his sleeves rolled to below his elbows and the collar unbuttoned showing a gold necklace. He wasn't wearing socks as he slid his feet into his expensive Italian loafers.

It seemed that Aléjandro convinced one of the drivers to leave a car, allowing Aléjandro and I to travel with Silas and Felipe. The lack of a stranger in the car brought back a bit of my confidence and eased my stretched nerves. My husband took my hand in his as Felipe drove us through a prestigious neighborhood filled with wrought-iron fences, walls of shrubbery, and gates.

Felipe approached one of the gates. As Gerardo's

monstrosity of a home came into view, I had visions of my mother's home, the one she'd had enlarged to keep her children from hearing her distress.

With Aléjandro's hand in the small of my back, we walked up the stairs to the main doors. A maid answered, smiling and bidding us entrance. Ángel was standing guard inside the foyer, managing not to make eye contact. I kept my smile in place at the sight of Gerardo towering next to Liliana. Her body language screamed as her lips remained still. She seemed to be thinner than she was at the wedding, and her eyes weren't reflecting the large smile she was projecting. Her dress was also long sleeved, but hers had tight cuffs.

"*Bienvenido*," Gerardo gregariously said. "*Señora* Roríguez" —he bowed— "an honor to have you visit our home."

"Thank you for having us."

"Come in," Gerardo motioned us away from the foyer to a stunning sitting room with a grand piano.

Immediately, two maids entered with trays of wine and water. I took a crystal flute of water as did Liliana. Both men took the wine.

"Do you play?" I asked, tilting my chin toward the piano.

"No," Gerardo answered, "but my wife is taking lessons." He turned to her. "Aren't you?"

"*Sí*," she said softly.

"*Inglés*," he reprimanded. "We want *Señora* Roríguez to feel comfortable."

"I'm sorry, *Señora*." Liliana paled and looked down.

Aléjandro reached for my hand as I bit the inside of my cheek. Taking a breath, I replied, trying to lighten the mood, "I'm learning to get used to it. Hopefully, my Spanish will improve." While Liliana was obviously chastised, I would suspect Ruiz's driver had done exactly as he'd been instructed. "Your home is lovely."

Gerardo nudged his wife, causing her eyes to come my way. "Thank you."

"Is Sofia home?" Aléjandro asked.

I recalled Sofia was Gerardo's daughter from his first wife.

"She's at university," Gerardo replied. "She has an apartment near the campus. Very safe."

And one less person to hide your abuse from.

Garnering my courage, I said, "If dinner isn't ready, I'd love to see more of your home."

"It will be soon." Gerardo looked at his watch. "A few minutes."

I stood. "Perfect, Liliana would you like to show me around?"

Her frightened eyes went to Gerardo's. The muscles in his cheeks pulled tight and his beady dark eyes came my way. Finally, he turned to Liliana and nodded. She stood. "We can start this way."

I could barely hear her meek voice as we walked

back toward the foyer and then turned right, into an opulent living room. "This is lovely. Did you decorate?"

"Oh no. Ximena, Gerardo's first wife. She was much better at that than I am."

"Did Ximena also play the piano?" I asked.

Liliana nodded. "I'm trying, but" —she lowered her head— "I'm not very good."

"Did you want to take lessons?"

She nodded faster as her cheeks paled. "Yes."

I called bullshit.

Forcing a smile, I walked toward the back windows. Beyond the glass and a story below was a large swimming pool. "That is big. You could swim laps."

"*Sí*." She shook her head. "Sorry. Yes, my husband swims every morning."

Cautiously, I glanced toward the front room where we'd left our husbands and spoke low. "Liliana, forgive me if I'm being forward, but as a recent bride myself, I'm finding myself lonely when Aléjandro is working. I suppose Gerardo also works long hours."

She nodded.

"Maybe we could exchange phone numbers and talk. I think we are going through many of the same things. It's always nice to have a friend to talk to."

By her expression, you would think I asked her the impossible. "I would need to ask Gerardo."

"To share your phone number?" I inquired.

"I have friends. He's...I'm..." Her voice trailed away.

I'd come prepared. I pulled a small paper from my pocket. "Take this. It's my number. Gerardo reminds me of my first husband, and I remember when I wished for someone to talk to, *really* talk. Thankfully, I had my cousin."

Her eyes met mine. "Could your cousin help?"

"No, but she listened and that was a help. In hindsight, I misjudged the people who may have been able to help. I should have talked to them."

Liliana looked down at the paper in her hands and back up, her voice was barely audible. "No one can help."

"I'm the wife of Aléjandro Roríguez."

"But you're not cartel." She looked down and back up. "I don't think Gerardo would approve."

"My last name is still Roríguez. Don't underestimate me." I forced a smile. "No pressure, Liliana. I think you have enough of that. Just remember that I'm here."

At the sound of our husbands' voices, she stuffed the paper into her pocket and began nervously describing the landscaping around the pool.

"Of course, the gardeners do the work, but the succulents and other drought-tolerant plants are..."

TWENTY-FIVE

"W hat did you decide?" Aléjandro asked once we were on the plane and in the air on our way home.

"Let me ask you: what is your impression of Gerardo Ruiz?"

"He's an arrogant prick. It revolts him to have to deal with me instead of *Padre*."

"Was he at least respectful?"

Aléjandro nodded. "As he was at dinner."

"Did you notice how he did all the talking? Liliana barely said two words throughout the meal."

"She's eighteen, Mia. She's intimidated. When it comes to the Roríguez cartel, we are royalty." His cheeks rose as his smile formed. "Like you appear." The brown of his eyes melded with the black of his pupils. "You only need a crown."

I shook my head. "It's more than that. She's frightened. She doesn't want to take piano lessons."

"That's your big find? Piano lessons?" My husband let out a long breath as he leaned against the soft chair. "Maybe because of your history, you're seeing things that aren't there."

Clenching my jaw, I stared out the small window as darkness prevailed. I wasn't projecting. In the depth of my marrow, I knew the hell Liliana was going through.

Aléjandro reached out his hand toward me. "You're a caring person."

I crossed my arms over my breasts, not taking his. "If I'm right, she needs help."

"Has she asked for it?"

"No," I said. "She won't. She'll suffer silently because Gerardo is a respected lieutenant. No one will stand up to him."

The cut of my husband's jaw sharpened, and tendons strained in his neck.

"I'm sorry," I said, lowering my arms. "I shouldn't push you to do something you don't want to do."

"It's not just that." His words were terse. "Remember when I told you about Dante's comments about Wanderland?"

"Yes."

"I've spoken to Nicolas multiple times. He talks a good game, but nothing is changing. Rei said there are two new whores on the payroll, and he's not certain they're participating willingly. Many of the cartel soldiers like the way things are, the way they have been. We're fighting the bratva. They're breaking into our homes. We need a united front. It feels like I'm butting heads over issues that may not matter."

"You don't think that forced prostitution matters?"

Aléjandro shook his head and his tone deepened. "It matters. Fuck, if someone reports us and we're linked to human trafficking, they'll shut down Wanderland and come for other cartel businesses." He lifted his glass of tequila and brought it to his lips. When he set it down, he exhaled. "It matters—they matter. Liliana matters, but making sure Wanderland isn't setting itself up for a raid is different than inter-fering in a marriage. Gerardo already doesn't want me to stay in the States. He was happy with the freedom he used to have."

"You can stay because of me."

"What?"

"You can stay in the States because you married me. I asked Dario about it before we were married."

Aléjandro nodded.

"The entire time Silas and I were with that driver, Ángel, he only spoke Spanish. Silas explained that it was Ángel's way of doing his job and protesting me at the same time."

"Mia, it's not—"

"Please." I shook my head. "I get it because now I see how I should have treated Catalina differently, but I just had another thought."

"What thought?"

"If I'm unhappy, if I feel threatened or unwelcomed...if I leave you, your ability to stay in the States is gone."

"You're not leaving me."

My lips curled. "I'm not. When I accepted Dario's decree, I didn't do it with the hopes of our marriage ending. I just didn't want it to ever start."

Aléjandro grinned. "Maybe if you'd said something."

"Yeah, I tried that." I relaxed against the seat. "Many of the cartel think less of me because I'm famiglia."

"You're now cartel."

"I am. But I'll always be famiglia. I don't want to leave you or for the cartel to fail or have Wanderland raided, but don't you see?"

"Someone wants me back in *México*, and one way to do it is to end our marriage."

I nodded.

Again, Aléjandro laid his hand palm up on the table. This time, I willingly placed my hand in his. Warmth filled my circulation as he closed his fingers, encasing mine. "They won't succeed."

"They won't."

"I just need to find out who is behind this."

The next few weeks flew by as the calendar changed and I concentrated on furnishing our home. While I'd decorated Aléjandro's office with the idea of him working from there, Silas used the room more than my husband. Other than Rei and sometimes Emiliano and Nick, no cartel soldiers came to our home.

Viviana and I scoured the hill where Silas found the jewelry box, but no more jewelry was found. Honestly, it could be right under our noses. As new vegetation came to life our chances of ever finding my grandmother's ring decreased.

I spoke almost daily with Giorgia and at least once or twice a week to my mom. I'd even added calling Catalina to my list of to-dos. She was feeling huge as her pregnancy progressed. She'd also given me some advice on reputable art dealers in the San Diego area. Silas and I visited a studio that offered her an internship after she graduated from college.

If there were any threats to our home or property, I wasn't informed. The new patio furniture turned our pool area into a resort, and I enjoyed spending my free time relaxing near the water with a book in my hand. I even convinced Viviana to allow me to help with the housework to give her time to relax. Slowly, she was finding her way out to the pool.

The other day she came out wearing shorts, a tank top, and a sheepish smile. "I don't own a bathing suit."

"We need to get you one."

She hesitated near a lounge chair. "I have things I should be doing."

"*Por favor*?" I asked with pleading eyes.

Viviana smiled and nodded before settling on the long chair. She didn't stay all afternoon, but I took even a short stay as a win.

Aléjandro spent his days and some nights doing whatever he did. He didn't hide what his work involved, but he also wasn't a big sharer. I knew a large shipment of drugs made it successfully to Kansas City, making both my husband and my brother happy.

I also knew Rei was often at his side as well as Felipe and Diego. Not since we were first married had he come home wounded. There were times when he was in a darker mood—days that didn't go as he'd planned. I'd come to recognize those as times he needed me, and with each passing day, I wanted to be there. During those darker states, my husband earned my trust. He could be passionate without crossing the line.

I continued to worry about Liliana. Periodically, she'd come to mind. However, I had no way of contacting her, and there was nothing I could do from five hundred miles away. Truthfully, I wasn't certain what I could do if we were in the same city.

The most surprising event was that Aléjandro followed through on his offer to teach me to drive. We'd only been out a few times—the first time was in an open parking lot—but I'd actually driven. It was much more nerve-racking than I anticipated. My fingers ached from holding so tightly to the steering wheel. The last drive originated from our garage. Thank goodness for the backup cameras. I wasn't certain how anyone went in reverse before those existed. As far as accidents were concerned, none had occurred. Both Aléjandro and I considered that a win.

We were into the month of July when one night as Aléjandro came to bed with his dark mane freshly washed and still damp, he announced, "We bought an apartment building today."

I laid my book down on the bedside stand. "Why?"

He sported a smug expression as he climbed under the blankets wearing only a pair of basketball shorts. "It has twenty units."

"Where is it?" I thought I'd try with a different question.

"Mission Valley."

"Not far from Wanderland?"

He nodded with a cat-who-ate-the-canary grin.

"Oh," I said excitedly. "You bought it for the Wanderland workers."

"*Sí.*"

I smiled at his expression.

"The system Nicolas had in place, hell, none of the workers would be able to afford their own place. This will provide them with a step away from Wanderland. No one should have to live where they work, especially in those conditions. I've revamped the payroll. Working at Wanderland is a job, and if the women want to do it, they should be rightfully compensated. If they save up and want to move somewhere else, they can. This will help them on their way."

This was more than he usually said, and I loved hearing his pride. I scooted closer and leaned against his strong arm and inhaled his fresh shower scent. "I'm proud of you."

"I've talked Nicolas into renovating Wanderland. The space that used to be where the whores lived is now available for better things."

"What do the women think about it?"

"Em said they're nervous and happy."

"I get that." I leaned close and kissed Aléjandro's cheek. "The renovation will help Wanderland. You made Nicolas see that."

He wrapped his arm around me. "I concentrated on that—improvements to increase business and productivity. Moving the whores out was the obvious answer to our space problem. I'm pretty sure he thinks he came up with the idea."

"What matters is that those women will have more humane living conditions."

"And freedom to come and go. In my opinion, they were prisoners. Once Dante opened my eyes, I couldn't unsee their reality."

"Will any leave?"

He shrugged. "If they do, they don't want to be

there. Those that stay will be treated better." He shifted, pulling my softness against his hard muscles. "I know something else that matters." His tone dropped an octave, and his accent became more pronounced.

It was crazy how only a minute change in his voice could affect me, sending volts of electricity through my body, igniting nerve endings, and twisting my core. "What would that be?"

He leaned closer and pushed me back until my head was on the pillow and he was over me, nose to nose. "I have a problem. My wife makes me hard as a rock, and I can't always fuck her when I want."

I giggled. "It seems as if you fuck her often."

"Never enough. There was this morning when she was still sleeping, tonight at dinner when Silas and Viviana were present, and there's now." He dropped his chin to the sensitive spot between my shoulder and neck and peppered my skin with his kisses, licks, and nips.

My insides melted as my flesh covered in goose bumps. "Now would be good," I panted as his hands began to roam beneath my nightgown.

Aléjandro lifted his face, meeting my gaze. "No."

"No?"

"Now will not be *good*. Now will be *extraordinary*."

"You seem pretty sure of yourself."

Sitting up, he reached for the hem of my night-gown and tugged. I wiggled, helping him rid us of the interference. Next to go were my panties, leaving me stark naked and fully exposed. His focus scanned over me, warming my skin. "Mine."

"Yours."

Wordlessly, he encouraged me to roll over and climb onto my elbows and knees. There was a time I had mixed feelings about this position. I preferred not seeing my husband's face while simultaneously fearful of one of Rocco's favorite punishments.

In my new life, my reasoning was different. I had no objections to my husband's handsome face, his protruding brow, huge dark eyes, slender nose, high cheekbones, strong lips, and chiseled jaw. I also trusted Aléjandro with access to my ass. We hadn't gone there yet, and I knew in my heart when it happened, it would be on my terms.

One of the reasons I enjoyed this position with Aléjandro was how incredibly full he made me feel. After teasing my folds and finding me wet and ready, he thrust deep within me, causing my back to arch. Another reason was from this angle, my husband was extra affectionate and attentive. From kisses over my shoulders and back to the way he caressed my breasts, taunted my nipples, and paid special attention to my clit. It was as if his electrifying touch was everywhere at the same time.

While deep within me, he tantalized my breasts, nipped my shoulders, and lavished me with praises. I was beginning to recognize phrases as terms of affection. I hadn't asked for translations, but there was the tone and timbre of his voice, the timing and accompanying actions.

My elbows gave out as my circulation caught aflame, singeing my insides as my body convulsed around his. Aléjandro didn't stop, his guttural growl growing louder and the pressure of his grip on my hips growing stronger. I let out a moan as he stilled, his cock throbbed, and he filled me to overflowing.

Breaking our union, Aléjandro rolled to my side. I rolled, facing him and laid my hands on his wide chest. His heart beat strong and steady beneath my touch. I faintly recalled hearing the vibration of my phone. He surrounded me with his arms as I curled into the cocoon that was only the two of us. If anyone called, they could wait for tomorrow. I didn't want to leave Aléjandro's embrace.

I was almost asleep when I had a thought. Lifting my face, I looked at his eyes. His long lashes fluttered as he opened them.

"Is everything all right?"

Nodding, I smiled. "I thought of something I wanted to tell you." He didn't respond, waiting for me. "I wanted to tell you that I don't regret our marriage."

Aléjandro's lips took mine, soft and slow, tasting and exploring. His fingers wove through my hair and his tongue tangoed with mine. The lingering kiss tingled my lips and warmed my soul in a way I'd never known.

A phrase with three words came to mind, but I couldn't say them. My husband deserved to hear them, whether he'd ever feel the same way or not. Nevertheless, as I curled against him in the safety of his embrace, I chose to keep the phrase to myself.

TWENTY-SIX

When I awakened, Aléjandro's side of the bed was cool. His lingering scent of body-wash and shampoo emanated from his pillow. Inhaling his scent, I smiled at the memory of him telling me about the apartment building. I liked seeing and hearing his happiness about something he'd done, something he used to think of as unimportant. I had no doubt that to the workers at Wanderland, this would be a monumental step.

After retrieving my nightgown from the floor and my panties lost within our sheets, I took care of business and made my way downstairs covered by a long robe. The blue sky over the ocean was mesmerizing as I stepped into the main area of our home. Viviana had the doors open to the pool, allowing a gentle breeze to fill the living area.

Viviana smiled and filled a cup with coffee and

cream as I approached the breakfast bar. Even with the large new table, I preferred having breakfast sitting at the bar and talking to Viviana.

"*Buenos días. Qué te gustaría para el desayuno?*"

"I'm not very hungry. How about fruit and a bagel?"

"*Ahora lo traigo.*" She smiled. "You're understanding more. Don't be afraid to respond. Learning the words and accents takes practice."

"*Gracias,*" I replied.

Viviana laughed.

Without me asking for assistance, Viviana had taken it upon herself to help me understand the Spanish language. My pronunciations were horrid and apparently, in some instances changed the meanings of my comments. Nevertheless, I appreciated her patience. In return, whenever she had a question, I helped her with English.

You know what they say about old dogs and new tricks.

My problem was that I didn't think in Spanish. Every sentence was constructed in English in my head and then I spoke. I thought out the words: Have you seen Aléjandro? And then, I spoke, "*Haz visto a Aléjandro?*"

Viviana shook her head. "He must have left early. He was gone even before Silas and I woke."

I wrapped my fingers around the warm coffee mug and looked out through the open glass doors toward the pool and ocean. With the summer months, the temperatures rose, but unlike in Missouri, the lack of humidity kept everything pleasant. As my focus came back indoors, I sat back contented with the way our home looked. The furnishings were quality yet not ostentatious, minimalistic yet warm and inviting.

As Viviana set a bowl of fresh fruit and a toasted bagel with cream cheese in front of me, she read my mind. "You've done a wonderful job. Your home is stunning."

"A while back, I spoke to Aléjandro about a housewarming party." I stabbed a piece of pineapple with my fork. "I think I've waited too long for Dario and Catalina to visit. With their baby only weeks away, I'd suspect my overprotective brother won't allow Catalina to travel."

"Who would you want to invite?"

I'd already given that plenty of thought. "Other members of my family. I want them to see that I'm all right, that Aléjandro and I are doing" —a smile came to my lips— "better than I could have imagined. That would include my mother, my brother Dante, my cousin Giorgia, and her husband, Antonio."

I'd thought about my uncles; however, I decided we didn't need their negativity. Uncle Carmine and Uncle Salvatore were still of the belief that Dario should have stepped aside, paving the way for one of them to be capo. They also didn't hold back on their misgivings about the cartel or their concerns that the alliance would end up harming the famiglia.

Viviana nodded, leaning against the counter and holding her coffee cup. Her outfit made me grin. Today she was wearing a faded pair of blue jeans, an orange top, and white canvas loafers. Her hair was pulled back in a loose ponytail, making her appear younger than her years. After she and Silas were with us for a few weeks, I mentioned that uniforms weren't necessary. Viviana took me at my word. She also explained that Silas's casual attire was a suit without a tie. I didn't expect to see him in blue jeans anytime soon. "And Jano's family?"

I nodded. I'd given them a lot of consideration too. Some in the cartel may protest my presence, but nothing said accepted like the drug lord himself being there. "Jorge and Josefina. I hope they can make it. I'll contact Josefina to find out when would be best for them. Rei, of course. Also, the Ruizes, all of them, Andrés's family, Nicolas's family, and Gerardo's family. I'd say Felipe and Diego, but I'm certain they'll be here in a professional capacity, as will you and Silas. Of course, Aléjandro wants to be certain everyone is safe."

"It sounds like you need to set a date and let the men worry about the guards. We'll have our hands full with the menu."

I liked the way Viviana never complained, taking my ideas in stride. "I'm certain you're better at that than I am."

She grinned. "You taught me how to make lasagna. I'd only eaten it before in restaurants. Yours was much better."

It was Chiara's recipe, my mother's cook. She'd even taught me to make the noodles from nothing more than flour and eggs. It was a rigorous process that left the kitchen covered in flour dust. With Viviana, we used store-bought noodles, but the rest was all Chiara's recipe.

"We can plan a menu of both traditional Italian and Mexican dishes," I said. "Serve it buffet style. No messing with formal dining. We'll hire staff to carry trays of drinks and keep the buffet filled. You'll oversee them if you don't mind. I prefer the casual approach."

"We can do it."

My smile grew. "We can. Now to set a date." I pulled my phone from my pocket and noticed I'd missed a call. My forehead furrowed as I stared at the unknown number.

"*Qué pasa?*" Viviana asked.

"I received a call late last night. I didn't answer it." When I looked up, the memories of what kept me from answering filled my cheeks with warmth. "I figured it was my cousin, but I was wrong. I don't recognize the number."

"Did they leave a message?"

I shook my head. "The area code is 916. I don't recognize that. Do you?"

"*No, lo siento.*"

"If it was important, they'd have left a message." I finished the rest of my coffee. My bagel was mostly gone as was my fruit. "I'll go upstairs and shower. We can look at the calendar and talk with Silas." My smile grew. "We're going to have a party."

My mother was always the one who enjoyed entertaining. My father enjoyed showcasing his wealth. It was why he insisted Dario's wedding take place in their Ozark mansion. I didn't try to host gatherings during my first marriage. Our townhouse was too small even when compared to my father's Kansas City apartment. As consigliere, Rocco's father also had a large home. Between our parents, entertaining was always done at one of their homes.

That didn't mean I didn't want to do it, only that we didn't have the means. If it made me a bad person or even a stereotypical Mafia/cartel wife that I was excited about bringing our family and friends into our beautiful new home, then so be it. The fact Aléjandro had allowed me to decorate was the icing on the cake.

After a call with my mother-in-law, we narrowed the party date down to two options in August and one in September. I told her I'd talk to Aléjandro and get back to her. Honestly, I was feeling almost giddy knowing that she and Jorge would attend. Josefina told me she couldn't wait to see what we'd done. Of course, they'd stay on Bella but come to our home for the gathering.

While Aléjandro wasn't as excited about the party

as I was, he didn't nix it either. The date was set for the second Saturday in September. That would be four months after our wedding. It was also one month after Catalina's baby was due. I had high hopes they would be willing to come and show off the baby.

Near the end of July, I began making the calls, inviting my family. Giorgia was overjoyed at the prospect of us seeing one another and her seeing our house that I'd talked so much about. Mother said she would come in bright colors. Her mourning period would be officially over, and she was already purchasing a new wardrobe. Dante asked if Andrés Ruiz's family would be in attendance. When I said they were invited, he sounded interestingly pleased.

Dario called me before I had the chance to call him. His news was more exciting than a housewarming party. Catalina was well and my brother was officially the father of a seven-pound, six-ounce baby girl named Ariadna Gia Luciano. Her name was the combination of the names of both Catalina's grandmother and Dario's. My new niece was undoubtedly the personification of our alliance. I made a note to send Catalina flowers.

Aléjandro provided me with the phone numbers of the lieutenants' wives. Valentina Ruiz and Maria Ruiz were both gregariously happy with their invitation. Of course, Valentina told me about her new grand-daughter and her planned trip to Missouri. Before we disconnected our call, my mother called me back, ecstatic about her new role as *nonna*.

It was as I began to enter Liliana's number that it appeared on my phone—the unanswered call from a few weeks earlier. The realization knocked a bit of my excitement out of me, replacing that emotion with something akin to fear.

What happened to make her call me?

Why didn't she leave a message?

Is she all right?

I hit the green button, the call connected and began to ring. After about three rings, the call went to a voicemail that wasn't accepting new messages. The next day I tried and had the same result. After a third attempt, I took my concern to my husband.

A little before dinner, I found Aléjandro standing at the vanity in our bathroom with a towel around his waist, his hair wet, shaving cream on his cheeks, and his bronze flesh covered in water droplets. Despite the fact he looked tired, I couldn't help pausing and taking him in. Heat began to build beneath my skin as I leaned against the doorjamb with my arms crossed over my breasts and scanned from his dark mane to his bare feet. My gaze no longer lingered on the silver scars but on the definition in his muscles and the indentations of his torso.

Aléjandro turned my way with a grin before turning back to the mirror. "I hope you like what you're ogling."

"I'm not ogling."

Completing his task of shaving, he reached for a towel and wiped the remaining shaving cream away. We met somewhere between the sink and door.

I wrapped my arms over his broad shoulders and inhaled the cool, clean scent. "I didn't realize you were home. I could have washed you." I let my hand float down his bicep to the place where he'd been stabbed. "This is healing well."

"You're responsible for that."

"I am?" I asked, surprised.

"*Sí*, it's a well-known fact that sex is good for the circulation. Circulation promotes healing. Thus, a regular and active practice of fucking will keep me healthy."

"*Estas loco.*"

Aléjandro laughed. "Your Spanish is improving." He kissed my cheek. "And I may be crazy, but you're okay with that."

I changed the subject as we walked into the bedroom. "I told you that I called around to see if the second Saturday in September will work for our families and friends." My mind blanked as my husband dropped the towel.

He nodded as he pulled up his silk boxer shorts and stepped into a clean pair of blue jeans.

Shaking my head, I continued, "I still haven't gotten an answer on the number you gave me for Liliana Ruiz."

Aléjandro tilted his head as his nostrils flared. "Mi-a..." The way he elongated my name was a warning not to revisit my crusade where Liliana was concerned.

"I'm not insinuating anything. I just can't get an answer. I spoke with Valentina and Maria a few days ago. I don't want Liliana to learn about our party and think we hadn't invited her and Gerardo."

"You could call Valentina again. She might be able to get through to Liliana."

"I could..." I tucked my chin and widened my eyes.

"Fuck, what does that expression mean?"

A giggle rolled from my lips. "How about you give me Gerardo's number?"

Aléjandro shook his head. "I'll call him."

"And tell him that I couldn't reach his wife? He could very well get upset with her that you became involved."

"You don't think receiving a call from *you* won't also upset him?"

"I won't tell him I haven't been able to reach Liliana. Instead, I'll invite them to our party and ask if Liliana could call me for the details."

Aléjandro huffed as he tugged a button-up shirt over his shoulders.

"Don't you see?" I asked. "I'm playing into him, as you did by stroking his ego. I'll be asking for his permission because he's the granter of all things." There was more than a little sarcasm to my voice. "Then Liliana will have his approval to contact me."

My husband sat on the long bench near the end of our bed and began putting on his shoes. When he looked up, I noticed the small lines near his eyes and the way he clenched his jaw.

"Is something wrong?"

"A few months ago—right after we were married —there was an incident with the bratva. Remember when Andrés's home was invaded?"

I nodded. Of course, I remembered. It was the same time our home was broken into.

"We retaliated."

"The cartel or you personally?"

"I was involved."

"I didn't know that."

He inhaled. "Yeah, it wasn't something I wanted to talk about. We kept waiting for a response from Ivan Kozlov, the boss of the bratva. The lack of reaction was grating on me—too quiet. You know what I mean?"

I sat at his side, the warmth of his leg against mine. "Did something happen?"

Aléjandro leaned forward, supporting his head with his hands, his elbows on his knees. "Our apartment building caught fire early this morning."

I gasped. "Oh my God. Is anyone...the women...?"

He sat straight and exhaled. "Three casualties, including one of the new girls." He stood abruptly, the muscles in his arms bulging. "She was only eighteen. A fucking kid. Most of these workers are runaways or disenfranchised from their family. We don't even have contact information to notify family. The fire started after Wanderland closed. The building went up like kindling. It's a total loss. Now the fucking authorities are involved. Some asshole detective made an offhand comment that we probably torched the place on purpose to hide our operations."

"Aléjandro, I'm sorry."

"A few other women were injured. They won't be able to work until their burns heal. The old dorms at Wanderland are gone. Renovation has started."

"You need a place to house the women, a place that's safe."

"Right now, they're staying at one of our halfway houses."

My eyes grew wide, recalling the hideout I'd seen. "Are they safe?"

"Probably not. Em is looking at a few options, but we can't get anything fast enough. And when we do, we don't want the building associated with the cartel. It's like putting a fucking target on the women."

"Are you sure it was the bratva?"

He nodded. "They left a calling card—a human finger." He shook his head. "Thankfully the police and fire personnel didn't find it."

I stood. "Can I help?"

"And do what?"

"I don't know, anything. I could help with getting the women settled into a new place. I mean, I'm sure Em and Nick are kind" —I wasn't sure— "but it might help to have a woman involved." I thought of shopping with Silas. "I could be the face of the purchaser of a new building. Again, I'm less intimidating, and unless they know me, they won't know I'm associated with the cartel."

Aléjandro shook his head. "I don't want you on the front lines. You're more important than all the whores."

It reminded me of something Dario had said. "I can also be more trouble, according to my brother. Really, Aléjandro. Our home is furnished. Other than planning for the party, I'm twiddling my thumbs."

"Go shopping. *Mi madre* enjoys that."

I went closer and laid my hand on his chest. "I want to help people. I've never truly been in a position to do that before now. You've given me the means. Let me use it."

"The philanthropic arm of the Roríguez cartel?" He shook his head. "Let me think about it."

CHAPTER
TWENTY-SEVEN

Two days later and over a month earlier than I planned, I met my brother as he and Diego entered the gate to our home. Dante looked as handsome as ever, and while dressing up wasn't his forte, he was impeccable in a custom suit. The months of separation came crashing down on me. I ran toward him, wrapping my arms around his neck. "I've missed you."

Dante reached for my arms and pushed me back, his eyes narrowing. "Who are you and what have you done with my sister?" He furrowed his forehead. "One of the last times I saw her, she wanted me to gut her fiancé."

I laughed. "Things have worked out better than I could ever have imagined." I lowered my voice. "Let's not talk too loudly about my murder-for-hire scheme. I'm no longer interested."

"I didn't figure you were, not with this wild request you made."

Locking my arm with Dante's, I led him into our home. "Thank you for accepting. Aléjandro approves. I thought it was a good plan and a way for the famiglia to show the cartel we're partners."

"It's a great plan, fucking bratva." Dante stopped, seeing Aléjandro on one of the stools at the kitchen counter. My husband was facing us, his expression unreadable as he casually sat, also handsome, filling out his black short-sleeved t-shirt and black jeans. Aléjandro stood and Dante went toward him, with his hand extended. As they shook, Dante said, "You must be doing something right. Mia's not only happy, but she also no longer wants you dead."

I shook my head.

My husband scoffed and reached for me, wrapping his arm around my waist and tugging me toward him. "You wanted me dead?"

"He wasn't supposed to tell you." I turned to my brother. "Thanks a lot."

"It wasn't much of a secret." Aléjandro's expression softened. "We appreciate you making the trip, Dante. Come in my office. Your first meeting is in less than two hours. I'll go through the plan and paperwork with you." He turned to me. "Do you want to hear it again?"

"No. I helped you come up with the plan. I know my part."

Aléjandro nodded and looked at Dante. "She did. She's smart and sexy, and since she no longer wants me dead, I think I'm going to keep her."

Dante grinned. "Miracles do happen."

My part in this plan was to accompany my business associate—enter Dante—to a meeting with a realtor, and then with an attorney on the famiglia's payroll, and also a city attorney representing an abandoned school located less than a mile from Wanderland.

It wasn't exactly an apartment building, but according to the MLA listing, the plumbing and electrical met code. There were seventeen classrooms, five bathrooms, two locker rooms with showers, as well as offices and a cafeteria/gym. With a little help, the building could house the women, and the minimal number of outside entrances made protecting the workers easier for the cartel. Dante and I were attending the meeting because we didn't appear to be associated with the Roríguez cartel.

Aléjandro provided me with a fake ID. When he opened the safe, I learned that he had multiple identities for both of us, complete with passports and cash. "Just in case," he'd said.

Dante would also be going by a different name. Together we would represent an LLC that had been in the famiglia's back pocket for years, filed and waiting for use.

As long as the money transferred without a hitch,

the cartel would have the building closed before dinner. I didn't understand all the legal maneuvers, but in essence, the closing was accelerated with both the seller's and purchaser's approval.

Another famiglia connection was waiting for the word; once the sale was complete, he would start the process of having the property rezoned. Hopefully, the Wanderland workers could have a new place to live within a month.

That was a longer timetable than we'd hoped, but the building would be a valuable investment that would solve our long-term problems.

The car in the driveway was supplied by the famiglia. We weren't taking chances with any connection to the cartel. Giovanni, a soldier from Kansas City, opened the driver's door and stepped out. "*Señora* Roríguez."

"Giovanni, it's nice to see you." I lowered my voice. "Dario let you off of diaper duty for a day?"

That made him grin, which as I recalled wasn't an easy feat.

"And for the next few hours, my name is Ms. Alessandra" —Aléjandro thought it was close to his name— "Mancini." I motioned to Dante. "And my business partner, Edoardo Barone."

Aléjandro reached for my hand. "You won't be alone." His gaze went to my brother. "Dante brought trusted soldiers with him besides Giovanni, and I'll have cartel eyes on you the entire time. You're meeting at the school first to do a walk-through. Stay at your brother's side. Then you'll meet the attorneys at the title company to sign the paperwork."

I nodded. "I know the plan."

Strain showed in the tightening of his facial muscles. "I fucking hate not being with you."

"I won't let anything happen to her," Dante reassured.

With Giovanni in the driver's seat, Dante and I scooted into the back seat. I knew my role. I was prepared. I'd even crafted the plan. What I wasn't expecting was the onset of nerves. Aléjandro had been the one to suggest Dante's assistance. Now that the plan was underway, I was thankful I wasn't on this mission alone. I turned to Dante. "Tell me about Ariadna Gia."

My brother smiled as we drove away from our property. "She's about the most precious baby I've ever seen."

"Is Dario disappointed that she's a girl?"

"Not in the least. He's not anxious to repeat our dear ole dad's fathering techniques. Ariadna will have him so wrapped around her little finger, he'll be softened when a son comes along."

"Oh jeez, Ariadna was just born, and he's talking number two?"

Dante scoffed. "No, that was me. Even with Contessa's and Jasmine's help, I think Catalina and Dario are suffering from sleep deprivation."

"It's a busy time. We appreciate you coming out to help the cartel."

"It's always a busy time." His nostrils flared. "Targeting women. Fucking bratva has no honor."

Shaking my head, I stared straight ahead. The surroundings alerted me that we were nearing Wanderland. The tires bounced on the uneven concrete. "Who would have thought this alliance would work?"

"I seem to recall *not* you."

I turned to my brother. "I was wrong. Your comments about Wanderland hit a chord with Aléjandro. He wants better for the workers than what they were getting."

"He's turned out to be a better man than I initially thought."

An unexpected sense of pride in the man I married flooded my system. "He has."

Dante squeezed my hand and let it go. "It's good to see you smile. Your home is beautiful. *This* is the marriage you deserve, Mia."

"Maybe I had to have the other one first to appreciate this one. Despite everything I said before the marriage, I'm happy, and I know that's because of Aléjandro."

Giovanni pulled the car into a parking lot in front of a long limestone one-story building. Weeds poked through cracks in the concrete, and there was graffiti on the exterior walls.

A petite woman in a sheath dress and heels waved as she scurried by our car on her way up the sidewalk to the front doors, juggling papers and a tablet in her grasp.

"That's our realtor," I whispered as Dante and I got out of the car. I brushed against his back, feeling his holster. "You're armed?" I whispered.

"Always."

"She's about one hundred pounds soaking wet. I don't think she's a threat."

My brother only growled, a low rumble that I remembered was his way of saying no one is safe. If I had to guess, besides the gun, Dante had at least two knives sheathed somewhere under his clothes.

"Mrs. Mancini," the realtor said as we approached, shoving her hand my direction. "Nice to meet you. I'm Rennie."

"Ms." I corrected. "And this is my business partner, Edoardo Barone."

She smiled approvingly at my brother, who had a way of garnering the attention of women of all ages. She offered him her hand.

"Thank you for seeing us," Dante said as they shook, his professional tone perfected by years of practice.

The petite woman spoke a mile a minute as she unlocked the front door to the school. "This was a shocker. The city closed this school a few years ago due to decreased enrollment, and there's been no activity or interest. You can imagine our surprise when we heard from Mr. Lombardi." Mr. Lombardi was the famiglia's attorney who specialized in real estate. Rennie continued talking, not pausing for either of us to comment.

The musty stench of an abandoned structure combined with what could only be described as the pungent ammonia scent of urine hit us as we stepped beyond the second set of glass doors. A knot caught in my throat as my stomach revolted. Dipping my chin, I fought the urge to cover my mouth and nose. It had obviously been a while since this place had seen life that wasn't of the rodent variety.

"I'm sorry about the odor," Rennie said. "We didn't have time to air out the building." She pointed to the glass separation. "Security doors. Of course you can do whatever you want with...well, anything, once it's yours. What are your plans?"

"We're working with the city on that," I said, not giving too much away.

She stared for a moment as if a pause would give us time to divulge more information. When neither of us spoke, she turned. "Follow me."

The hallways were covered with the kind of carpet that was laid in squares to be easily replaced. Mouse droppings and dead insects littered the path. Pieces of the suspended ceiling dangled while others were missing, exposing pipes, wires, and a vast network of thick spider webs. I tried to imagine what would be required to make the building livable space—my month timetable seemed suddenly out of reach.

"As I'm sure you read in the description, there are seventeen classrooms, five bathrooms..."

I tried to block out her constant chatter as we stepped into the front-office suite. There wasn't any furniture. The built-in desks and bookcases were in tatters. Exposed wires led to where computers, televisions, and other technology had once been.

Within one of the bathrooms marked 'boys,' the realtor went on about the plumbing. According to her, it was in working order. However, before that could be verified, the city would need to turn on the water. Dante and I exchanged glances at the wall of urinals only inches above the ground. Down one hallway, Rennie opened classroom doors. They were all about the same size. Faded paper covered bulletin boards, and the outlines from where pictures once hung were visible. I was certain that more than once I saw something or many somethings scurry into the shadows.

Our shoes echoed throughout the cavernous gymnasium. Basketball backboards hung folded above, and lines could be seen through the debris on the wood floor.

"The school used this room as a lunchroom too. Let me show you the kitchen."

Dante and I followed. The kitchen was bigger than I'd anticipated. While many of the appliances had been stripped away, the few that remained gave a good indication of what this room was capable of being again with the right amount of workmanship and money.

Lots of money.

"The building was constructed in 1978," Rennie said, referring to her tablet. "It is fifty-two thousand square feet. The lot is nearly two acres. It was larger when the school was open, but the city sold off a parcel on the west boundary."

"We read the specs," Dante said.

"Yes," she replied, somewhat flustered that he would interrupt her spiel. No doubt she'd been studying since she learned that there was interest in this old building. "And the asking price is $2.3 million."

"That was the asking price," I said. "Mr. Lombardi offered $1.5. If Mr. Barone and I approve of what we see today, we'll pay $1.5. Cash."

"I-I," she stuttered. "I'm not able to speak on behalf of the seller."

"The seller is the city," Dante said, flashing his smile. "This project will obviously take money to renovate. No one is going to pay the asking price, or they would have done so years ago. Mr. Lombardi has taken time to negotiate."

That wasn't the full truth. Instead of negotiating, it could be better described as pulling strings. A friend of a friend—the way our businesses operated.

"I've seen enough," I said, looking to Dante,

silently praying to get away from the disgusting odor. "Shall we let Mr. Lombardi know our thoughts."

Rennie walked us back to the front of the school, talking the entire way. "You're right about the work needed. The structure is sound..."

Gulping the fresh air as we stepped out onto the sidewalk, I scanned in all directions, wondering where our soldiers were hiding. Everything was quiet, no one walking on the sidewalks and very few cars. Goose bumps scattered over my arms as I stepped closer to Dante and turned to Rennie. "Thank you. We have an appointment at the title company. Mr. Lombardi will be meeting us there."

"So, do we have a deal?" she asked, hopeful.

Dante replied, "If Mr. Lombardi's offer is still acceptable, yes."

As soon as we were safely in the back seat, I ran my hands over my arms.

"You did great," Dante said.

"She wasn't hard to fool. Thankfully, Mr. Lombardi will be doing most of the talking during the closing." My phone rang. I pulled it from my purse, happy to see Aléjandro's number. "We're on the way to the closing."

"I was watching you go in and out of the school. If I haven't told you today, you're beautiful."

Warmth filled my cheeks as I looked over to Dante, who was looking out the window, pretending he couldn't hear. "It may take longer to renovate than we hoped."

"Silas is already working with Hugo, the man who built our bookshelves."

I grinned, knowing he didn't say *secret room*.

"Once the building is ours, they'll get working."

"I'm warning you," I said, "it smells." I sniffed my shoulder and Dante's. "I think we smell now too."

My husband laughed. "This is why you shouldn't be on the streets and why I shower so many times a day."

"I'm glad it's not for another reason," I said, referencing his showering.

"Me too."

"Where are you?" I turned in all directions.

"We're a few cars behind you. Don't try to find me."

A sigh of relief loosened the knot in my chest. "I'm glad you're close."

"You can't get rid of me."

"I'm not trying."

"Pass the phone to Dante."

"Okay. Bye." I handed the phone to my brother. "He wants to talk to you."

Dante took my phone. "Dante here."

I was wrong about Dante pretending not to hear. I couldn't make out what Aléjandro was saying on the other end of the call. Instead, my imagination ran wild as Dante's posture stiffened, and he lowered his voice.

When he finally handed me back the phone, the call was disconnected. "What was that about?"

My brother's lips thinned as he pressed them together. "Precaution. Making sure our men are on the same page." He began sending text messages.

I'd known him my entire life.

Dante might be damn good at lying to other people, but it didn't work with me. He was being less than truthful.

After a few miles on the freeway, Giovanni pulled into a parking lot in front of a tall building. A quick look out the window reassured me that we were no longer in the middle of nowhere at an abandoned building. We were in the heart of San Diego. People were coming and going, and the parking lot was filled with cars.

Dante sent another text message.

It didn't take a genius to realize the silent form of communication went to Giovanni in the front seat. He read from his phone, met Dante's stare in the rearview mirror, and nodded.

"What's going on?" I asked, my voice an octave higher.

Dante laid his hand on my thigh. "We're staying in the car a minute while Giovanni checks something out."

My palms grew clammy as the goose bumps returned. "Tell me."

CHAPTER
TWENTY-EIGHT

D ante nonchalantly opened his suit coat. He removed his gun from the holster.

My mouth grew instantly dry as my heart rate accelerated. "No. There's no danger." My volume rose. "No one knows about this transaction." Fidgeting, I twisted my wedding rings. My hands trembled and my knee bounced, wanting and needing to move.

Dante's hand again came to my thigh. "Sit still, Mia. If we're being watched, we need to appear calm."

"I'm not calm," I growled in a low whisper.

The click as Dante released the safety on his gun reverberated like thunder through the car, competing with the thumping in my ears.

"Where is Giovanni?"

"He went to check on something."

"What if...?" I had too many questions to finish this one. What if someone shot Giovanni? "Should one of us get in the driver's seat?"

"Probably, but I'd rather concentrate on my target if I need to shoot."

"I can drive."

Dante turned toward me for a millisecond and then back to the view ahead. "Since when?"

"Aléjandro's been teaching me."

"License?"

"No, but so what? You're ready to shoot somebody. I think driving without a license is the least of our concerns." As I spoke, I contemplated my ability to climb into the front seat. The skirt of my dress wouldn't help, but if flashing my brother saved our lives, I'd worry about his therapy another day.

I slipped my feet from my pumps.

"Wait," Dante said. "Giovanni is coming back."

"How can you...?" I realized my brother was watching the mirrors, seeing in all directions.

Giovanni opened the driver's door, bringing an acid scent with him as he laid his gun equipped with a silencer on the front seat, sat down, and closed the door. His eyes met Dante's.

"Go," Dante said.

Giovanni calmly started the car, backed out of the parking space, and drove around the back of the building. There were fewer cars on this side. We exited the lot from a different place than where we'd entered, merging into traffic.

"Someone talk to me. What about our meeting? What about the building?"

Dante still had his gun in his lap as he quickly typed out a text message.

Giovanni was silent, his attention on the city streets.

Finally, my brother spoke. "I texted Lombardi. He's up in the title office."

"Don't we need to sign?"

"He's taking care of it."

"How? What happened?"

Dante looked around, seeing that Giovanni had managed to get us back on the highway, headed north toward my home. My brother locked the safety on his gun and placed it back in the holster. He shrugged his suit coat back into place and turned my direction. "Someone found out about your plan."

"Bratva?"

Dante looked up at Giovanni.

He nodded. "I'd say yes. Two of them."

My mind was having difficulty comprehending. "Did you shoot them?" My voice went higher. "Are there two dead men in the parking lot?"

"Not for long. Mr. Roríguez called for a cleanup crew," Giovanni said.

"Aléjandro. He knew that someone was there." I

turned my attention on Dante. "That's why he wanted to talk to you."

"He was tipped off. One of his men reported a suspicious car."

"Oh my God. He knew and he let us go…like bait?"

"No. You were never in danger." Dante laid his hand on my thigh. "We had to show up to find out if they were a threat. If we never arrived, we'd never know."

Laying my head back on the seat, I exhaled. "How? This whole thing was planned as recently as the last few days. Only the men you brought with you and Aléjandro's most trusted men were informed." Tears stung the back of my eyes. I'd wanted to help the workers. "What about the school?"

Dante looked at his phone. "Lombardi will make an excuse for our absence from the closing. He has people faxing power-of-attorney paperwork. He won't need us. He can act in our stead with the POA."

My brother's smile broke through. "Were you really going to drive us out of there? Bonnie-and-Clyde style?"

"I don't know. It seemed like a good idea at the time." My phone rang. The trembling in my hands was gone, leaving them cold as ice. Seeing my husband's number released the dam I'd put on my tears. "Aléjandro?"

"You were always safe, Mia. I want you to know that. You were safe. You are."

Tears slid down my cheeks as I nodded.

"If I could have stopped them without the two of you...but we needed to know."

"Who?" I asked. "Who tipped off the bratva?"

"We have fewer possibilities."

This was too real. My thoughts went to my husband. "We're okay. What about you? Are you safe? Rei? Diego and Felipe?"

"We're all good, and you are too. I wish it had been me, but Dante knew what could happen. He was ready."

I looked over at my brother, grateful that he was here and spoke into the phone, "Come home when you can."

"Mia, I'd never let anything happen to you. That's why we had so many eyes on both buildings. I'll fucking find the mole and when I do, I'll lay his head at your feet."

Swallowing my tears, I scoffed. "I don't want that. I just want us to be..."

What was the next word?

Happy?

In love?

"...to be safe," I said.

"I'm calling a meeting at our house tonight. I'll tell Silas to be ready." The call disconnected.

I turned to Dante. "Aléjandro is calling a meeting. Will you stay?"

Dante nodded. "I'm not leaving until Aléjandro has

his answer. If I did, I'd take you with me, and I would suspect your husband wouldn't be too happy about that."

"I'm not leaving him."

"Mia, you're still famiglia." He nodded. "I know how this works, you and Catalina. You're both important to both sides of this alliance. Hurting either one of you would hurt the alliance. It sucks and I'm sorry you're in this position, but you are. You were the target today."

My stomach churned as acid made its way up my throat. We rode in silence as Giovanni drove us back to my home. My turbulent thoughts added to my distress. Today's meetings were supposed to be safe. It was all about helping the workers at Wanderland, and in the process, I'd been targeted. I didn't relish hearing Dante's truth. Who would? Yet he was right. Hurting Catalina or me would result in fracturing our alliance.

I kept my composure as Giovanni pulled the car beyond the first gate and into the driveway. Not waiting for anyone to help, I opened the car door and made my way inside, not stopping until I was upstairs, my head over the toilet bowl, expelling what was left of my breakfast.

Perspiration dotted my skin and the permeating odor of the school lingered on my clothes. Quickly, I stripped, pushing everything I'd worn into the corner and stepping into the shower. More tears coated my cheeks as I stood beneath the hot spray.

I was a target.

Aléjandro had mentioned the possibility. Today was more than a possibility; it was reality.

Scrubbing my skin raw and washing my hair multiple times, didn't fully cleanse me of the smell. I was pouring more bodywash onto the washcloth when the bathroom door opened. Aléjandro didn't slow. He came straight for the shower, opening the glass door, and stepping under the spray fully clothed.

I crumpled against him, my body trembling and sobs coming from my chest.

One hand came to my hair as he held me upright with the other. "You are safe."

"I'll never be."

He turned off the shower and helped me from the enclosure. I shivered at the loss of heat. My husband wrapped me with a towel and lifted me to his chest. His canvas loafers squeaked over the bamboo flooring as he carried me into the bedroom. "Mia, you said something a while ago that has stuck with me. The only reason I allowed you to be out today and part of this plan was because I knew you were protected."

I leaned my aching head against his chest.

Aléjandro threw back the blankets on the bed and laid me on the sheets. After covering me, he sat at my side. Droplets dripped from his dark hair, and his features were stark with emotion. The furrow of his forehead and sharpness of his jawline displayed his concern. His black t-shirt was wet and plastered to his muscles, and without seeing them, I knew his jeans and shoes were also wet. "Someone wants me back in *México*. They've decided to fuck up my plans, maybe to make me look incompetent so *mi padre* would call me home. In case that didn't work, their plan B is to take away my ability to stay in the States."

"Me," I said, my voice hoarse.

He ran his hand over my hair. "Yes. You. I fucking hoped I was wrong. If I couldn't be with you today at your fucking side, I chose the one person who I could trust and who wouldn't give away the cartel's connection."

I remembered that when we'd originally come up with the plan, I'd offered to do the business deal alone. I reached for my husband's hand and intertwined our fingers. "Their plan won't work. Jorge believes in you. I believe in you."

He leaned down and kissed my forehead. "What can I get you? Aspirin? Water?"

"Don't bring it to my feet but the head of the mole." I squeezed his hand. "I know you have momentous plans, and you're capable of leading when Jorge is ready. We can't keep living like this. We need to know who's undermining you."

Aléjandro nodded. "I've called a meeting. I want you to go to Nicolas's house." Before I could question, he went on, "Valentina's in Missouri with Catalina and the baby. Nicolas and the other men will be here. All the other women will be there. Take Viviana."

Alarm bells sounded. "Why? Who will be at the meeting? Why can't I stay here?"

"Because watching you today, so fucking brave and beautiful, was torture. During the meeting, I need to concentrate on those around me. The only way I can do that is to know you're safe."

"Dante?" I asked.

"He'll be with you. I don't think his presence at the meeting will facilitate open disclosure."

"Because he's famiglia?"

There was no need to pretend Dante or I were welcomed by all of the cartel. Aléjandro's expression was somber. "Yes."

Later that night, Aléjandro walked with Dante, Viviana, Giovanni, and me into the garage, Dante smiled. "Mia, do you want to drive?"

"I think we've had enough excitement for one day."

Aléjandro reached for my hand, tugging me to a stop. "I probably could have chosen a more private or romantic setting to say this."

I tilted my head.

"Mia, I love you. I think I have since you slapped me at Cat's wedding."

My tears were back, burning my eyes and streaming down my cheeks. "I love you, too." I forced a smile. "I didn't then, but I do now." I wrapped my arms around his shoulders.

He rubbed circles in the small of my back, his lips

blowing his warm breath near my ear. "I wanted you to know that. To hear the words from me."

I felt my pulse quicken as I pulled back and met his dark stare. "You're scaring me."

"That's not my intention."

"This meeting is with the Ruizes. How is that dangerous?"

"It's not." He brushed my lips with his. "I'll see you once the meeting is over."

Swallowing my fear, I nodded as Dante led me to the car.

Viviana and I rode in the back seat as Giovanni drove and Dante rode shotgun. Instead of the famiglia's car, we were in one of Aléjandro's bullet-proof cars. The doors were extra thick and heavy. The windows were dark except for the windshield.

I closed my eyes, wishing I'd accepted a painkiller earlier in the day. My temples throbbed. While Viviana had convinced me to eat a little, nothing tasted right. And now we were headed to Maria's home where I would be expected to be polite and talkative. Those weren't qualities I currently wanted to display.

The gate to Nicolas and Maria's property opened after Giovanni said my name into a small box. By the time we made it up the driveway to the house, Mireya and Camila were standing on the steps. I gave Viviana one last glance, wishing we could avoid this evening's gathering, and knowing we couldn't.

I tried to convince myself that this was for Aléjandro. He could concentrate on his meeting and not worry about my safety.

"*Hola,*" Mireya said as we approached.

"Hi," Camila said softly, her cheeks pinkening before my eyes.

It didn't take me long to figure out who had her attention. I wanted to jab Dante in the stomach and make a wisecrack about him breaking children's hearts. Camila wasn't exactly a child. I think she was near twenty, still a decade younger than my brother.

"Come in," Mireya opened the door. "*Mi madre* isn't home. I guess I'm hosting." She giggled. "I know where she keeps the wine."

"She isn't home?" I questioned as we crossed the threshold. "I thought Aléjandro said all the women would be here."

Camila spoke, "He probably didn't know. At the last minute, Aunt Maria decided to travel with *mi madre* to Kansas City."

I nodded. "Ariadna Gia."

"I can't wait to meet her," Camila said. "Isn't she just perfect in the pictures?"

"She is," I concurred. I gestured toward Dante. "Mireya and Camila, this is my brother Dante."

"We've met," he said, his deep voice more of a purr.

I looked his direction, but honestly, my mind was too cluttered to decipher whatever secret discussion was occurring in my presence.

"I'm going to have a talk with your bodyguards," Dante said as he walked toward the man stationed by the front door.

"This feels very weird," Mireya said, taking my arm. "Do you know what's happening?"

Camila's lips parted as she stared in a trance, watching Dante walk away.

I wanted to tell her that he was too old for her, but instead, I responded to Mireya, "Only some of it."

Viviana left us to help the Ruizes' cook in the kitchen.

"We've been sitting out back," Mireya said. "Sofia and Liliana are here."

"Really?" I asked. "Gerardo brought them all the way here for a meeting?"

"Sofia said Aléjandro demanded they come." She shrugged. "Like I said, it feels weird."

Stepping out onto the back deck, I was enthralled by the kaleidoscope of colors: reds, purples, and pinks filling the sky above the distant mountains. As it was the last time I was here, the patio was lit like daytime in the twilight. The two young ladies were seated on a sofa that was situated around a firepit. Liliana looked up as we approached. Her expression was as lifeless as it had been during our visit to Sacramento.

"It's nice to see you again," I said. "I've been trying to reach you." I took a seat on the other side of the flames.

"I must have missed your call."

"It was a couple of calls. Your voicemail box is full."

Her eyes went to Sofia and back to her lap.

Sofia sat back and pressed her lips together as Mireya and Camila joined us.

"It's not a big deal," I went on. "Aléjandro and I have our house decorated, and we'd like to invite you, Sofia, and Gerardo to a housewarming party."

Liliana looked at Sofia.

Part of me wanted to walk over and shake Liliana. Another part of me wanted to wrap her in a hug. By the doe-in-the-headlights expression she was giving her stepdaughter-slash-friend, either of those actions could send her spiraling.

"*Mi madre* told me about the party," Camila said, her smile growing. "Will your family be there?"

"Yes. I'm not sure about Dario and Catalina. That will depend on Ariadna Gia."

For a few minutes the conversation went to the new baby. Camila had new pictures on her phone from Valentina. She handed me her phone. Ariadna was wrapped in a pink blanket and held by a different person in each picture. I came to a picture of Catalina. "Catalina looks amazing," I said.

"Oh, I didn't see her picture," Liliana said.

"Here," I handed her Camila's phone.

As she reached for it, my breathing stopped, and my stomach twisted. It was the sight of the large ruby ring on her right hand. The nearly two-carat ruby on yellow-gold prongs had always been too small for me, but Liliana was more petite.

No, it couldn't be my ring.

"What a lovely ring," I said, reaching for her hand. "Where did you get it?"

"Gerardo. It's my birthstone."

TWENTY-NINE

Aléjandro

Gerardo was the least happy about my emergency meeting. In his defense, he had the farthest to travel, I hadn't given him the option of declining, and taking orders from me was not my strong suit. After what we'd learned over the last few days, his presence was mandatory. This meeting had to take place with the attendance of the men congregating in my home. That included our personal guards. There was little that they didn't know. That was why I also asked for their presence.

Andrés and Em brought Sergio. Nicolas and Nick brought Carlos. Gerardo brought Ángel. I recalled he was the one who drove Mia all day and never spoke

English. He didn't look any happier to be here than Gerardo. Rei, Felipe, Diego, and Silas were also present.

"Sit," I said, gesturing toward the long dining room table as our meeting progressed in Spanish. I remained standing. "The Roríguez cartel is being attacked."

"Down here. Things are good up north," Gerardo grumbled, leaning back and crossing his arms.

Andrés and Nicolas quickly refuted their brother, naming a series of incidents that had occurred in our northern region as well. I stood back for a moment until voices became raised.

"This isn't about who's doing what. When Andrés's home was invaded, we stood together and delivered a loud message to Ivan Kozlov. We waited for him to retaliate. Fuck, we'd delivered three of his men to his personal property in pieces. Instead of going after our men, he retaliated against our women."

"Whores," Nicolas said.

"Women," I repeated. "They work for us. We're responsible for them."

"You can always get more," Gerardo said. He laughed. "I can send down a few from up north. Checked them out myself. Three willing holes."

My gaze met Rei's, Em's and Nick's. They were seated at the kitchen bar, away from their fathers, uncles, and guards, facing us. The younger men had clenched jaws and stern expressions. It wasn't a secret

355

that there was an ongoing clash between the two generations.

"How did Kozlov learn about the new housing for the women?" I asked. When no one responded, I continued. "Who shared that information?"

"It could have been any of the soldiers on the street," Andrés said. "Word spreads fast when there's a shake-up." He shrugged. "Change causes resistance."

"And the soldiers give a shit where whores live?" Rei asked, walking toward the table, and leaning against the wall between the closed glass doors.

"It's not only the whores," Gerardo said. "It's other changes. My men report to me. My brothers haven't complained, but they should. You've come up here, overruling the only real bosses the soldiers have known."

"*Mi padre* is the real boss, the one they've known."

"Known *of*," Gerardo said. "Yes, Jorge is the boss, but you can't expect men to treat you with respect when you haven't earned it. The men talk."

Though my expression remained unchanged, the small hairs at the base of my neck stood to attention. "I see. You're blaming the fire at the apartments on our own soldiers?"

"No," Andrés and Nicolas said at the same time.

"Which is it? Our soldiers are at fault because they don't respect me, or our soldiers are at fault because they talk?"

"Ja-no," Nicolas said in a pacifying tone and cadence.

That tenor pissed me off more than Gerardo's blatant disrespect.

"Men talk," Nicolas went on. "They're on the streets, in the hideouts, on assignments. The bratva men are on the same streets. Fuck, the whores themselves could have said something to the wrong customer, one associated with the bratva. That one customer goes back and tells Kozlov he has intel to share. There's no way to know. The fucking Russians found out. It happens."

"Four women were killed."

Gerardo stood, scooting back his chair. "Tell me, son. Did you really call this emergency meeting to discuss dead whores? Because if you did, I wasted cartel profits on a plane and fuel. And ruined an evening I could be spending with my new wife."

"Sit down, Gerardo."

At the sound of my command, the room grew deathly silent as the older man stared my direction. I took a step toward Gerardo with my fingers itching for the handle of my knife. Gritting my teeth, I took another step. "Sit down or back up your words."

At his side, Ángel flinched, ready to attack me. Hatred shone like beacons in his eyes.

Gerardo laid his hand on Ángel's shoulder and retook his seat.

I resumed my position, standing near the end of

the table. "Today's attack was different. The soldiers didn't know our plan."

"The fucking famiglia did," Gerardo said. "You talked to Luciano. You know they can't keep a secret."

Andrés pressed his lips together.

"Do you have anything to say?" I asked Catalina's father.

"The famiglia has kept their word," Andrés said. "Dario and Dante," he added, "have helped the cartel. Their pull with government agencies has opened passageways for our product."

"One of your men was arrested," Gerardo reminded us. "Lost product."

"You're right," I replied, moving around the table. "Coincidence. He made it over the border but was pulled over by Highway Patrol because his car was on an APB." I inhaled. "Here's the thing, *mi padre* doesn't believe in coincidences and neither do I."

I went to a small table near a chair next to the fire-place, grabbed a plastic bag containing two cell phones, and carried it to the table. "These phones were with the two Russians who were at the title company today." My focus went to each man sitting at the table. "As you know, we have some fucking great hackers. The thing is, we didn't need hackers. These phones contain the numbers of people who they've recently communicated with. The numbers of their informants."

Everyone's attention was on me. Rei's nostrils

flared, knowing what I was about to say. Andrés and Nicolas sat straighter. Gerardo's and Ángel's Adam's apples bobbed as their expressions remained stoic.

I measured my words carefully. "Our soldiers, the ones on the street, didn't know about the plan to secure the school building. The whores didn't know about the plan. Only you here around this table" —I looked around— "all of us in this room."

"No one in this room would go against the cartel," Nicolas said.

"What about the famiglia?" Gerardo asked. "You stand there accusing us, men who would die for your father, and you don't accuse the men who hate us?"

"Did I accuse you?"

"Yes," Gerardo answered, his eyes wide and agitation growing.

"It was one thing when our product was disrupted. It was a whole new issue when our homes were broken into and our families threatened" —I moved next to Rei who was now standing behind Ángel— "and a fucking different matter when my wife was targeted."

Rei and I moved in sync. My blade was against Gerardo's neck. Rei's blade was against Ángel's. The older generation sitting at the table jumped back, chairs screeching on the tile, and knives and guns unholstered.

Em and Nick were both standing, their guns

pointed. Silas, Felipe, and Diego also had guns aimed at the table.

"What the fuck, Jano?" Nicolas yelled. "You've lost your fucking mind."

Gerardo slammed his chair back, knocking me off balance as he pulled his own knife from a sheath on his ankle. He swung toward me. I dodged the first swing. Silas turned his gun toward Gerardo while Rei kept Ángel pinned to the chair.

"You're a fucking liar," Gerardo screamed.

He lunged again, narrowly missing my torso. I moved, a dance choreographed by fighters for centuries. One of Mia's new tables overturned, the sound of glass breaking echoed as the contents crashed to the floor.

Silas's aim was beyond compare. His shot rang out, hitting Gerardo's arm and causing him to drop the knife. He screamed in pain as I wrestled him to the floor with my knife back at his throat.

"Kill me, you coward."

A smile curled my lips. "I will watch you take your last breath, but it won't be now. You're going to suffer as you've made others suffer."

"Jano?" Andrés questioned.

Nick lowered his gun and stepped forward. "Jano is right. Those phones prove it. Gerardo has been plotting against Jano since he moved to California. We didn't see it at first."

Andrés and Nicolas lowered their weapons as did their guards.

"We didn't want to see it," Em said. "Gerardo's been working with Kozlov. The people we found in the desert a few months ago. The whole stealing of product was a setup. We were supposed to be caught with them and made to look like we were trafficking people over the border." He stepped closer, staring at his father and Nicolas. "What we didn't realize until today, until those phones, is that he's also been working with Herrera."

"That's a lie," Gerardo screamed.

I held him down, my knife still at his throat.

Andrés and Nicolas looked at their sons.

"It's the truth, *Padre*," Em said. "I wouldn't lie to you. You know that."

Andrés and Nicolas cursed under their breath. Andrés turned to me. "Patrón? Does he know?"

"*Sí.*"

Gerardo was pinned to the floor and Rei's knife was still at Ángel's throat. Everyone else turned to the sound of *mi padre's* voice. *Mi padre* walked into the dining room with two of his guards, coming from the direction of my office. He shook his head at the chaos. Gerardo quickly lifted his head, pressing against the blade. If you asked me, he was throwing himself on my knife. There was no way he'd get off that easy. He'd targeted my wife.

Gerardo and Ángel had a long night ahead of them. Their deaths wouldn't be quick or painless.

"Aléjandro is in charge of this region, this state," *mi padre's* voice boomed against the glass doors. "My word is still final. If anyone else has a problem with his command, now is the time to voice your opinion while you still have a tongue." He walked closer to where I had Gerardo on the floor and kicked him with the toe of his boot. "I knew you were a problem when you continued to call me even after I told you to call Jano."

"Patrón, this is all a lie," Gerardo said. "I haven't hidden my displeasure with Aléjandro, but I'd never go behind your back with Kozlov or Herrera."

Mi padre motioned to his two guards. Rei and I stepped back. One guard hauled Ángel from his chair and the other lifted Gerardo by grasping his injured arm. The guards twisted the moles' hands behind their backs and secured them with zip ties. Both men continued their claims of innocence as the guards removed Gerardo's and Ángel's weapons and walked them into the garage.

Once they were out of the house, Andrés and Nicolas turned to me and then to *mi padre*. "We didn't know."

Mi padre looked at me.

"I believe them." I lifted my chin toward Rei, Nick, and Em. "We've suspected for a while, but we couldn't prove it until now." The world around me blurred. I reached for the back of a chair, knowing my circulation was racing with adrenaline.

"You should have told me," *Padre* said.

"I wasn't going to sentence an innocent man to death without proof."

"You've seen the proof?" Nicolas asked Rei.

"I have seen it," Padre said.

Rei nodded. "I have, too." He turned to our *padre*. "Gerardo has a wife and a daughter."

Padre inhaled, his nostrils flaring. "The wife is young, no?"

"Too young," I said.

Padre turned to Nicolas and Andrés. "The girls will stay with one of you until everything is sorted out. Keep them safe."

Both men agreed.

Looking down, I saw the pool of red. Lifting my foot, I saw the bloody shoe print. My knees wobbled as I reached for my side. To my dismay, I found my shirt sticky, clinging to my skin. I splayed my fingers, now covered in warm crimson. "Fuck, he got me."

I hadn't felt the wound, not until now. I pressed my hand against my side as blood continued to drip onto my shoes.

How much blood had I lost?

Rei rushed my direction. "Jano."

The adrenaline from earlier was gone, leaving the room around me spinning as I collapsed. The world went black.

THIRTY

Mia

Dante held me as I walked by his side, up the metal stairs in the hideout. Rei was leading the way. All I'd been told was that the mole was found, and my husband had been stabbed.

Again.

Without my brother's strength, I'd still be lying on the floor of Nicolas's house, in the same spot I fell when I was told that another husband was in jeopardy of losing his life. Blood loss.

Till death do us part.

I couldn't do this again. I wouldn't.

Aléjandro and I found one another, two unlikely

people who when we were together made the world, our lives, everything better. Our too-brief relationship played on a loop in my mind as I was driven to the hideout. Each smile. Each word. Each kiss.

There weren't enough. I wanted more.

I'd been told that he was being attended to by one of the cartel doctors. The man at the door didn't hesitate to allow us entrance.

I scanned the room, seeing a different scene than I'd seen the last time I was here. The mood was somber, and the men were quiet. A few even bowed their heads. Not one made a comment about me, Dante, or the famiglia.

My heart thumped wildly against my breastbone as I clung to Dante. "Why are they looking down?" I asked between sobs. "Why won't they look at us?"

"*Señora.*"

"*Muerte.*"

The words were muttered as we made our way back to the room where the doctor worked. The guard at the second door turned the knob, opening the barrier. While the scent of perspiration and disinfectant was present, it was the prevailing odor of copper that filled the air. My gaze went to the spot where I'd found Aléjandro the last time.

The cot was empty.

A woman in scrubs stepped out from behind a curtain. "*Señora* Roríguez?"

"Where is he? Where's my husband?"

She pulled the curtain back. Tears clogged my throat as I ran toward the man lying on the gurney. I threw my arms around him. "Don't you dare leave me."

Aléjandro's arms wrapped around me. "You thought you were free."

"No." My tears dampened his shirt. "I don't want to be free."

As I stood to see him better, his hands framed my cheeks. "We found the mole."

I nodded. I'd heard them talking to Liliana. "What about you?"

"A little scratch," he said, feigning a smile.

I turned to the woman. "May he go home?"

"His wound isn't life-threatening, but he did lose a lot of blood. We have someone securing his blood type. After a transfusion, he can go home. He needs to rest."

"Fuck no," Aléjandro said. "I'm going where they have Gerardo." He grunted as he sat up and swung his legs over the side of the gurney.

Rei came forward. "You're listening to the doc."

"No. That fucking scum targeted my wife. I'm going to watch him die."

I lifted my husband's hand, and his dark orbs came to me. "I don't need a head. I just need you."

Aléjandro's stare searched my expression as time forgot to tick by. Finally, he looked over at his brother. "Go. You're my second. Make him pay."

Rei nodded. "I will."

Dante stood with his back to the wall and his arms crossed over his chest as I sat on the gurney beside my husband. The transfusion took over two hours. By the time Aléjandro was released, it was somewhere between midnight and morning light. Once we were home, Silas helped me get Aléjandro upstairs and into bed. They'd given him something for pain and to help him sleep. He was out within seconds of his head hitting the pillow.

I went back downstairs, finding Dante in the living room with a glass of tequila. "I didn't think you were a tequila drinker."

He turned, flashing his smile. "You need bourbon in your liquor cabinet." He tilted his head. "Shouldn't you be upstairs?"

"Aléjandro is asleep. I'm ready to be too, but I wanted to thank you."

"I was thinking, you almost got your wish—the gutted part."

I laid my hand over my stomach. "It's not my wish. I love him and the idea of going on without him makes me ill."

Dante's eyes went to my hand. "Oh shit. I know that gesture."

"It's nothing."

Dante slowly shook his head. "Catalina did it before they announced..."

A tired smile curled my lips. "I'm not sure. I'm only

a week late. I haven't told Aléjandro because if I had, he wouldn't have wanted me to carry out our plan."

My brother's eyes shone. "You and Dario are making this marriage thing seem like it could work."

"Don't tell me that you're considering it."

"I called Dario earlier." He lifted his eyebrows. "Asking for my capo's approval."

"Who?"

His smile grew. "The next step is Dario's. If my offer is accepted, I'm sure you'll hear."

"Accepted by whom?"

"Now that would give it away."

"Patrón?"

Dario finished his tequila and set the glass on the table. "I'll see you in September for your house-warming."

"Yeah, I don't know."

He grasped my shoulders. "You have a beautiful home, a husband you love and who loves you, and maybe a little person on the way. Celebrate, Mia. You've lived through enough hell. It's time for a bit of heaven."

"I love you."

He kissed my cheek.

"Hey," I said, "don't tell anyone. I want to tell Aléjandro first and maybe I'm not pregnant."

"My lips are sealed." He waved. "Giovanni is waiting and so is the plane. You know, you can always visit Kansas City."

"I know." I waited until Dante left and tiredly made my way back upstairs. Aléjandro was still sleeping in the same position. After washing my face, brushing my teeth, and changing into a nightgown, I climbed into bed. Scooting closer to my husband, I whispered, "I love you."

After I thanked the heavens that Aléjandro was alive and the mole was uncovered, sleep came with my head on his chest, listening to the steady beat of his heart and his measured breaths.

I should be concerned about Liliana, but I wasn't. She would survive. I had. Maybe one day she'd find that not all marriages are horrible. Some are...as Dante said...heaven.

EPILOGUE~

Mia

Second Saturday in September

Standing on a chair, I secured the welcome sign above the table with a pink-icing cake decorated with 'Welcome, Ariadna Gia' scrolled in white frosting. While this gathering was to be our housewarming party, it would also be Ariadna's first visit to the West Coast. She had an entire side of her family anxious to meet her.

"*Qué estás haciendo?*"

I turned and smiled at the deep voice.

His brow furrowed as he looked in my direction. "No." He reached for my waist and lifted me, helping me down. My shoes landed on the tile floor. "Don't do things like that."

Tilting my chin up, I grinned. "It's a chair. I was what, two feet in the air?"

With his hands still on my waist, he tugged me close. "You have Viviana, Silas, and me." He released one hand and splayed his fingers over my stomach. "And our *bebé*. Your number-one job is to be careful."

My cheeks rose as my smile grew. I looked down at his large hand and back to his stunningly protective gaze. "I'm well. The doctor has reassured us that the baby is too. Everything is on schedule as much as it can be for only eight weeks."

"You're going to stay that way even if I have to cover you in bubble wrap."

"Bubble wrap may be a hindrance to my new addiction." I'd read that an upsurge in hormones can cause an increased sex drive. Whatever the cause, as of late, my libido had been insatiable. That's not exactly true. I'm satisfied and satiated but always wanting more.

Aléjandro's smile grew. "If anyone would have told me four months ago that I was marrying a nympho-maniac, I wouldn't have believed them."

"Me either." Warmth climbed from my décolletage to my cheeks. "You're responsible for my addiction."

He kissed my nose. "I'll shoulder all the blame."

If the cartel was selling whatever magic Aléjandro had, they'd be set for life.

"Everything is ready," I said, looking around our living room and out to the pool deck. "Viviana and I have been cooking for days. Currently, she's meeting with the hired waitstaff."

"Silas has the house well-guarded. Even though Gerardo is no longer a threat, having *mi padre* and the Kansas City capo in the same home is reason for precaution." He tilted his head. "Have you decided if we can announce our news tonight?"

"I know some people like to wait, but I don't want to." I was practically buzzing with excitement. "I want to tell my mom and Giorgia in person. Jorge and Josefina too. I never thought I'd have a child and now we are." Lifting my touch, I cupped my husband's freshly shaved cheek. "Four months ago, I never dreamed I'd be this happy."

"Then it's settled. The other announcement can wait."

Dropping my hand, I pinched my eyebrows together. "What other announcement?"

"*Mi padre* has approved another marriage."

My stomach sank. "Not Liliana."

Aléjandro shook his head. "No."

"Good. I'm hoping I can convince her to help me at the new housing units. If she stays in San Diego."

"She doesn't want to go back to Sacramento. *Padre* is sending Rei up there for the time being. I'm going to miss him, but I know he'll do well."

"Is he going to live in Gerardo's home?"

"For now." My husband grinned. "It's bigger than Andrés's pool house."

"Is *he* marrying...someone from the famiglia?"

"No, and I'm not saying more. I hear things are coming along at the school."

He'd changed the subject to my other new passion.

"Things are progressing. Gutting the place took longer than planned, but now the renovation is moving quickly." I was particularly pleased with all that had been accomplished in a relatively short time. We were already beyond the one-month schedule, but the end was near. To my delight, Aléjandro offered me the position of overseeing the school-slash-new housing.

I didn't think he expected me to take to the project with so much enthusiasm.

I'd met with the Wanderland workers multiple times at the halfway house where they were staying. The place was cramped. Once the school was done, it would be as if they'd moved to a mansion.

Silas didn't hover, but he was always nearby. My husband didn't want me to go to Wanderland, and I respected his wishes.

This was the first time the women had had someone who cared about their day-to-day lives, someone who listened without 'checking out' the merchandise. Nicolas wasn't exactly happy about my position. Surprisingly, Em and Nick were fine. By taking on the role as their advocate, Aléjandro said I was the new humanitarian and philanthropic wing of the Roríguez cartel.

My husband and I discussed me continuing my education. He brought it up one night, saying he remembered me mentioning it. His thoughtfulness never ceased to amaze me. There might be a time I'd want to follow in Catalina's and Camila's footsteps, but for now, I was plenty busy with the workers, getting them moved into their new housing, and planning some new endeavors. "Have you thought any more about my idea for tutoring?"

Aléjandro exhaled. "Nicolas is concerned about turnover. He thinks if you educate the women, they will want to leave."

"So?"

My husband grinned.

"Over sixty percent of them don't have a high school diploma. Tutoring them and encouraging them to get their GEDs will open more possibilities to them for their future. If that means they move on to another profession, good for them. If they choose to stay because the cartel is giving them opportunities they couldn't get elsewhere, that's good too."

"What about after the *bebé* is born?"

"That isn't until late April. By then, we will have a better idea who is needed at the school and employ more people. And like I said, I'm hoping to involve Liliana."

"When Dario told me that you'd be a handful, I never expected that you'd cause disruption with Wanderland workers and lieutenants."

"I'm not a disruption," I said with a grin. "I'm the humanitarian arm of the Roríguez cartel, remember? Maybe we should advertise." I batted my eyelashes. "I'd promise to be less trouble if you told me about this upcoming wedding, but I probably won't. I'm excited about doing something that's meaningful for others."

I recalled the last time I'd seen Dante. "Is it Dante... the marriage?"

Aléjandro didn't verbally respond, but I was getting to know this man well enough to read his body language. A solid muscular book that I enjoyed reading from cover to cover. "I'm right. Who does he want to marry and has she been told?"

"She hasn't."

"That is bullshit," I said. "The men making the plans without the woman's knowledge is archaic and misogynistic."

"Guilty as charged," he said, flashing his smile. "Watch at tonight's party and let me know if you have a clue."

"She'll be here?"

Aléjandro nodded.

Biting my lower lip, I mentally did a rundown of guests. "I'm going to figure this out."

"If you do, don't say a word. It will come out soon enough."

"Maybe I'll warn her that her future is being planned without her consent."

Aléjandro shook his head. "If you do, I'll enjoy reddening your ass."

The threat shouldn't melt my insides and put a smile on my face, but it did.

We couldn't have asked for more beautiful weather to have our home opened and on display. With extra outdoor tables, our guests milled both inside and outside. Viviana had the serving staff ready and accessible with trays of champagne, wine, and sparkling water. There was a bar set up on the pool deck stocked with the best tequila and bourbon known to enthusiasts of both liquors.

After Dario and Catalina arrived and said their hellos, I was able to hold Ariadna Gia for the first time. Catalina laid her in my arms.

I stared down at the beautiful baby in my grasp and imagined one of my own. Ariadna's eyes were dark brown like Dario's, shaped big and round like her mommy's. Inhaling, I savored her sweet scent of lotion and sunshine. "She's so tiny."

Catalina teased some of Ariadna's dark hair into a curl on the top of her head. "She's gained three pounds since she was born."

Tears blurred my vision. "She's perfect."

"She is." Catalina lowered her voice. "Do you have an announcement?"

I opened my eyes wide. "Did Dante tell?"

"Did Dante know something and not tell us?" She smiled. "No. In the few minutes we've been here, you've repeatedly touched your stomach. It's a telltale sign. Stop if you're not wanting anyone to suspect."

My smile grew. "April. We decided to tell everyone tonight."

She reached for my elbow. "I suggest you invite Arianna out when the baby's born."

Invite my mother. "To help me or to get her away from you?"

Catalina laughed. "A little of both."

I couldn't help thinking of how much Catalina had changed and grown in her confidence since her wedding day. She'd not only accepted her place as the wife of the capo dei capi, but she also shone brightly as the woman meant to stand at his side.

As if conjured by my thoughts, Dario appeared at my side, looking down at his daughter in my arms. "Don't get any ideas, Mia. You're still a newlywed."

Catalina looked at me and grinned.

Dario studied his wife and then turned to me. "Well, shit. I guess I'm too late. Congratulations?"

"Do I have my capo's approval?"

"Of course, Ariadna Gia will have a cousin."

It seemed that amongst our closest family and friends, news traveled lightning fast. Finally, I stood at Aléjandro's side as he lifted his hands, quieting the guests. He wrapped his arm around my waist. "If you haven't already heard, Mia and I have an announcement."

"*Bebé* Roríguez," Rei said loudly to a hearty round of applause.

Mom and Josefina immediately descended upon us with hugs and kisses. It was later when I heard Jorge and Dario talking that I knew in my heart of hearts that our alliance would work. It had to. In another seven months, we'd have two children who were both cartel and famiglia. A new generation to witness the success that can be had when unlikely partners worked together.

Near the end of the evening, Dante found me in the kitchen. "Congratulations, Mia. I didn't say a word."

"I hadn't known for sure when you were here."

"I'll tell you what I said before; *this* is the marriage you deserve."

"You kept my secret. Now tell me who you want to marry."

He pressed his lips together.

"I heard your request has been approved. Don't you think you should clue the future bride in?"

"Tonight is your night."

"Does she even know you?"

"What's not to love about me?"

I laughed. "Seriously. This misogynistic—"

Dante laid a finger on my lips and spoke in a whisper. "Here's my secret, Mia. Don't tell anyone."

"I can't keep a secret from Aléjandro."

"He knows."

That means he'd kept a secret from me. My curiosity was getting the better of me. "Spill."

"My future bride knows. I asked her before I asked Dario."

My eyes flew open. "Rebel."

"Don't tell Dario or Jorge. The marriage couldn't happen without their approval, and we both knew that."

I turned, taking in the guests. In the category of unwed cartel women present, there were four: Mireya, Camila, Sofia, and Liliana. Aléjandro had told me it wasn't Liliana. "Are you going to tell me?"

"No, I don't trust your poker face."

"What?" I asked with a gasp. "I have a great poker face."

"Aléjandro will tell you once we're all gone." He kissed my cheek. "Great party, Mia."

Later that night, as soon as Aléjandro and I settled into bed, we both scooted toward the middle of the mattress.

"Mireya, Camila, or Sofia?" I asked.

Aléjandro didn't hesitate. "Camila."

My smile grew as I thought about Dante asking her before getting approval. "Dante is a good man. If he wants Camila, he'll take good care of her." I thought of something else. "And Camila will move to Kansas City. Catalina will be happy."

"The biggest sticking point in the negotiations was

about her schooling. She has two years left at university, and Andrés wants her to finish."

"Surely, Dante doesn't want to stop that."

"Transfer. Kansas City has multiple options." Aléjandro rolled me to my back and leaned over me, staring down. "If Dante loves Camila even a tenth of how much I love you, they'll be good." He grinned. "*Padre* and Dario don't know what I'm about to say."

It was my turn to smile.

"This relationship apparently started when Valentina and Camila went to Missouri after their home was invaded. The idea of marriage is very much mutual."

"Then I'm glad everyone agreed."

He teased the strap of my nightgown and flashed his sexy smile. "It's been a busy day." His lips peppered my collarbone with kisses, sending a wave of goose bumps down my legs. "I was wondering about something else mutual."

I licked my lips. "My nightgown is all I'm wearing."

My announcement about my lack of panties was all the incentive my husband needed before my nightgown and his basketball shorts found their way to the floor, and my new addiction was being supplied by my favorite dealer. Aléjandro was a high I'd never grow tired of experiencing. He'd smashed my walls, fears, and doubts to smithereens while treating me as I'd always imagined a husband should.

We were meant to last...until death do us part.

Thank you for reading TILL DEATH DO US PART, Aléjandro and Mia's story. If you haven't read NOW AND FOREVER, Dario and Catalina's story, you can read it today at your favorite retailer.
Coming September of 2024, BOUND BY A PROMISE, Dante and Camila's story.
If you've enjoyed Brutal Vows, check out all of Aleatha's titles here.

What to do now

LEND IT: Did you enjoy TILL DEATH DO US PART? Do you have a friend who'd enjoy TILL DEATH DO US PART? TILL DEATH DO US PART may be lent one time. Sharing is caring!

RECOMMEND IT: Do you have multiple friends who'd enjoy my dark romance with twists and turns and an all new sexy and infuriating anti-hero? Tell them about it! Call, text, post, tweet...your recommendation is the nicest gift you can give to an author!

REVIEW IT: Tell the world. Please go to the retailer where you purchased this book, as well as Goodreads, and write a review. Please share your thoughts about TILL DEATH DO US PART:

*Amazon, TILL DEATH DO US PART, Customer Reviews

*Barnes & Noble, TILL DEATH DO US PART, Customer Reviews

*Apple Books, TILL DEATH DO US PART Customer Reviews

* BookBub, TILL DEATH DO US PART Customer Reviews

*Goodreads.com/Aleatha Romig

Books by
ALEATHA

BRUTAL VOWS:

NOW AND FOREVER

TILL DEATH DO US PART

BOUND BY A PROMISE

READY TO BINGE

SINCLAIR DUET:

REMEMBERING PASSION

September 2023

REKINDLING DESIRE

October 2023

ROYAL REFLECTIONS SERIES:

RUTHLESS REIGN

November 2022

RESILIENT REIGN

January 2023

RAVISHING REIGN

April 2023

RELEVANT REIGN

June 2023

SIN SERIES:

RED SIN

October 2021

GREEN ENVY

January 2022

GOLD LUST

April 2022

BLACK KNIGHT

June 2022

STAND-ALONE ROMANTIC SUSPENSE:

SILVER LINING

October 2022

KINGDOM COME

November 2021

DEVIL'S SERIES (Duet):

DEVIL'S DEAL

May 2021

ANGEL'S PROMISE

June 2021

WEB OF SIN:

SECRETS

October 2018

LIES

December 2018

PROMISES

January 2019

TANGLED WEB:

TWISTED

May 2019

OBSESSED

July 2019

BOUND

August 2019

WEB OF DESIRE:

SPARK

Jan. 14, 2020

FLAME

February 25, 2020

ASHES

April 7, 2020

DANGEROUS WEB:

Prequel: "Danger's First Kiss"

DUSK

November 2020

DARK

January 2021

DAWN

February 2021

THE INFIDELITY SERIES:

BETRAYAL

Book #1

October 2015

CUNNING

Book #2

January 2016

DECEPTION

Book #3

May 2016

ENTRAPMENT

Book #4

September 2016

FIDELITY

Book #5

January 2017

THE CONSEQUENCES SERIES:

CONSEQUENCES

(Book #1)

August 2011

TRUTH

(Book #2)

October 2012

CONVICTED

(Book #3)

October 2013

REVEALED

(Book #4)

Previously titled: Behind His Eyes Convicted: The Missing Years

June 2014

BEYOND THE CONSEQUENCES

(Book #5)

January 2015

RIPPLES (Consequences stand-alone)

October 2017

CONSEQUENCES COMPANION READS:

BEHIND HIS EYES-CONSEQUENCES

January 2014

BEHIND HIS EYES-TRUTH

March 2014

STAND ALONE MAFIA THRILLER:

PRICE OF HONOR

Available Now

~

STAND-ALONE ROMANTIC THRILLER:

ON THE EDGE

May 2022

***

017//7081004157807

TALES FROM THE DARK SIDE SERIES:

INSIDIOUS

(All books in this series are stand-alone erotic thrillers)

Released October 2014

ALEATHA'S LIGHTER ONES:

PLUS ONE

Stand-alone fun, sexy romance

May 2017

ANOTHER ONE

Stand-alone fun, sexy romance

May 2018

ONE NIGHT

Stand-alone, sexy contemporary romance

September 2017

A SECRET ONE

April 2018

MY ALWAYS ONE

Stand-Alone, sexy friends to lovers contemporary romance

July 2021

QUINTESSENTIALLY THE ONE

Stand-alone, small-town, second-chance, secret baby
contemporary romance

July 2022

ONE KISS

Stand-alone, small-town, best friend's sister,
grump/sunshine contemporary romance.

July 2023

INDULGENCE SERIES:

UNEXPECTED

August 2018

UNCONVENTIONAL

January 2018

UNFORGETTABLE

October 2019

UNDENIABLE

August 2020

ABOUT THE
AUTHOR

Aleatha Romig is a New York Times, Wall Street Journal, and USA Today bestselling author who lives in Indiana, USA. She has raised three children with her high school sweetheart and husband of over thirty years. Before she became a full-time author, she worked days as a dental hygienist and spent her nights writing. Now, when she's not imagining mind-blowing twists and turns, she likes to spend her time with her family and friends. Her other pastimes include reading and creating heroes/anti-heroes who haunt your dreams!

Aleatha impresses with her versatility in writing. She released her first novel, CONSEQUENCES, in August of 2011. CONSEQUENCES, a dark romance, became a bestselling series with five novels and two companions released from 2011 through 2015. The compelling and epic story of Anthony and Claire Rawlings has graced more than half a million e-readers. Her first stand-alone smart, sexy thriller INSIDIOUS was next. Then Aleatha released the five-novel INFIDELITY series, a romantic suspense saga, that took the reading world by storm, the final book landing on three of the top bestseller lists. She ventured into traditional publishing with Thomas and Mercer. Her books INTO

THE LIGHT and AWAY FROM THE DARK were published through this mystery/thriller publisher in 2016.

In the spring of 2017, Aleatha again ventured into a different genre with her first fun and sexy stand-alone romantic comedy with the USA Today bestseller PLUS ONE. She continued the "Ones" series with additional standalones, ONE NIGHT, ANOTHER ONE, MY ALWAYS ONE, and QUINTESSENTIALLY THE ONE. If you like fun, sexy, novellas that make your heart pound, try her "Indulgence series" with UNCONVEN-TIONAL. UNEXPECTED, UNFORGETTABLE, and UNDENIABLE.

In 2018 Aleatha returned to her dark romance roots with SPARROW WEBS. And continued with the mafia romance DEVIL'S DUET, and most recently her SINCLAIR DUET.

You may find all Aleatha's titles on her website.

Aleatha is a "Published Author's Network" member of the Romance Writers of America and PEN America. She is represented by SBR Media and Dani Sanchez with Wildfire Marketing.

facebook.com/aleatharomig

x.com/aleatharomig

instagram.com/aleatharomig

Made in the USA
Middletown, DE
04 October 2024

61976227R00232